S. SUMMERS

D1097546

TALISA'S SONG

LINDA SMITH

TALISA'S SONG

Book Two of the TALES of THREE LANDS *trilogy*

Edited by Barbara Sapergia.
Cover painting by Stella East.
Cover and book design by Duncan Campbell.
Typeset by Karen Steadman.
Printed and bound in Canada by Gauvin Press.

Library and Archives Canada Cataloguing in Publication

Smith, Linda, 1949-
Talisa's song / Linda Smith.

(Tales of three lands ; bk. 2)
ISBN 1-55050-327-8

I. Title. II. Series: Smith, Linda, 1949- . Tales of three lands ; bk. 2.

PS8587.M5528T34 2005   jc813'.54   C2005-904904-9

10 9 8 7 6 5 4 3 2 1

2517 Victoria Avenue
Regina, Saskatchewan
Canada   S4P 0T2

Available in Canada & the US from:
Fitzhenry and Whiteside
195 Allstate Parkway
Markham, Ontario
Canada   L3R 4T8

The publisher gratefully acknowledges the financial assistance of the Saskatchewan Arts Board, the Canada Council for the Arts, the Government of Canada through the Book Publishing Industry Development Program (BPIDP), and the City of Regina Arts Commission, for its publishing program.

*To the Grande Prairie Cygnets Writers Group
for their help and encouragement*

MIDSUMMER NIGHT

TALISA DODGED A CARTWHEELING ACROBAT, then darted around a clump of men who stood, ale mugs in hand, laughing uproariously at some joke. She needed to reach her inn. To get away from this tumult. To let her bitter tears flow.

She rounded the corner into Fallmart Square and stopped. The streets she'd just walked through were packed, but they were nothing compared to the wall of people and noise that met her here. How was she to make her way across the square to the streets on the other side that led to her small, solitary room?

She should never have come here. She should be at home, in Uglessia, where the only lights on Midsummer were the long, lingering rays of the sun, followed by the glimmer of stars, where her family gathered on the hillside to sing the ancient songs of the season and share the old legend about the sun's promise to the mountain spirits. For a moment, she could almost hear her father's quiet voice, her Aunt Gwynne's bubbling laugh, almost see her uncle's slow smile and her cousins' fiery hair, almost feel Welwyn's fingers as her sister touched her arm.

A man bumped into her. "Oops. Sorry." His words were slurred, his breath heavy with wine fumes.

Talisa jerked backwards and bumped into someone herself. She mumbled a hasty apology, took a deep breath, and inched her way through a crowd gawking at a juggler's silvery arc of balls.

Earlier, she would have stopped and watched. Walking to the palace as the pink of the western sky deepened into mauve, her heart had quickened, seeing lanterns lit and people spill into the streets, singing and laughing. Now...

Why had she come here? To this land of Freya, where wizards and courtiers hated Uglessians and hatched plots against them? To this city of Freyfall, where noise assaulted her ears and it seemed that more people jammed into the streets to celebrate Midsummer than existed in all of Uglessia?

She knew the answer, of course. She had come for the music competition. She had wanted to impress others. To impress herself. To prove that she had a gift. Not the one she wanted, but a gift.

Her plan had succeeded. She'd been chosen as one of the five best musicians. Tonight, she'd sung before the Freyan queen and the assembled wizards of three lands, including her beloved grandparents. She should be happy.

But her moment of glory had been eclipsed by a deadly plot. She stopped as images surged over her. An outraged giant of a young man striding towards Queen Elira. Courtiers in silk and satin, wizards in sombre black, clustered around her. A small, tawny cat, sinking its teeth into the arm of a Freyan soldier whose hand, unknown to most at the time, had been reaching for a long, curved knife.

A conspiracy to destroy peace had failed. It shouldn't matter that her achievement had been brushed aside like some unwanted present.

But it did.

Talisa clenched her jaw. She *had* to get to her room in the inn. She took a few steps, then stopped again, barred by a line of weaving, laughing dancers.

A tall, burly man darted out of the line and grabbed her hand. "Come on, sweetheart," he bellowed. "Join the dance."

She tried to pull her hand free. "No! No, I –"

"Come along. Midsummer comes but once a year."

He was a great brown bear of a man and immensely strong. Before she could protest further, he had swung her into the line. A younger, slighter man grasped her left hand, then started and looked at her with wide, surprised brown eyes. He almost stumbled as the woman on his other side tugged at him.

Yes, I'm Uglessian, Talisa thought bitterly. *Do you think your five-fingered hand doesn't feel as strange to me as my six fingers do to you?*

The young man regained his footing, tightened his grip, and smiled at her. The brown bear man roared with laughter as the music grew wilder and wilder, the dancing faster and

3

faster, and kept flying in and out of line to add yet more dancers. He was drunk, Talisa thought, more on excitement than on wine or ale.

As the pace quickened and, with it, her breath and heartbeat, Talisa felt everything slip away except the music pulsing through her blood and the rhythm pounding through her feet. She had no idea how long the dance lasted, but when it ended with a final, frantic burst of energy, she found herself panting and laughing with the rest of them.

The young man beside her dropped her hand and wiped his sweating face. "I've never danced so fast in my life."

She nodded, smiling, and tucked some strands of long red hair back behind her ears.

"I think a drink is called for." He grinned at her. "Want one? There's a vendor selling water over there."

Sure enough, there was a stall not far off with a sign of a man holding a glass. Along with the wine casks and beer kegs on the counter, there were jugs of water.

She hesitated. Earlier, all she had wanted was to get away from this place. But she *was* thirsty, and music still tingled in her veins. She went with him. They snaked their way through the crowd and joined those waiting in front of the stall.

Her companion turned to her. "I'm sorry I reacted the way I did. When I took your hand, I mean. I guess... Well, I haven't met many Uglessians before."

Talisa's face stiffened. "It's all right."

He looked uncertain, then smiled, a bit tentatively. He was younger than she'd first thought. A boy, really. About her age. "I'm glad you joined the dance. Is this your first Midsummer in Freyfall?"

"Yes."

"Have you been here long? Do you like it?"

She was about to say something polite and noncommittal when a woman beside them said, "Look," and pointed.

Halfway across the square, a man stood on an overturned box. He waved his arms wildly, his mouth opening and closing as he yelled something no one could hear above the roar of the crowd. As he continued, however, those closest to him turned their heads and listened. Silence spread, like a ripple from a stone flung into a pond, until some of his words could be heard in the growing pool of quiet.

"The queen...assassination..."

Talisa blinked. Didn't they already know about the attempt on the queen's life?

No. Of course not. She'd left the palace soon after calm had been restored. Word would only now be trickling into the streets.

Cries of horror. Shocked disbelief. Beside her, the boy gave a retching gasp as though he'd been kicked in the stomach.

From somewhere to her left, a woman shouted, "Is the queen dead then?"

The man on the box shook his head. "No."

"Who did it?" someone else called.

"Dunno. I heard it from my cousin, who heard it from a friend."

"But *why* would anyone want to kill her?" a woman wailed. "She's a good woman, is our queen."

Talisa saw heads nod all around her. The quiet was deepening as news was called to revellers further away. A jig screeched to a jarring halt.

She should explain what had happened. She opened her mouth.

Then someone behind her said loudly, "The Uglessians." The anger in the voice hit her like a brutal slap across the face. She turned and looked at the speaker, a man with the small eyes and plump pink face of a pig.

Others were staring at him too. "What do you mean, the Uglessians?" demanded a man with a pointed black beard.

"They were there, weren't they? Uglessian wizards right alongside our own wizards and those from the Islands. What better chance to kill our queen?"

Silence. Talisa's skin pricked. She shivered, despite the warmth of the night.

"They'd no reason to kill her," a man said. Talisa couldn't see who it was, but she let out her breath in relief as he continued, "She's their friend. She's always wanted us to have better relations with them."

A man with sense. Thank you, spirits of my mountains.

But there were other voices too, voices that seemed to swell like overheated wineskins.

"Queen Elira should never have trusted them."

"My grandda always said they were bloodthirsty beasts."

"I never did like them. No, nor trust them neither. Long-haired, six-fingered creatures. Unnatural."

"We should never have sent them our rain in the first place."

No! It wasn't Uglessians who tried to kill the queen! She must tell them. She *must*. She opened her mouth again, but fear seemed to have wedged a huge fist in her throat.

"Put your hands in your pockets," said a quiet voice.

Startled, she looked at the boy beside her. She'd forgotten he was there.

"Quickly."

"But —"

"You're unusually tall for a girl, and your skin is paler than ours, but no one will know you're Uglessian unless they see your hands. Not for sure."

"But there's no need. If they knew..." Her words died, struck down by the anger she could hear around her. The anger she could *feel*. She looked down at her hands, with their betraying sixth fingers. They were trembling. She stuffed them into her pockets.

"Let's get out of here," he muttered.

She shook her head. She must stay. Tell them what had really happened. What would they do to other Uglessians if she didn't? Surely they would believe her. She looked around.

The festive mood had vanished like a pricked bubble. The air felt as heavy as it did when a storm was brooding. A short distance away, a woman stared at her, suspicion darkening her face.

The boy flung his right arm around her waist, drawing her close. She jerked.

"Throws off suspicion," he murmured.

It did. The woman turned away to listen to what a bearded man was shouting. Something about "punish." Talisa shuddered.

"Come on," the boy said in a low voice. "We'd better not look as though we're running away though. Walk slowly."

Unless they'd elbowed and shoved to plough a path through the crowd, they couldn't have walked quickly anyway. They dodged and wove their way past clots of people, clumped together not to laugh, not to sing, not to applaud cartwheeling acrobats or balls circling a juggler's head, but to exchange information – and misinformation. To stoke the fires of their suspicion and their rage. Talisa's heart thumped so loudly she wondered they didn't turn to stare at her. Her skin was clammy with cold sweat. Every time people glanced her way, she was sure their eyes narrowed. After a while, she stumbled along with her head down, letting her companion guide her steps.

Gradually, the sounds around them changed. Shocked, angry voices gave way to laughter, music, all the cheerful chaos of a Midsummer celebration. The news must not have reached this far. Not yet. How long before it did?

"We'd better keep going," the boy muttered.

The night seemed to stretch out around her, an endless blur of noise and cobblestones and people. She was vaguely aware of the weight of the arm around her waist, the body beside her, the faint smell of sweat coming from that body. But mostly she was conscious of fear. Fear, and the thought that drummed through her head. *I should have told them what really happened. I should have told them. I should have told them.*

The streets grew narrower, darker, less crowded. Talisa raised her head and gazed about, seeing shabby buildings and a few tattered banners, forlorn attempts at Midsummer cheer.

She stopped. "Where are we?"

"Barrow Road. Just two more blocks and we're home."

Home. His home. Did he think...?

She stepped backwards. His arm dropped from her waist.

"I should go. Surely now... It must be safe."

The street was too dark to see his face, but concern was sharp in his voice. "Go where?"

"To my inn."

"Where's that?"

"A few blocks east of Fallmart Square." She had been glad to find the room when she first arrived in Freyfall a fortnight ago. It was small and cramped, but there was a slit of a window, and it was clean. And cheap.

He was silent, but she could almost hear his thoughts. Or maybe they were her thoughts. If she went back to that area, she'd be walking into danger.

"Do they know at your inn that you're Uglessian?"

She stared at him, even though all she could make out was his shadowy outline. She hadn't thought of that.

Her silence must have answered for her. "I think you should come with me. We don't have much, my sister and brother-in-law and I, but we can find room for you to sleep.

Better that than returning to a place where you might not be safe."

The mention of a sister was reassuring. Talisa nodded and walked silently beside him up the dark street.

THE UPPER ROOM

THEY STOPPED IN FRONT OF A TALL, SKINNY building on the corner. Windows stared down at them like dark, empty eyes. The boy opened the door and ushered her inside.

Total darkness. Talisa stopped.

Beside her, she heard a muttered curse, then the rustle of cloth and the strike of spark on flint. A moment later, a feeble light cast shadows in a large, dusty hall.

"Lucky I had a candle stub in my pocket. There's supposed to be a lantern in the hall, but it must have burned out. Either that, or someone's stolen it. Sorry."

She murmured reassurance.

"Our room's at the top of the house, I'm afraid."

She trailed him up a winding stone staircase that seemed to go on forever. The echo of their footsteps was the only sound Talisa could hear. Everyone must still be out celebrating Midsummer.

Celebrating – or killing Uglessians.

No! She flinched away from the thought, tried, instead, to identify the smells.

Dust. And the faint, disagreeable odour of mildew.

On the top floor, the boy dug in his pocket, produced a key, and unlocked a door. She followed him inside and looked around as he lit another candle from the stub of the one he held.

"It's not much of a place," he said apologetically.

"You forget. I'm Uglessian."

"Huh? What – ?"

"It's fine."

It was. The room wasn't big, but it was spacious enough to hold a table and chairs, a loom, some shelves, and two chests. Brightly coloured curtains hung in front of two alcoves, providing separate sleeping quarters. There was no smell of dust here, or mildew. Even the shadowy corners looked as though they'd been scoured by a cleansing wind. Not big. Certainly not luxurious. But fine. Better than most Uglessian homes.

Her eyes were caught and held by a tapestry on the wall. The woven strands showed a young girl in a red dress, running through a field of golden grain, her arms upflung, her face alight. Talisa took a couple of steps forward and stood in front of it.

"Do you like it?"

"It's beautiful." How inadequate! She tried again. "It...sings. With life. And joy."

"My sister made it." The pride in his voice was undisguised.

"Your sister? She must be a very good weaver. Has she made more like this?"

"No." His voice had changed, hardened. Talisa turned and looked at him.

He shrugged. "Work like this takes a long time and doesn't pay well. Rina mostly makes clothes for Bart to sell at his stall. Bart's my brother-in-law."

"Where are they? Your sister and brother-in-law?"

"Still out celebrating, I imagine. Here, have a seat." He drew out a chair from the table.

She hesitated. Should she stay here? He was a stranger. She knew nothing of him. His sister might not return for some time. She studied him carefully.

He was about her age, sixteen or perhaps seventeen, with long, lanky limbs. Shoulder-length brown hair swung around his face. He certainly wasn't handsome. All his features were just a little too large: the nose too long, the mouth too wide, the brown eyes too big. And his ears stuck out.

He grinned suddenly. "You look like a bird watching a creeping cat. Don't worry. I won't pounce."

There was no reason to believe him, but she did. She sat. He took the chair opposite her. Neither of them spoke for a moment. It was quiet. Inside the room. Inside the building. In the street beyond the building. But what about the streets beyond that? Were Freyans hunting through them for Uglessians? Killing Uglessians?

"What is it?"

She said nothing.

"What's wrong?"

She ran her finger along a crack in the table. "I should have told them."

Her voice was so low she was surprised he heard her, but he must have. "Told who what?"

"The people in the square. I should have told them it wasn't us."

He was silent for a moment, then said, "They wouldn't have believed you. Anyway, are you sure?"

Her head shot up. "Of course I am!"

He held up a restraining hand. "I didn't mean you were involved. I'm sure you weren't. But can you speak for all your countrymen who were in the palace tonight?"

"Yes! I know them all. None of them would do such a thing."

He said nothing, but there was no misreading the doubt on his face. She leaned forward.

"I was there. I *saw* what happened. It was Freyans, not us, who tried to kill your queen."

"Freyans?" He stared at her.

"Yes, Freyans."

"But..." He stopped and wet his lips. His face had turned a strange shade of sickly green. "You said you were there. Why? What...?"

"I was singing."

"Singing?" he asked blankly.

"I was one of the winners of the music competition."

"Music competition?"

"You must have heard of it. All the musicians in Freyfall – maybe half the musicians in Freya – took part. I came from Uglessia to enter the contest. And I was one of those chosen to perform." For a moment, some of the fierce pride she had

14

felt when she saw her name on the notice filled her and rang in her voice.

"Perform?"

Did he have to echo every word she uttered? "Yes. Perform. Tonight, at the opening of the wizards' meeting. So I was there. And I *know* who it was who tried to assassinate Queen Elira. It was Freyans."

"I see," he said slowly. He looked down. Now it was he who was tracing a crack in the table. "Do you know who it was? Their names?"

"Not their names. Some wizards, and men in the queen's court. At least one army officer." Again, she saw a picture of a cat digging its teeth and claws into the arm of a tall man in a green uniform. "I think the queen's cousin was involved. I saw guards lead him away."

His head came up. He stared at her, eyes wide. "Count Varic? And wizards? But *why?*"

Talisa frowned. "There's a lot I don't know, but from what I saw and heard, I believe they wanted to wreck the wizards' council and destroy goodwill between Freya and its neighbours. Maybe even cause a war. One of the musicians sang a song that insulted Uglessians. I think they were trying to anger us and, in all the shouting and confusion, kill Queen Elira and lay the blame on us."

His face had regained a healthy touch of colour. "But they failed."

She looked away. There was a small square window in the wall, but she could see nothing except black night beyond the glass. "Did they?"

He was silent. Perhaps he was remembering, as she was, the suspicion that had narrowed eyes, the anger that tightened voices, the hate that throbbed in the air in Fallmart Square.

Suspicion. Anger. Hate.

Blood. The blood of Uglessians. Of her grandparents.

Without knowing how she got there, she was at the door, her hand on the knob.

"Wait!" He grabbed her arm. "Where are you going?"

"Out! I must... My grandparents are here! They'll be killed!"

"Where are they?"

"I... Grandmother told me the name of the inn they're staying at. It's..." She couldn't remember. Couldn't think. "With the others."

"What others?"

"The Uglessian and Islandian wizards who are here for the council."

"Oh." He released his hold on her arm. "They'll be safe."

She kept her hand on the knob. "How can you say that? You saw those people in the square."

"Your grandparents and the other wizards are important. They'll be well guarded. The important always are."

There was a note in his voice that she didn't like. But it didn't matter. All that mattered was the relief singing through her.

She dropped her hand, but remained facing the door. "There are other Uglessians, people who have moved here, hoping for work."

"Do you know where they live?"

She paused. "No."

"Then you won't be able to find them to warn them."

"I can tell the Freyans what really happened."

No, screamed a voice inside her. *They hate you. They'll kill you.*

"There's no sense in going out there. You're a Uglessian. You're the last person they'd believe. All you'd do is put yourself in danger for no reason."

She mustn't listen to him. She took several deep breaths and raised her hand again.

"Look," he said. His voice had changed again, was very gentle now. "They'll have sent a crier into the streets with the news of what happened. Everyone will know by now that your people weren't to blame."

Surely he was right. He *had* to be right. Slowly, she turned, walked back, and sat down.

"How about that drink we were talking about before all this started?" he asked, a shade too brightly. "What would you like? Water? Ale?"

"Kala, please, if you have any." The room was hot, but kala was a reminder of home, and the plants growing wild on the mountains. Right then she needed that reminder badly.

He smiled. "We do indeed. Bought specially for Midsummer."

"Oh. Don't waste a special treat. Water will be fine." She'd forgotten that kala was a luxury in Freya.

"No waste." He smiled again and went to prepare the drink.

She opened her mouth to protest, then closed it, suddenly too tired to argue. She watched him as he shook some grounds into two cups, stirred the embers in the hearth and placed a kettle over them. Despite his lanky limbs, he moved with grace, and his large hands were quick and precise. He brought the steaming drinks back to the table.

"Here you are, Mistress... I'm sorry. I don't know your name."

"Talisa."

"That's a pretty name."

"Thank you. I was named after Talis, a boy my grandparents knew when they were about my age." *But I'm not like him. He died trying to stop Uglessians from killing Freyans, Freyans Uglessians.* She looked away.

"I'm Cory."

She murmured something polite and took a sip of her kala. They were both silent then. Cory frowned into his cup. Talisa felt too drained to speak. A question kept nagging at her, though.

"Why did you do it?"

The question seemed to drag him away from somewhere. He shook his head, then shook it again. "Do what?"

"Save me. Especially since you believed that Uglessians were responsible for the assassination attempt."

He thought for a moment, then shrugged. "I don't know."

She raised her eyebrows. "You don't know?"

He laughed. "I guess I wanted to save a good dancing partner."

She looked at him.

He shrugged again. "I don't know. You were there. You needed help. Anyone would have done it."

No, Talisa thought. Many would not have wanted to help her. Many more would not have dared. What would have happened to *him* if they'd been caught?

"Thank you," she said gravely.

Pink stained his cheeks. "You're welcome."

They lapsed into silence. She finished her drink and yawned.

He jumped to his feet. "I'm sorry. You're tired. It's time to sleep."

She watched him take a couple of blankets from one of the chests and arrange them on the floor in a corner.

"Thank you. That looks comfortable." She rose.

"No, no. I'll sleep here. You take my bed."

"I can't do that."

"Please. It's more comfortable. Though it's not really a bed, just a straw mattress," he added apologetically.

Talisa smiled faintly. "I'd never even *seen* a bed till I came to Freya. A straw mattress is fine. So are blankets on the floor."

"It's true, then? Everyone in Uglessia is poor?"

"We're certainly not rich," she said dryly.

He looked as though he wanted to ask more questions, but all he said was, "It would be better if I'm out here, not you, when Rina and Bart come home."

Talisa's mouth went dry. Her stomach tightened into a knot. Would Cory's sister and brother-in-law be angry when they found a stranger in their room? A Uglessian in their room? She stared at Cory.

"Explanations and introductions will be better in the morning," he said.

She nodded silently and entered the curtained alcove he indicated. It was very small. The only objects it contained, aside from a narrow straw mattress, were the pitcher, basin, and pan that stood on the floor at the foot of the bed. She removed the green festival dress she'd worn for the performance. How long ago was it that she'd put it on, so proudly, so lovingly? Five hours? Six? It seemed like days. Placing it carefully on the end of the mattress, she crawled in under the covers.

She was so tired. Weariness dragged on her like a heavy stone around her neck. But she couldn't sleep. She lay in the unfamiliar bed, in the unfamiliar room, and listened to the sound of footsteps on the stairs, voices in the hall, the doors to other rooms opening, closing. Perhaps an hour after she'd gone to bed, the door of Cory's room opened. She stiffened.

Someone must have lit a candle, for light glimmered beyond her curtained wall.

"Cory!" exclaimed a woman. "What are you doing out here?"

"Huh?" came Cory's sleep-filled voice.

"What are you doing sleeping out here?" the woman repeated.

Cory sounded more awake. "Someone – a guest – is in my bed."

"Who?" It was a man's voice this time. Curt. Sharp.

"Someone. You'll meet her in the morning."

"If it's someone from that group of yours –" There was anger in the man's tone, and something else that she couldn't quite identify. Fear?

"It's not." Cory sounded wide awake now.

There was silence. Then Talisa heard footsteps coming towards the alcove.

"Bart!" the woman protested. "Let her be. Whoever she is, she'll be sleeping. It's late. Time we were in bed ourselves." She yawned.

"We could be in danger."

"Cory said –"

"Bah!"

Another silence. Then the woman said, very slowly, with muted anger of her own. "My brother does not lie. And this is no time to pick a fight – or to wake sleeping guests. We'll meet her, whoever she is, in the morning. Come to bed."

After a moment, the man said, "Very well." Grudgingly.

Talisa lay rigid. The man had spoken of danger. What danger? The danger of harbouring a Uglessian? But they didn't know she was Uglessian. Did they?

She should go out, introduce herself, explain why she was there, ask them what had happened tonight in the streets. She dreaded what they might tell her, but she needed to know.

But what if they turned on her? Threw her into the street?

Go out. Ask.

No!

The candle must have been extinguished, for there was no light now. She stared into the darkness, hating herself.

She didn't dare leave the alcove and speak to them just as, earlier, she hadn't dared speak to the Freyans in Fallmart Square.

Had people died tonight because of her cowardice?

THE BERRYMORE HOUSEHOLD

TALISA'S EYES FELT AS THOUGH SHE'D RUBBED sand into them. She pressed the heels of her hands against her eyelids, then removed them and, reluctantly, opened her eyes.

She blinked in surprise. Sunlight filtered through the curtain and splashed onto her blanket. The last time she'd had her eyes open, the darkness had just begun to thin. She must have slept after all.

Noises came from the outside room – voices, the clatter of dishes. The pungent aroma of kala was strong and heady. She breathed it in and reached for her festival dress.

Then she remembered. These people were hardly likely to welcome her. Last night, Bart had sounded suspicious. Hostile. How would he react this morning when confronted by a stranger? A stranger who was Uglessian? Worse: what news did they have? News of carnage? News of her people, slaughtered? Her hand dropped.

But she had to face them sometime, had to face their news. She closed her eyes tightly, whispered a prayer to the mountain spirits, and reached for the dress again. Pouring water into the basin, she washed her face, but the water did little to remove the grey layer of weariness that clung to her.

Three heads turned her way as she inched the curtain aside and stepped into the room.

Cory jumped to his feet. "You're awake."

"I... Yes. Is it very late?" She looked uncertainly at the light streaming into the room, then at the three people in front of her. The two men were dressed, but the woman standing by the hearth, brown hair tousled, spoon in hand, was still in her nightgown. She smiled at Talisa.

"Don't worry. It's almost noon, but we just got up too. I'm making porridge. Want some?"

Did she? She should be hungry. She'd been too nervous last night to eat much before the performance, and she'd had nothing since. But her stomach was jumping up and down now too. And Rina and Bart might not know she was Uglessian. She should tell them before she accepted their food.

Rina misread her hesitation. "There's plenty," she assured Talisa. "It will be a few minutes before it's ready. In the meantime, would you like some kala?"

"I'll get it," Cory volunteered before Talisa could respond. She watched him pour the dark drink into a cup and bring it to the table.

"Please have a seat," the other man said. She sat on the edge of a chair and reached for the cup.

Was it her imagination, or did Bart's eyes stop and rest on her hand? Her six-fingered hand?

Well, better he know now. She took a deep breath, then raised her eyes and looked at him. He was a dark-haired, lean-faced man with bushy eyebrows and high cheekbones, who seemed to be in his early or mid-twenties.

He met her eyes and smiled faintly. "Sorry for staring. Cory didn't tell us you were Uglessian."

She swallowed. "I am."

"So I see. Welcome to our home. My name is Bart Berrymore and this is my wife Rina. Cory you already know."

Was this the same man who had sounded so suspicious, so angry, last night? Talisa took a gulp of kala, trying to clear her head. Then she remembered her manners.

"I'm glad to meet you. My name is Talisa." He seemed to be waiting, so she added, "I'm sorry. I always forget that two names are used in Freya. At home, they simply call me Talisa, or sometimes Talisa of the red hair or Talisa, daughter of Davvid. I'm Talisa Thatcher."

That brought a reaction. Rina turned and stared at her, and Bart raised his eyebrows. "A Uglessian named Thatcher? Are you related to Alaric Thatcher, by any chance?"

"He's my grandfather."

"You didn't tell me that," Cory exclaimed.

"No. Well... There really wasn't time."

Rina clapped her hands. "We have a living legend in our house!"

Talisa stared at her. "I'm scarcely that."

"No. But your grandfather is. And if he's your grandfather, then Redelle must be your grandmother and Yrwith your great-grandmother. And *they're* all legends."

Cory started to whistle a tune. After a few bars, he stopped. "It's 'The Rains of Uglessia,'" he explained. "The song tells the story of how Yrwith, trying to help her country, shifted the winds to bring more rain to Uglessia, and how Kerstin Speller broke the spell that had caused drought in Freya and torrential downpours in Uglessia, then persuaded Freyan wizards to shift the winds again so that Uglessia could get enough rain to be productive. I'll sing it for you if you like."

"No, don't!" Rina said. "Cory's singing sounds like a seagull squawking," she told Talisa, "or maybe the caw of a crow."

Cory made a face at his sister.

"Are you a wizard, like they were?" Bart asked.

Talisa felt her face go stiff. She gazed down at her cup. "No."

"She's a singer," Cory said. He turned to the others. "Talisa was one of the five musicians chosen to sing before the queen and the wizards at the opening of the council last night." He sounded as proud as though he'd been the one chosen.

Bart whistled. "Quite an honour."

Rina clapped her hands again. "You must be very good indeed."

"All the more reason why you don't want to hear Cory sing," Bart said.

Talisa glanced quickly at Cory, but he just grinned. All the antagonism she'd sensed between the two men last night might never have been. In fact, the room was so filled with warmth that all her fears almost seemed like phantoms of the night.

Almost. She wrapped her hands around her cup and asked, "What happened last night? In the streets." She closed her eyes.

There was a brief pause, then Rina said, "A lot of singing. A lot of dancing. A lot of drinking. The usual Midsummer celebrations. Why?"

"We heard a rumour that someone had tried to kill Queen Elira," Cory explained. "Then there was nasty talk about Uglessians being responsible and how to punish them."

Another silence. Then Bart asked, "Is that why you brought Talisa here?"

"Yes."

Talisa's hands clenched more tightly around the cup.

"Good for you."

Her eyes flew open. She stared at the man's lean face.

Rina walked over and covered Talisa's hand with her own. "But you thought other Uglessians were hurt? Don't worry. We'd have heard if there'd been any violence, and there wasn't even a whisper of it."

"We *did* know about the assassination attempt," Bart said. "An official crier was sent out from the palace with all the news, including the identities of the conspirators. Those who thought Uglessians were responsible must have had their suspicions squashed before any harm was done."

"The news caused quite a stir, especially when we heard the queen's cousin was in on it," Rina added. "If it hadn't been Midsummer, there would have been even more talk. But none of your people were hurt, I'm sure. Now, how about some porridge, before it's burned?"

Talisa discovered that she was hungry after all. She even accepted a second helping.

Breakfast over, she looked up to thank her hosts, and found Rina studying her thoughtfully. "I wish I could make a picture of you," Rina said. "That red hair and green dress. And your pale skin. It would be lovely."

"I... Thank you," Talisa stammered. She added, "You're a fine weaver. That tapestry on the wall... It makes my heart sing."

Rina nodded absently, her eyes still fixed on Talisa's face. Those eyes were as large and brown as Cory's. Indeed, she looked much like her brother, though with a small, pert nose and ears neatly pressed to her head.

Cory leaned forward, eyes eager. "Could you stay for a while, so Rina could make some sketches?"

"I'm sorry. I told my grandparents I'd call on them early in the afternoon."

Rina smiled and nodded, but her eyes were wistful. Then she shook her head, as though shaking off a dream. "Oh well. It would have taken too much of my time anyway."

"It would have been beautiful," Cory protested.

"But not brought in much money," Bart said.

"And we must think of money, mustn't we?" Cory muttered.

"I haven't noticed you refusing to eat any meals lately."

Cory shot Bart a look hot with resentment. "I bring in my share."

"Do you? How many carvings have you given me to sell lately?"

"It takes time to make a good carving."

"And you have other things to occupy your time, haven't you?"

Cory said nothing, only stared at his brother-in-law, who stared back. After a quick glance at both their faces, Talisa averted her eyes, wishing she wasn't there.

"We have a guest," Rina said. Her voice was quiet, but Talisa thought she heard a tautness there, as of a string stretched too tightly.

A wave of colour swamped Cory's face.

"Sorry," Bart said shortly.

Cory stood up, his face still red. "I'll escort you to your inn. Or to your grandparents', if you'd rather."

"Thank you." She would need his guidance. She had no idea how to find her way back to Fallmart Square.

As she rose, a ray of sunlight touched a small statue on the shelves that stood to the left of the hearth. Two figures, a man and a woman, were carved out of dark wood. They stood looking straight ahead. Their hands barely brushed against each other's, but somehow Talisa felt a deep connection between them. They drew her, the way the sound of water on a hot day would. She moved forward.

They were middle-aged, the man and woman, and plain, their faces thin and etched with fine lines. There was strength there, in the squared shoulders, the set of the heads, the way they looked outward, steady, direct. And there was love there too, in the tender upward tilt of their lips, in their hands, in the way their bodies curved, almost unnoticeably, towards each other. Talisa reached out to touch the figures, caress the wood, then drew her hand back out of respect.

"It's..." She fumbled for the right words. It wasn't beautiful in the strict sense of the word. "It...moves me. Very much."

"Thank you," Cory mumbled.

She turned around and looked at him in wonder. "This is yours? You made it?"

"Yes."

"Are there others?" Her eyes scanned the shelves, but found only the usual assortment of plates and bowls and cups.

"We usually sell Cory's carvings," Rina explained. "But not this one. Cory gave it to Bart and me for a wedding gift."

Talisa looked back at the figures. "Are they your parents, yours and Cory's?" She thought she caught a resemblance, in the woman's broad forehead and wide mouth, the set of the man's eyes. And his ears stuck out a little, just like Cory's.

"Yes," Rina said. She came over and picked up the carving. Her fingers traced the lines of the faces. Watching her, Talisa thought that Rina's fingers must know those lines by heart. "Cory made this from memory. They died, two years back."

"I'm sorry." And she was, not just for Rina's and Cory's sake, but because she would have liked to know this man and woman. She added, impulsively, "My mother died when I was five. I wish I had a carving of her."

Her memories of her mother were so vague: a woman's face, bending over her; a woman's voice, singing a lullaby; a woman's hand, stroking her hair. Not enough. Not nearly enough.

"I'm sorry," Rina said in her turn. The men were silent, but Talisa felt their sympathy. For a moment, she wished she could stay there, warmed by their sympathy as much as by the sunlight bathing the room.

She shook herself. "I must go. Thank you so much for all you have done for me."

Bart rose and bowed. "You are most welcome," he said formally, but Rina returned the statue to its shelf and hugged her.

"I'm so glad to have met you, Talisa. May Freyn be with you."

Talisa returned the hug, surprised and pleased.

As she descended the stairs with Cory, she noticed dust-balls in corners, cracks in the stones, a damp stain on the ceiling that had been hidden the night before by the kindly darkness. The smell of frying sausage couldn't quite mask the odour of mildew. Yet the Berrymores' room had been a haven of cleanliness, colour, and warmth – except for the brief sharp clashes between Cory and Bart. She glanced at Cory and saw that he was frowning down at his boots. As though feeling her eyes on him, he looked up and flashed her a bright smile.

"I'll have you home soon," he promised. "The streets should be almost deserted today."

So they were, if the streets of Freyfall could ever be said to be deserted. Even when they left the narrow, shabby roads that surrounded Cory's home and walked down the broad thoroughfares, usually thronged with shoppers and noisy with rumbling carts, the pace was subdued. Shopkeepers were just beginning to raise their shutters, stallholders to lay out their wares. Some were taking down the sad remnants of last night's gaiety. The rush of water that fell from the cliff above Freyfall and gave the city its name could be heard more clearly than usual. Talisa raised her eyes to the shimmering wall of water.

Cory's eyes had followed hers. "It's magical, isn't it? It almost makes living in Freyfall worthwhile."

Talisa looked at him, startled. "You don't like living here?"

"Would you?"

"Well...no, though I do find it fascinating in many ways. But then, I'm not used to cities."

"Nor am I."

A cart loaded with potatoes and onions blocked their way. She waited till they'd dodged past it, then asked, "You don't come from here?"

"No. Until two years ago, we had a farm in the hills." He jerked his head towards the east. She was about to ask more when they turned a corner and Cory stopped. "Where now?"

They were in Fallmart Square, though it looked like a plucked bird without its bright plumage of lanterns and jugglers, acrobats and dancers.

Talisa hesitated. She'd like to go to her inn to change into a plainer dress. Festival gowns were no more appropriate today than the banners and garlands that had decorated the square last night. It would be good to go to the stable and give Merisha a pat too. But her grandparents would be waiting for her, and it would help to have a guide to their lodgings. She might be in more familiar territory here, but Freyfall's streets were a twisting maze.

"Could you take me to my grandparents' inn? Grandmother said they were staying at The Golden Pheasant on Courtway Avenue." Now that she was no longer in a panic, the names came back to her clearly. "Do you know it?"

He nodded. "Not that I've ever been inside it. They wouldn't let the likes of me in the stable yard, much less the back door."

He led the way through streets that were growing crowded. Talisa recognized some landmarks. Above slanting slate roofs, she saw the elegant stone facade of the upper floor of the palace. How her heart had thudded, approaching the palace last night! How she'd worried. Would she forget the words of her song? Would her mouth go as dry as the brook at home had the summer no rain fell for two months?

Well, she hadn't forgotten her words. Her mouth hadn't gone dry. But the knowledge of that was as flat as a note sung off-key.

They turned a corner. Cory came to an abrupt halt. Talisa glanced at him in surprise, then followed his gaze.

Halfway down the block stood an imposing building, with a smaller, if no less imposing, stable beside it. Above the door, a wooden sign swayed gently in the breeze. It bore a picture of a bird whose feathers gleamed like gold. An impressive number of green-uniformed Freyan soldiers stood in a large, cobblestoned courtyard.

"There you are. The Golden Pheasant."

"Yes. Thank you." She started to walk forward, then stopped and turned around. Cory had remained where he was. "Won't you come with me? My grandparents would be happy to meet you."

He smiled. "And I'd love to meet them. I've never spoken to living legends." He hesitated, then shook his head. "Better not."

"Why not? They'd want to thank you, for my sake."

He glanced at the courtyard. "No. I'd better be on my way. Will I... Will you be here for a while? In Freyfall, I mean?"

"No. I just came for the competition. Now that it's over, I'll be going home." The thought should have made her happy. It didn't.

"Oh." He looked at her blankly.

She gazed back at him just as blankly. "Well... Thank you. For everything. Your hospitality. Your... You saved my life."

He shook his head. "From what Rina and Bart said, things settled down pretty quickly. You probably would have been perfectly safe, staying where you were."

She thought of the anger that had swept through the square like storm clouds rolling in across the mountains, and shivered. "No."

34

He shrugged. "Maybe not. Anyway, I'm glad everything ended well."

"Yes." Where were her words, to thank him as he should be thanked?

"I'll be going then." He stared to turn away.

"Wait!" He did. "I just wanted to say thank you."

He grinned. "You already have. Several times."

"Yes. Well... Thank you again." She fumbled for other words. Finally she said, "I'm glad we met."

His smile faded. He stared at her, his brown eyes solemn. "Me too." His Adam's apple bobbed. "May Freyn smile on you."

"May the mountain spirits guide your steps." It seemed a foolish thing to say, so far from the mountains, but it was the usual Uglessian blessing and all she had to give.

He smiled, nodded, half-raised a hand in farewell, and strode away. She watched his lanky form disappear around the corner, then turned and walked slowly towards the inn.

The Golden Pheasant

A SOLDIER WITH A SWIRLING GINGER MOUSTACHE stopped her in the courtyard. "Your name?"

"Talisa."

He waited, but she said nothing more. She didn't like the way he was eyeing her up and down. Anyway, one name was good enough at home. Did she have to change the way she did everything just because she was in Freya?

"What's your business here?" His voice was a growl. He reminded her of the large mastiff she'd seen guarding a cart in the street two days ago. The dog had bared its teeth as she walked past. She raised her chin.

"To see my grandparents."

He scowled. "And who might they be?"

"Redelle and Alaric." He didn't move aside. She added, reluctantly, "Thatcher."

He still didn't move. "Do you have proof?"

She blinked. "Proof?"

"That they're your grandparents. That you're not here to cause trouble."

What proof could she have? "No."

He grabbed her arm. Not gently. She refused to wince.

"Let her go, Carter," said the soldier standing next to him.

The man holding her didn't let her go or remove his eyes from her face. "Orders are we're to stop everyone trying to enter the inn, especially after last night. How do I know she's who she says she is?"

"Use your eyes. She's Uglessian, isn't she? And the spitting image of the woman upstairs, the one she claims is her granny."

After a moment, the first soldier dropped his hand and stepped aside. She walked forward, not letting herself rub her arm where his fingers had dug into it, not letting herself quicken her pace, even though she sensed his eyes on her back all the way to the door. She felt soiled, not so much by his touch as by his suspicion.

She stopped just inside the hall. It was large and well-lit, but her eyes needed to adjust after the bright afternoon sun. And her nerves needed to relax.

She had no time for that, however. A neatly-dressed, grey-haired man was approaching her. Was he too going to demand proof of her identity? Question her motives?

"Talisa!"

Startled, she whirled around and saw a woman descending the stairs that led to the upper floor.

"Mistress Brooks." Talisa bobbed a quick curtsy. She wanted to laugh. If Cory and his family thought her grandparents were living legends, what would they say about Kerstin Speller – or Brooks, as she'd been known since her marriage almost forty years ago? But she certainly didn't look like a legend, only like a rather tired woman in her late fifties with greying brown hair tied back in an untidy bun, dressed in a plain, serviceable navy dress.

The grey-haired man melted away as Kerstin Brooks came to a halt in front of Talisa.

"Congratulations."

Talisa stared at her.

Kerstin laughed. "Your song. Surely you haven't forgotten already?"

"Oh. No, of course not. It's just that it was rather...overshadowed by what happened later."

"True. The evening did take a rather exciting turn, didn't it, what with insulting songs, disrupting spells, and a cat stopping an attempt on Queen Elira's life. Still, everything worked out well, and the council can go ahead as planned."

Talisa looked at the floor. She knew her song had been eclipsed. All the same, it hurt to have this woman agree with her.

"But what came later doesn't alter the fact that you were chosen to sing and that you sang beautifully."

Talisa flushed. "Thank you."

Kerstin nodded, and tucked an errant lock of hair back behind her ear. "I'd better be on my way. The council is due to start soon. You'll find your grandparents on the second floor, third door on the right. I just left them. Redelle's still spluttering about that hot-tempered young man, Thannis, who reacted so foolishly last night. But she'll get over it when she sees you. If I don't meet you again before you leave, may Freyn and all your mountain spirits guide you on your path home." She left, her mind, Talisa knew, already on the meeting ahead.

Talisa climbed the broad marble stairs slowly. Was she that transparent? Had Kerstin Brooks seen how much it bothered her that her triumph had been overwhelmed by the assassination plot? She pressed her hands against hot cheeks.

The door was opened quickly to her knock. Her grandmother flung her arms around her. "Talisa! Come in, come in. I was getting worried. It's well past midday."

"I'm sorry I'm late," Talisa mumbled.

Her grandfather smiled at her. "Don't apologize. We're all late after the events of yesterday. We were just concerned that we might not have time for a proper visit before we had to leave for the council. But there's plenty of time. Sit down."

He waved towards a rose-coloured, comfortably cushioned chair. Talisa looked at it, then around the spacious, richly furnished room, so different from everything she was used to. She perched on the wooden window seat.

Redelle sat on one of the two high-backed chairs facing her granddaughter. Its arms were ornately carved. Talisa wondered what Cory would think of the work.

"We were so proud of you last night, Talisa," Redelle said. She might have been spluttering a few minutes earlier, but now her grey eyes were alight, her face glowing.

People were wrong, Talisa thought. All her life, they had told her she looked just like her grandmother. She didn't believe them. Oh, they shared the same height and build, the same red hair – Redelle was only now beginning to show a few strands of grey – the same arched eyebrows and fine features. But there was something more in her grandmother that shone through and made Talisa catch her breath whenever she saw her. She would never have that, she knew, just as she knew she would never possess her grandmother's poise and confidence, no matter how old she got.

"We *are* proud of you," Alaric corrected softly. "Very proud."

"Yes," Redelle agreed. "Your song touched me deeply. And your voice... I have never heard you sing so well."

The sun coming in through the paned glass warmed Talisa's back. But it was nothing compared to the warmth that spread inside her. She felt like a child, safe and at peace in the shelter of their love and pride.

"I'm glad you liked it," she murmured.

"We did," Alaric said. "Very much. And to think you were one of only five who were chosen." He shook his head in wonder.

This was what she had wanted. She should be content. She should let it rest there. But something made her prick, made her prod.

"My song seems so unimportant, compared to what came afterwards."

"Nonsense," Redelle said, but Talisa could almost see her mind flicker to those events. "Your song was – your singing *is* – very important. And the plot failed, thanks be to all the spirits that are and ever were and ever will be."

And if it hadn't failed, nothing else would have mattered. Talisa knew that. It shouldn't bother her. The friendship between Freya and Uglessia should be as important to her as it was to her grandparents and all the rest of her family. It *was* important to her. She forced herself to ask, "What exactly did happen? There's a lot that I don't understand."

Alaric leaned on the back of his wife's chair. "That's not surprising. Things were just a mite confusing last night." He grinned, then sobered. "You know, of course, that the musician Bellmore sang a song that was not quite – flattering, shall I say? – to Uglessians."

Talisa nodded, remembering her shock and outrage as the singer's words turned from honey to venom. "But I don't understand why none of us could understand his words the first time he sang them."

Redelle laughed. "It was the boy. Konrad's grandson."

"Garth Spellman," Alaric explained. "One of your fellow musicians. He cast a disruption spell that made the words incomprehensible to everyone but the singer himself."

"Oh." Talisa digested this. She shouldn't be surprised. She had known that the thin-faced, dark-eyed boy was involved somehow. After all, it was the cat that accompanied him everywhere that had sprung at the captain. And Garth had told her he was an apprentice wizard. But she had thought he hated magic, that all his love was given to music.

She missed what her grandmother said and had to ask her to repeat it.

"The disruption spell worked at first. But when the conspirators insisted that Bellmore repeat the last verse, Garth didn't have time to renew it. But at least that forced those in the plot, including the queen's cousin, into the open. We knew about the plot –"

"You did?" Talisa stared at her.

"Yes. Konrad had warned us. The conspirators thought he hated Uglessians enough to be sympathetic to their cause."

Talisa thought about this for a minute. Vague memories of stories she'd heard as a child came back to her. "Is Konrad Spellman the one who almost caused your death when you were both students at the College of Wizards?"

Her grandmother nodded. "Yes. But he's changed since then. Luckily for everyone, the conspirators didn't know that."

"Is that why Garth cast this spell then? Because his grandfather asked him to?"

"No," Alaric said. "Garth found out about the plot and about his grandfather's involvement in it. Since he didn't know Konrad wasn't *really* in it, he decided to stop the plot by himself rather than go to the magistrates with news that might endanger his grandfather. He thought a disruption spell was the best solution, not realizing that we'd been warned."

"A warning that did little good, thanks to that fool Thannis," Redelle said tartly.

Her husband placed a hand on her shoulder. "Now, Redelle..."

"I know, I know. He thought, as we all did, that the assassin would kill Bellmore, not the queen. He didn't realize that to attack someone in the group around Queen Elira was to play into the conspirators' hands. But to lose his temper after he'd been warned... If he weren't such a promising wizard, I'd send him home right now."

Talisa thought of big, bumbling Thannis, with his burning eagerness to learn more magic, and winced. "He'd feel as though he'd lost..." His best friend, she'd been going to say, but that wasn't quite right. "He'd lose his dream."

Redelle sighed. "I know. Don't worry. I'll let him stay. But I *will* have a talk with him later."

Talisa winced again. Her grandmother was one of the kindest people she knew, but she'd hate to be on the wrong side of her tongue when she was roused.

"We were worried enough when we thought the plan was to kill the musician and blame it on angry Uglessians," Alaric said. "But to kill Queen Elira with one of our knives..." He shivered.

"It would have meant war," Redelle said grimly. "And they might have succeeded if it hadn't been for Cat."

"Cat? Do you mean Garth's cat, the one that sprang at the captain?" Talisa leaned forward. "That's one of the things that puzzles me most. Why did it do that? Was that a spell too?"

Her grandfather laughed. "Yes indeed, though not the kind you're thinking of. You see," he paused dramatically, "Cat is not a cat. She's a girl."

"What?" Talisa stared at him, mouth agape.

He laughed again. "We were just as surprised when we found out. Her name is Catrina Ashdale. She came to Freyfall to look for her father, whom she hadn't seen for twelve years, and went to Konrad for a finding spell. But Konrad wasn't there, only his apprentice. Garth got the spell just a little wrong."

Talisa shook her head. "He told me he wanted to be a musician, not a wizard. But to turn a girl into a cat... How could he do that, even if he's a terrible wizard?"

"Oh, he couldn't have if he were a terrible wizard. Only a very powerful magician could change a person into a cat, then transform her back into a person, which he did last night with a little help from the rest of us."

"The sad thing is that he isn't going to use his talent," Redelle said. "Last night Konrad agreed, with a better grace than I would have expected, that his grandson could become an apprentice musician. What a waste!"

Talisa turned her head towards the window, not wanting them to see her face. Vaguely, she heard her grandmother say something about Catrina's father: Bellmore...a pardon...sick wife...money...Raven, the Islandian Healer. But the words were a blur, as was the view from the window of the top of soldiers' heads and the street beyond.

So Garth Spellman, who had the ability to become a powerful wizard, who already *was* a powerful wizard, had turned his back on magic.

And she, who would do anything, give anything, to be able to use spells to help her land, as her family had done for generations, had not the smallest, not the *tiniest,* drop of magic in her.

Garth had asked her, as they sat waiting for their names to be called in the competition, if her grandparents minded that she was a musician, not a wizard. She had said no. It was true. They didn't mind. Her father didn't mind. After all, her cousins could use spells. Her sister Welwyn viewed magic the same way she viewed climbing the mountain behind their hut. You had to work hard at it if you wanted to reach the peak, but it was the natural thing to do, the *inevitable* thing to do, if you had legs to climb with.

They said they were proud of her gift of song. They asked nothing more of her. Expected nothing more of her. But her grandmother's words made it very clear that wizards were more valuable – much more valuable – than musicians.

She realized that her grandfather had asked a question. "I'm sorry," she said, face still averted. "Could you repeat that?"

"Will you stay here with us for the duration of the council? We hope you don't want to go home immediately without us."

She had insisted, against all arguments, on coming here alone. She had intended to go home as soon as the contest – and, hopefully, her performance – were over. Now...

Now the thought of going home filled her with dread. She would tell her father and sister what had happened. They would smile and hug her and tell her how proud they were. Then they would return to their work, their important work. She could picture them, their heads bent over their few, precious books, her father's capped with red, like her own, Welwyn's a net of pale gold. They would try to include her, as they always had, would tell her what they were reading, what they were working on, as simply and clearly as they could. And she would nod and smile and understand nothing. Then she would go outside where she could sing to the mountains, and know that she had sung before the Freyan queen – and that her singing meant nothing.

Her throat hurt, her eyes were hot with unshed tears.

"Well?" Alaric asked. "Do you want to stay here or return home immediately?"

A man left the inn. She couldn't see who he was. But then, she couldn't see anything clearly. The green of the soldiers' uniforms and the grey of the cobblestones blurred together.

"I don't ever want to go home," she heard herself say. "I want to stay here."

APPRENTICE

ER WORDS ECHOED IN THE ROOM. IN HER mind. Redelle started to say something, then stopped. The silence deepened.

"Talisa," Alaric said. He cleared his throat. "Did you mean what you just said?"

She stared out the window.

"Talisa?"

"I...I don't... Yes."

"But why...?" Redelle's voice trailed off, lost, like a frail flower choked by weeds. Talisa couldn't look at her.

"Why?" her grandmother had asked. What could she say? That she didn't belong at home? That she wasn't needed there? They would protest that she was wanted. That she was loved. She knew that. It didn't matter, any more than her longing for her mountains, for her family, mattered.

"Child..." Alaric took a deep breath. "Talisa, look at us."

Reluctantly, she turned her head.

They were staring at her with shocked eyes. Redelle's skin, always pale, had taken on the bluish tinge milk has when cream is skimmed from it. New lines dug into her face. She looked old. Talisa had never seen her look old before. Alaric was sitting now, his green eyes strained, his eyebrows drawn in a frown. A worried frown, not an angry one. She would have preferred anger.

"Talisa," he said, as though he were dragging each word through thick mud, "do you really mean that you never want to return home again? That you never want to see your father, your sister, any of us, ever again?"

She closed her eyes tightly, heard her father's quiet voice, whispered secrets shared with Welwyn late at night when they were supposed to be asleep, her cousins' teasing laughter as they raced her up the mountain paths.

Other memories: leading ursells to pasture high up on the slopes, watching peak after grey-purple peak change colour as they reflected the glory of the setting sun, returning home to be greeted by Welwyn's and her father's welcoming smiles.

"No! No, I do want to go home. I do want to see everyone again. It's just..."

"Just what? What do you want?"

What did she want? She wanted to be like her father, her sister, her cousins, her aunt, her uncle, her grandparents. She wanted to be able to use magic to help Uglessia. To be needed. Only that. Only the impossible.

She had to say something. They were watching her intently.

48

Should she say she hadn't meant what she had said?

But she *had* meant it. She didn't want to go home. At least not yet. Not until she could feel needed, or until she could accept the fact that she never would be needed.

"I want to study music." She didn't. Not really. But she had to say *something*.

"Study music?" Redelle echoed.

She nodded.

"You don't have to study it," her grandmother protested. "Songs come as naturally to you as to a skylark. You've never studied it in your life, but you were picked as one of the finest musicians in three lands."

Alaric's frown had returned, but this time it was a thoughtful one. "Talisa's right, Redelle. She has a gift. It should be nurtured and developed."

"But –"

"I remember how empty I felt, when I wanted to be a wizard and thought there was no hope for me, not until the Spellers found a runaway apprentice in their stable loft and took him in."

The heaviness had left his voice now that he thought he understood his granddaughter's motives. Talisa could almost see him thinking, the way he did when puzzling over a problem he knew could be solved by the right spell.

"We could have you – not apprenticed exactly, that's too long a process and I hope you'll want to return to us before seven years have passed – but you could study with a master musician, perhaps the same one Garth Spellman is being apprenticed to. I'll speak to Konrad."

Talisa inspected her hands. She didn't want to be with Garth Spellman – Garth, who could be a wizard and chose not to. But she couldn't explain that, not without revealing too much.

"But where would she live?" Redelle demanded.

"With the musician, if he has a good wife and home. It's the usual way with apprentices. I'm sure arrangements can be made, even if Talisa isn't *really* an apprentice. Don't worry, Redelle."

"Easy enough to say." Redelle rubbed a hand across her face, then smiled at her granddaughter. "I can't say I'm happy about this, Talisa. I'll miss you. We'll all miss you. But I'll try to be glad for your sake if it's what you really want."

Talisa returned her smile and said nothing.

FIVE DAYS LATER, she went to see Master and Mistress Coyne. Redelle was at the wizards' meeting, but Alaric had insisted on accompanying Talisa, despite her protests.

The musician and his wife lived on Gleeman Street, not far from the Musicians' Guild Hall where the competition had been held. It was a quiet road, lined with two- and three-storey wooden houses. Talisa noted with pleasure that it contained some traces of green: two yew trees, a few bushes, and a tall hedge across the street from the Coynes' home.

The door was opened by a small, birdlike woman.

"Mistress Coyne?" Alaric asked.

"Yes. And you must be Master Thatcher." The woman surveyed him with bright, interested black eyes.

"Yes. This is my granddaughter, Talisa."

The woman's attention shifted to the girl. She studied her for a minute, then said, "You'll be wanting to see my husband. Come this way."

They followed her down a short hall to a room at the far end. It was large, airy, and filled with sunlight and musical instruments. Talisa recognized some of them, though she'd never played them: a lute, a harp, a flute, some pipes, a horn. But there were others she couldn't even begin to guess at. She gazed around the room and said, more to herself than to anyone who might be listening, "Surely no one could play all of these."

A deep, rumbling laugh answered her. "Not all at once," said a bass voice with a chuckle in it.

Talisa blushed and turned to face the speaker, a man who sat in a wine-coloured chair by the window. He was as comfortably cushioned as the chair, and as tall as his wife was short, with a round belly and a cherubic face topped by a balding head. Spectacles perched halfway down a bulging nose.

She bobbed a curtsy. "I'm sorry, sir."

He chuckled and waved a benign hand. "No need to be, I assure you. Honest awe never hurt my feelings." He laughed again. "Please have a seat, both of you."

She sat on a chair opposite him. Her eyes shifted to the window. A rose bush heavy with yellow blossoms stood just outside. Beyond it, she could see more flowers and a small patch of green, the first real garden she'd noticed in this city of wood and stone.

"So, Mistress Thatcher, I understand you want to learn more about music."

She returned her attention to the musician. "Yes, sir."

"A fine voice you have, I know, a very fine voice. Have you had any training?"

"No, sir."

He raised his eyebrows. "None at all?"

"Not really, though I've always been surrounded by songs." She thought of her mother, singing her to sleep.

"A great many Uglessians sing, and sing well," Alaric said.

Master Coyne nodded. "What about musical instruments? Do you play any?"

She shook her head.

"Can you read music?"

"No."

He sighed. "We'll have to start at the beginning. Would you like to play an instrument, as well as sing?"

"I... Yes."

"Which one?"

Her eyes roved around the instrument-filled room. "All of them."

He laughed. "In that case, you'll be here much longer than the usual apprentice."

"As for that," Alaric interjected, "we were hoping for a much shorter time. Perhaps some lessons instead of the usual apprenticeship."

"Well..." The musician rubbed his chin. "I don't know. I've never had a student before except as an apprentice, with all the duties and responsibilities involved on both sides. Just a student... I don't know. I'd have to charge."

"How much?"

"No!" Talisa cried. "You can't pay for my music lessons, Grandfather." They didn't have the money for such luxuries, none of them. How could they, since the only coins they had were the small sums Freyans paid them for the kala roots that grew on the mountainsides?

"But, Talisa –"

"No!"

Master Coyne had been studying their faces. "I tell you what. How about an apprenticeship of two years, to be extended at the end of that time if both parties agree? It's not normal, mind, but I don't see what's to stop us. Then all the usual rules will apply, and no coins need change hands. What do you say?"

Alaric hesitated. "You're sure it's all right with you?"

"It's fine with me."

"Talisa? What do you think?"

Two years. She'd be eighteen before she saw her home or family again. But this was what she had wanted. Wasn't it?

"Yes." She cleared her throat. "Yes," she said again, more loudly. "Thank you. It's very kind of you."

"I'll have a clerk draw up the contract tomorrow. I presume Talisa will want to live with us? We have two apprentices staying here already, but there's a spare bedchamber since I understand the Spellman boy will be living at home."

Mistress Coyne stirred. "I'm not sure that's a good idea, William." It was the first time she'd spoken since they'd entered the room. Talisa had forgotten she was there.

Master Coyne looked at her, eyebrows raised. "Why not?"

"Use your eyes, William. You may only care about her voice, but Lem and Shep won't. Nothing against you," she said, nodding towards Talisa. "But facts are facts and boys are boys, especially where a pretty girl is concerned."

"They may have trouble concentrating," her husband agreed. He laughed. "On the other hand, it might have good results. They may compete to show who can play better and impress my new apprentice the most. Don't worry, Lizbet. We'll manage."

Talisa didn't think Mistress Coyne looked convinced, but she said nothing more.

Master Coyne turned back to Talisa. "That's settled then. When would you like to move in?"

"Tomorrow." Before doubts had time to overwhelm her.

He blinked in surprise but nodded. "Very well. We'll expect you then. And if your grandfather comes with you, he can sign the apprenticeship agreement." He rose.

Talisa did too. Her knees wobbled.

She had committed herself for two years to this man, this house, this life. Not because she wanted to, but because she couldn't think of anything she wanted more. Except one thing, of course.

Her eyes moved around the room. Could she learn to play any of these instruments?

Well, if not, she'd still have her voice.

Her gaze flickered to the window and the garden and rose bush beyond. They should make life here more bearable.

And... She caught her breath. Surely, during her two-year stay in Freyfall, she would meet Cory again.

LIFE ON GLEEMAN STREET

TALISA STIRRED BUT DIDN'T OPEN HER EYES. The house was quiet. It must be early still. She had a few minutes before she'd have to swing her legs out from under the covers and set her feet on the cold floor.

She'd been here four months now. It was hard to believe.

Or maybe not so hard. She'd fallen into the rhythm of the Coyne household and been absorbed by it. First, there were household chores, followed by lessons and hours of practice and copying music, then more chores. It was no wonder she fell asleep each night too tired even to think about the day's activities. Now at least she had a little time to reflect on her life here. She pulled her blankets higher. The autumn air was chilly.

She certainly didn't *dislike* life here. She was used to hard work, and helping around the house didn't bother her, though she wished she could do more in the small garden. Lem and Shep tended to claim those tasks. "Women's work," they grumbled when asked to do indoor chores, though never loudly enough for Mistress Coyne to hear. As for her lessons... True, singing scales over and over again was monotonous, but she trusted Master Coyne when he told her they would add strength and range to her voice.

She should be practising her scales now, before she had to help with breakfast preparations. She stirred again, then huddled deeper into her blankets.

She was learning so much. She'd been proud at how quickly she'd mastered the skill of reading music, though that meant that now she, along with Master Coyne's other apprentices, had to spend hours copying sheets of notes. Her first fumble-fingered attempts to pluck the lute had been embarrassing, but that was months ago. Now she could actually play simple tunes on it, and was even beginning to learn – a little – how to play the harp.

How could she dislike a household where music shaped their lives? Even Mistress Glover, who came twice a week to scrub sheets and floors, hummed as she worked. And always, in late afternoon, Master Coyne would set aside whatever else he was doing and play one of his many instruments as though he and it were one.

No. Life here wasn't bad.

But she was far too busy to do anything else. To explore Freyfall. To... Well, to see Cory.

Talisa sighed. Even if she had the time, she had no idea how to find her way to the street where he lived.

Garth. She could ask him. She opened her eyes at the sudden thought.

Funny. She'd been so resentful of Garth, who could have been a wizard if he'd wanted. She winced, remembering how hurt he'd looked when she greeted him politely but coldly on their first meeting as fellow apprentices. But that had soon changed. Garth was the only one she could really *talk* to. Oh, Master Coyne talked to her a lot, mostly about music. Mistress Coyne gave instructions about her daily tasks. But Lem and Shep... Talisa groaned. If they spoke to her at all, it was only with stammers and blushes.

"Lovesick," Mistress Coyne said.

Not really lovesick, Talisa thought. Eyestruck, as they called it at home. She'd had to turn to Garth if she wanted to be with someone who didn't turn into a red-faced idiot any time she addressed him. Not that Garth wasn't capable of blushing. Talisa smiled, remembering.

Yesterday afternoon, the four apprentices had been copying music at the large pine table. Talisa had paused to flex her fingers, and noticed that Garth had shoved the sheets aside and was scribbling furiously on a blank piece of paper.

"Are you composing a new song?"

He'd glanced up guiltily and nodded.

"Will you send it to Cat when you write her next?" A while back, he'd told her shyly that he often wrote to Catrina Ashdale, who'd returned to her home on a farm near the village of Frey-under-Hill.

He'd nodded again.

The other apprentices had raised their heads. Shep nudged Lem. "Garth's rather fond of felines, isn't he?"

Lem laughed. Garth had turned the colour of ripe tomatoes.

Yes, she might ask Garth if he knew where... What was the name of the street Cory had mentioned on their way to his home? Barrow. That was it. Barrow Road. Garth always did his best to answer her questions about Freya, though if it were up to him, all his talk would be devoted to music. That he could speak about endlessly, his dark eyes bright, his thin face alive with excitement. At first, Talisa had listened to him, to all of them, with amazement. At home, music wasn't something to be studied and discussed. It was simply there, like the air she breathed. But as she learned more and fell into the pattern of life in the Coynes' household, it began to fill her thoughts and words too.

Why, then, did new songs not come to her? They always had before. When tending ursells, or weeding the usit field, or walking on the mountain, or looking up to see Welwyn's hair shining like spun gold in the light from the hearth, tunes and words had sprouted in her heart and sprung to her lips. Now, they didn't. Now there seemed to be a hollowness inside her that would not allow songs to take root and grow.

She had not realized, even as she'd said farewell to her grandparents, how homesick she would be. They had left at the end of the council, taking Merisha with them. She had tried to tell herself she was glad that her beloved ursell was going home to the mountains. But she missed her so much – her small triangular face, her pointed ears, her habit of nudging Talisa to get her attention. But then, she missed everything. She missed the mountains. She missed her family.

Her grandparents had been pleased with the results of the council. "Once Queen Elira departed for Freybourg and all the conspirators were caught, including one of the royal musicians, the flurry over the plot died down and we were able to get on with talking and making some important decisions," Redelle had said. "New trust has been established and new plans formed. Two of our young people, Thannis and Branwen, will go to the College of Wizards in Freybourg, as will two Islandians. The Freyans are happy about that. They've been wanting to learn more about Islandian magic for years. Now Raven, the Healer, will be at their College to teach them. I wish I could study under him." She looked wistful. Then she shook her head. "Branwen and Thannis can learn from him, and Griffin and Morag will go to the Islands to learn other magic, as will the two Freyans who are also going there. Best of all, from our point of view, two Freyan wizards are coming back to Uglessia with us."

"Surely they can't teach you anything," Talisa protested. "You're both great wizards."

Alaric shook his head. "You can always learn from others. And we're so isolated and have so few books in Uglessia. The knowledge and ideas they'll share with us will be a great help."

They'd ridden away with Merisha, the two Freyans, and high hopes. And she'd been left here alone. It was, after all, what she'd asked for.

That was the last she'd heard from them, though a box of winter clothes had arrived from her father a month ago.

The box had contained a short letter from him and one bubbling with news from Welwyn. Both had ended the same way. They missed her. They wished her well. They loved her.

Below, she heard the rattle of pans in the kitchen. She sighed and threw her blankets aside. Time to get up.

"I was wrong about you," Mistress Coyne said.

Startled, Talisa glanced up from the bread dough she was kneading.

"I thought William shouldn't take you as his apprentice, but he was right. He usually is, when it comes to apprentices."

Should she say something? What? Carefully, Talisa removed pieces of dough from her fingers. The spicy, grainy usit cakes they ate at home couldn't compete with the smell and taste of fresh-baked bread. She even enjoyed the effort involved in kneading. But she wished the dough didn't stick so.

"I thought the boys would lose their heads over you, and so they have, the silly lads. But you handle them well. You're polite but give them no encouragement. I'm tired of their heavy sighs, mind, but they'll get over it. And there's no fighting between them, which is what worried me most. They know there's no point, poor things." She smiled. "No, William was right. You're a great help about the house, too, and pleasant company. I must admit, I was a mite troubled at first, you being Uglessian and all. Not that I've got anything against Uglessians. Still, having one in the house... But

I was wrong there too. It's almost like having a daughter around."

She stopped, staring down at her flour-coated hands. Talisa resumed kneading, but kept her eyes on the woman, who stood in a patch of early morning sunshine. Her grey hair was bound in its usual braid, her small frame wrapped in the white apron she always wore when working in the kitchen.

Talisa cleared her throat. "Do you have any daughters?"

Mistress Coyne shook her head. "I was never able to have children. Not that it's mattered much. We've had enough apprentices, over the years, to fill the house. But they've always been boys, or great louts of young men, never girls."

She sighed and plunged her hands back in her mound of dough. "And you? Do you have any brothers or sisters?"

"One sister, two years older than me."

"Does she look like you, your sister?"

"No. I take after Father and Grandmother, but Welwyn looks more like Mother."

"She must miss you, your mother."

"She's dead."

"I'm sorry."

"It happened a long time ago, almost twelve years now. She died trying to have another baby." It happened a lot, in Uglessia.

"I'm sorry," Mistress Coyne said again.

"It's all right."

They worked on in silence.

"Did you inherit your voice from your mother?"

Talisa looked up. "I never... I don't know. Perhaps. I know she used to sing. I remember her singing to me."

"You have a beautiful voice. William says you have great talent for music, and not just for singing either. A true ear, he says you have, and a fine touch on the lute."

He had never told *her* that. Talisa felt her lips curve in a broad smile.

"It's no wonder you were chosen to sing at the opening of the council."

"Why didn't Master Coyne enter the contest?" It was a question that had niggled at the back of Talisa's mind for some time.

"He did."

"He did? But... Why wasn't he chosen? I'm sorry," Talisa stammered. "Maybe I shouldn't ask. But he has such a rich voice, and he plays as I could never even dream of doing. As most musicians couldn't dream of."

"You made up the song you performed, didn't you?"

"Yes, of course."

Mistress Grove sighed. "The contest rules said that musicians must perform songs they had composed themselves. William has a great gift for singing and playing. And he knows everything there is to know about the patterns of music and how songs should be put together. But his melodies never soar, and as for his words..." She shook her head. "It is the greatest sorrow of his life that he, who loves music so, cannot make it. Not as it should be made."

"Oh." Talisa stared down at the dough. Until a few months ago, she would not have known what that felt like.

Tunes and words had always come unbidden into her mind, sometimes in fragments, sometimes as whole songs. Not now. Would she be like Master Coyne one day, knowledgeable, skilled, but unable to create?

"Here, that dough's ready to go in the pan. No sense in pummelling it to death." Briskly, Mistress Coyne shaped the dough into loaves and set them to rise. "Time for your lesson."

It was. She could hear voices in the music room, and the rippling of harp strings. Master Coyne had been out late last night, performing for a banquet at the Stonemasons' Guild Hall. He was much in demand at feasts for lords, wealthy merchants, and guilds. But no matter how late his return, lessons in the morning were never delayed by so much as a minute. Talisa headed for the kitchen door.

She stopped, hesitated, then came back and hugged Mistress Coyne. "Thank you."

The woman looked startled. "For what?"

"For...everything." For accepting me, Talisa thought. For sharing your sorrows with me. For giving me hope.

All her life, she had felt inadequate because she had no gift for magic. She had never wondered how others coped with their lack of ability. Yet here was Mistress Coyne, unable to have the children she wanted. Here was Master Coyne, unable to compose the music he loved. Despite that, they seemed happy enough. Maybe one day...

Maybe. But she wasn't ready to go home. Not yet.

SINGER WITHOUT SHOES

THE LUTE WAS OUT OF TUNE, THE SINGING slightly off-key. But there was a sweetness in the voice that caught Talisa's attention and drew her, the way the sound of running water drew ursells. She picked her way through the throng of shoppers on Weavers Street to find the source of the music.

The singer was in her early middle years, dressed in a patched brown dress that looked as though the wind blew through it at will. She stood on the corner, singing and accompanying herself on a lute that needed restringing. A scattering of copper coins lay on the cobblestones at her feet.

Her feet were bare.

Talisa drew in her breath. It was too cold for bare feet. This far into autumn, the frost that touched the ground at night lingered well into mid-morning. And though the sun shone brightly, it gave little warmth.

The woman finished one song and started another. A man beside Talisa tossed a few copper coins on the ground and left. Talisa reached into her pocket.

Three silver coins. The money Mistress Coyne had given her to pick up the cloak she had commissioned for her husband. Nothing else.

A cool breeze puffed past. Talisa shivered and pulled her cloak tighter. She glanced at the singer again. Her forearms were bare and covered with goosebumps.

She had some money in her room. Her grandparents had left it with her, not wanting her to be totally dependent on the Coynes. If she gave this woman the three silver coins in her pocket, then hurried back to Gleeman Street, could she be back in time to buy Master Coyne's cloak?

She looked up. The sun was halfway down the western sky. It was a good mile and a half to the Coynes', through crowded streets. By the time she returned, the shop would be closed.

The singer looked so cold. And so thin. Her eyes seemed very large, and very dark, against the pallor of her face. Her skin was so taut that it looked as though it might crack at any moment, letting the prominent bones break through.

Talisa bit her lip.

If she gave the woman the coins now, she could come back tomorrow for the cloak. It wasn't as though Master Coyne *needed* his new cloak today. True, he wanted to wear it to the Musicians' Guild Hall tonight. But his old one would do. It was warm enough. She reached into her pocket again.

But Mistress Coyne had entrusted her with the money. This was the first such errand she had sent Talisa on. To break that faith...

Talisa's shoulders slumped. She removed her hand and started to turn away. The woman's eyes rested on her a moment before they moved on. The eyes weren't angry. They weren't pleading. They asked for nothing, expected nothing. They were just...sad.

This woman needed the money far, far more than Master Coyne needed to impress his fellow musicians at the Guild Hall. Without giving herself time to think further, Talisa drew out the coins and tossed them onto the cobblestones by the singer's bare, dirty feet, then hurried away. Was it her imagination, or was there a catch in the woman's voice, a new joy in her song? .

It was going to be hard to tell the Coynes she didn't have the cloak.

"It's almost like having a daughter around," Mistress Coyne had said.

Talisa stopped.

Perhaps the owner of The Silver Thread would let her take the cloak tonight if she promised to bring the payment tomorrow. She walked along slowly, hunting for the sign of a needle and silver thread.

She saw something else first. Or, rather, someone. Bart Berrymore. He was standing beside a stall, calling out the virtues of his wares. It was hard to distinguish his words from those of all the other stall owners crowded along Weavers Street.

"Shawls! Skirts! Shirts! Not only warm, but beautiful as well. Step up for the finest clothes in all Freyfall, for the lowest prices. Bargains all. Step up!"

His eyes roved the crowd, searching for likely customers. They swept past Talisa, then returned to her face and stopped. She smiled and edged her way over to his stall.

"Well met, Master Berrymore."

"Bart," he corrected. "I didn't expect to see you again. Cory said you were returning to Uglessia."

"I was, but then I decided to stay here and study music."

He raised his eyebrows. "I wouldn't have thought you'd have much to learn. Not someone who wins a coveted competition."

"Oh, but I have. I didn't know how much I didn't know until I started studying under Master Coyne. I'm his apprentice, at least for the next two years."

"Are you enjoying it?"

She hesitated for a moment, considering. "Yes. Yes, I am."

He smiled. "Good." His attention swerved to a woman fingering a blouse on the counter. "Beautiful blouse, isn't it, Mistress? A work of art, I call it."

She eyed him suspiciously. "How much are you charging?"

Talisa waited for Bart to finish with his customer, only half listening to the bargaining. Was Cory around? Her own eyes roved the crowd, without success. Then she spotted a small wooden carving standing among the brightly woven clothes. She picked it up.

The woman carved out of dark wood was old, not middle-aged. Her shoulders were bent, her face deeply lined. Her hand was held out in a begging gesture, not plucking a lute. But it was the street singer all over again: the same thin face, the same bare feet, the same eyes.

"Do you like it?"

Startled, Talisa glanced up. Bart's customer was gone and he was pocketing some coins.

"Yes. Did Cory make it?"

"Mmmm. One of the few he's carved lately. It's sat here for a month now. No one wants it." His voice was flat.

"But why? It's beautiful." That was the wrong word. "Moving."

Bart eyed it. "Maybe. But not very happy, is it?"

"Well, no. But –"

"People want things that make them feel good. Puppies, small children, beautiful women, cuddly lambs. Not beggar women."

Her hands curled protectively around the carving.

"Do you want to buy it?"

She shook her head. "I'd love to, but I don't have the money."

He nodded, as though expecting her answer. His eyes left her and searched the passersby again.

"How is Cory? And Rina?"

"Fine," he said shortly. His attention was on a man who had stopped to examine a blue shirt embroidered with stars.

"Please tell him – them – that I asked after them."

His eyes returned briefly to her. "I will." He smiled. "Freyn be with you."

"Thank you." She lingered for a moment, but he had no more time to spare her. Slowly, she walked on.

Weavers Street was lined with fine shops and cluttered with stalls. It seemed to Talisa that anything and everything that anyone could possibly want to buy was on display here – not only the clothes and blankets that had given the street its name, but fruit, vegetables, cheese, meat, pots, saddles, harness, knives, dolls, wooden toys. When she'd first arrived in Freyfall, she had stared, goggle-eyed, at the wealth of goods available here, some of which she couldn't even name. Now she was more accustomed to the abundance, though still awed. But *none of these things are as fine as Rina's weavings or Cory's carvings,* Talisa thought.

The shop with a sign of a needle and silver thread glowed with new paint and freshly scrubbed windows. Talisa hesitated in front of it, then took a deep breath and entered. A short man with narrow shoulders and well-tailored garments hurried up to her.

"May I help you?"

"I'm here to pick up a cloak for Master Coyne."

He beamed. "Ready it is, and a fine cloak if I say so myself. Made of the softest wool, and with a warm lining too."

Talisa swallowed. "I'm afraid I don't have any money with me. Can I take the cloak now and return tomorrow to pay you?"

His smile disappeared. "Take the cloak now? Just when would I see my pay? What kind of fool do you take me for?"

"But I promise I'll bring it tomorrow. Mistress Coyne gave me the coins today. It's just –"

He was eyeing her up and down. Sewers at the back of the store had raised their heads and were watching avidly. "Just that you spent your mistress's money on the way here. It's an old story." His eyes stopped on her hands, then leaped back to her face. "Get out of here!"

Talisa felt colour flame through her face. She turned, blinking hard to stop her tears.

"Tell your mistress to send someone else next time," the shop owner called after her. "Someone trustworthy. And not a Uglessian."

She stumbled back down Weavers Street. Several times, she almost bumped into someone. Her eyes kept blurring. But she wouldn't cry. Not here. She ached, how she ached, to be alone. To be home, where only the wind and mountains would witness her tears.

She hated this city, where the only thing anyone cared about was money, where a woman could stand barefooted on cold cobblestones, and six-fingered hands were greeted with suspicion and rage. She *hated* it.

Her feet dragged, slower and slower, the closer she got to Gleeman Street. The sun was just a red glow on the horizon by the time she reached the Coynes'. Talisa stopped and breathed deeply, the way she would before beginning a song, then turned the knob.

The sound of a harp came from the music room. She walked to the door and slipped inside. They were all there, watching Master Coyne's hands move, precisely and lovingly, over the strings of his harp. Not a head turned. Shep and Lem might believe they were in love with her, Talisa thought, but they were far more passionately involved with music.

As the rippling notes died away, the listeners stirred like sleepers waking from a dream. Mistress Coyne turned and smiled.

"You're back then. Good. Let me see the cloak."

Talisa cleared her throat. "I don't have it."

"You don't?" Mistress Coyne frowned. "It wasn't ready? I'll have to give them a piece of my mind. They solemnly promised it would be done by today."

Talisa wished – *how* she wished – she could leave things there. She cleared her throat again. "It was ready. They wouldn't give it to me."

"What?" Mistress Coyne stared at her. They all did. Even Master Coyne had stopped in his work of putting away his harp.

"Why ever not?" he asked.

She wanted to close her eyes. She didn't. "I...I didn't have money to pay for it."

"But I gave you the three silver coins they demanded." Mistress Coyne sounded bewildered.

"Yes." She was doing this badly, so badly. She wet her lips. "I saw a woman singing on a corner. She had no shoes. I gave her the coins."

The silence that followed hurt. She rushed to explain. "I have money. Grandmother and Grandfather left me some. I'll go tomorrow and buy the cloak." She thought of returning to the shop and gulped. "I'm sorry I used your money. I'm sorry I don't have the cloak. But she looked so cold. So hungry."

"Probably left her shoes at home to make people feel sorry for her," Shep said. Talisa looked at his large, well-fed body and his face, rosy with health, and wondered if he'd ever been cold or hungry in his life.

"Talisa didn't know," Lem said. He smiled kindly at her. "When you've been here longer, you'll learn that you don't give away silver coins to every whining beggar you meet in the streets."

If he'd been closer, Talisa would have been tempted to kick him.

"You certainly don't give away other people's silver coins," Mistress Coyne said. Talisa looked at her face, then away. It was so hard not to cry.

"I'm sorry. If I'd had my own money with me... I'm sorry. I promise I'll go back tomorrow and buy the cloak."

"William was to wear it tonight. What impression will he make dressed in the cloak he's worn for the last five years, and it faded and smudged with that wine stain I couldn't get out, no matter how much I scrubbed?"

Bruised by the hurt in her voice, Talisa couldn't answer for a moment. Then an image of the barefoot woman revived her.

"At least he'll be warm. The singer only had a thin dress to protect her from the wind and cold. Her arms were covered in goosebumps."

Shep shook his head. "Another trick. You'll learn, Talisa. These street people will do anything to win sympathy and get money."

"No," Garth said. "Cat lived on the streets when she first arrived in Freyfall. She had to sing on corners, like this

72

woman, just to earn enough to buy a crust or two. It's no trick. There are many people in need out there."

"Still, to give away three silver coins..." Lem clucked his tongue. "It's too much. It was very generous of you, Talisa, but you really can't give people like that so much money."

Talisa glared at him. "Too much? Too much to give a cold, hungry woman who is forced to sing on the street in hopes that strangers will toss her a few copper coins, the way they toss scraps to stray cats? Have you no hearts? In Uglessia, we have little, very little, but if we saw someone standing on the cold ground with no shoes, going without food to put in her empty belly, we would share the little we have." She was shaking. She hadn't known she could be so angry. Her family had always said she'd inherited her grandmother's looks but not her temper. They'd be surprised if they saw her now.

Lem stared at her, slack-jawed.

Shep's face was red. "Of course we have hearts. But we have heads too. If you give away so much money to every beggar, you won't have enough for yourself."

"She wasn't begging, she was singing," Garth pointed out. "From what Talisa says, she was trying to earn a living through music. Just as we hope to do," he added.

Lem turned on him. "It's not the same. You know it's not."

"Do I?"

"You're pretty stupid if you don't."

Garth's voice rose. "Who's being stupid? Look –"

"Stop it." Master Coyne spoke softly, but his words cut through the heated air like a knife though soft butter. "I will not have my apprentices fighting or calling each other names." His voice was tight with anger. "Expressing contrary opinions is one thing. Calling each other stupid –" he glanced at Lem – "or heartless –" his gaze rested on Talisa – " is something quite different. And unacceptable. Is that understood?"

Lem nodded. After a moment, Talisa did too. Her face felt hot.

"As for giving this woman the money, Talisa... The cloak is no matter. I can wear my old one tonight. But to use money entrusted to you, even though you meant well, is..." He paused. A minute ticked by. Another. "It was not well done."

Talisa was no longer red, but white. Her hands felt clammy. What had he been going to say, before he stopped? A crime? A betrayal of trust? Her throat hurt, but she managed to say, "I'll go tomorrow and buy the cloak."

"Shep will go."

"But –" She stopped. Swallowed. Swallowed again. "I'll give Shep the money then."

Master Coyne hesitated. Was he going to refuse to let her repay her debt? Then he nodded.

It was time for Garth to go. "You did the right thing," he muttered before he left. His words helped, a little. They would have helped more if he'd spoken so the others could hear.

Dinner was strained. Lem and Shep kept glancing uneasily at Talisa. Master and Mistress Coyne were unusually silent. Talisa tried to choke down her food, but the mutton stew kept sticking in her throat.

Later, as she thumped her pillow and turned over in bed yet one more time, unable to erase memories of the shop-keeper's sneer, Master Coyne's words, the disappointment on Mistress Coyne's face, another thought hit her. Since she wasn't allowed to return to Weavers Street tomorrow, she wouldn't see Bart again. Bart...or Cory, who just possibly might be there.

Even so, she couldn't be sorry she had given the money away. Not really.

A MORNING'S SHOPPING

"TALISA!"

Startled, she jerked her head around. At first, blinded by the bright sun, she didn't see the figure standing among the orange and yellow leaves of the hedge across the street. Then...

"Cory!"

He loped across the road and came to a halt, grinning. He looked much as she remembered him, his lanky frame perhaps a bit lankier, his long brown hair a shade longer.

She smiled at him. "It's so good to see you. How... Where did you come from?"

He gestured towards the hedge. "Over there."

"But why –"

"Bart told me he'd seen you and that you were apprenticed to Master Coyne. I went to Weavers Street, thinking you might go back there. I even looked after the stall for a few hours, though I'm afraid Bart didn't appreciate my bargaining skills." He laughed. "When you didn't appear, I found out where Master Coyne lives and came here. I've been waiting, hoping you'd come out."

"But why not just come up to the house and ask for me?"

"I didn't think I'd be welcome."

"Of course you would be."

"Dressed like this?" He glanced down at his clothes.

Talisa looked at them too. She was still unused to Freyan garb. In Uglessia, everyone wore clothes made from ursell wool. Except for festival dress, they were all uniformly grey. But even she could see that Cory's shirt and trousers were made from poorer, thinner material than that used in her fellow apprentices' clothes. And Cory's were faded. And patched.

"Your clothes wouldn't matter."

"Wouldn't they?"

She was silent, remembering the reactions to her encounter with the street singer.

"I'm glad you finally came out. I was beginning to think you never would."

"How long have you been here?"

He shrugged. "A few days, on and off."

"Oh." A smile tugged at her lips.

He nodded at her basket. "Where are you going?"

She'd almost forgotten the basket. "To Portby Square, to do some shopping for Mistress Coyne." She'd felt a rush of relief when Mistress Coyne asked her to run this errand. Perhaps, after ten days, some trust was creeping back.

"May I walk with you?"

"Of course."

They walked in silence down Gleeman Street, then rounded the corner onto Hallmark Way, which was broader and noisier. There were so many questions she needed to ask him, so many things she wanted to tell him. Then why this sudden shyness that seemed to have trapped her tongue, the way stone walls blocked water? She glanced sideways at Cory and found that he was looking sideways at her. They both laughed. Talisa relaxed.

"Do you like it here?" he asked.

She tensed again. "Yes." What else could she say? How to explain?

He must have heard the hesitation in her voice. "Really?"

"Yes. Yes, of course. I'm learning so much. I can read music now, and even play tunes on the lute that don't make everyone within earshot wince."

"And the Coynes? They're good to you?"

"Yes. Very good." They were. And perhaps it was just her imagination that there was a new wariness in their eyes when they looked at her, that their silences were prickly with unvoiced reproaches.

Cory said nothing. They walked on. Talisa raised her eyes to the waterfall in the distance. The sun danced on the silver drops, wove rainbows through the mist. If only everything in Freyfall were so lovely.

They passed the ornate gate of the Musicians' Guild Hall. As Talisa glanced through it into the courtyard, memories surged back: the competition, the night she sang before the queen, her first meeting with Cory. How kind he'd been, rescuing a stranger, reassuring her that her grandparents were safe.

"It's just... Things are so different here. It's hard getting used to them. And I'm homesick. For my family. And the mountains."

He looked at her and smiled. "I can understand that."

"I forgot. You said you came from the hills."

"Yes. We had a farm there. The mountains seemed very close, especially on clear days like today." He was quiet a moment, then said softly, "I remember so many days in autumn, when I'd be out early, tending sheep or picking berries. Suddenly the mist would lift and there they'd be." His voice was full of dreams.

"Why did you leave? Did you think life would be better here?" As soon as the question was out, she wished she hadn't asked it.

He laughed. The sound grated. "We'd have been fools if we'd thought that, wouldn't we?" He looked away. "No. We were kicked off our land."

Talisa gaped at him. "Kicked off? But –"

"We didn't own it, only rented it. Oh, my family had lived there for generations, as had the Berrymores on the farm next to ours, but that didn't matter. Not to the Count of Eastlands."

A deep scowl dug into his forehead. Talisa looked at him and said nothing. After a moment, he continued, "He decided he could make more money grazing sheep than gathering rent from his tenants. So he ordered us all to leave."

Talisa tried to imagine what that had been like. In Uglessia, people often said all Freyans were rich. But no

Uglessians had ever been ordered off their poor, parched land. "And you left? Just like that?"

He laughed again. Talisa flinched at the bitterness in that laugh. "We didn't have much choice. He brought a squadron of the queen's soldiers with him when he came riding up to our farm to tell us we had a day to gather our possessions and go. He looked very grand in his red cloak, mounted on his black stallion. Very powerful. So did the soldiers."

The breeze felt colder, the sun less warm. Talisa shivered. "I'm sorry," she said. She hunted for better words but couldn't find them. "Is that when you came to Freyfall?" she asked at last.

"Yes." Cory's voice was flat. "We thought we'd find work here, but there were too many like us. The Count of Eastlands had a lot of tenants. There were some farmers who'd sold the land they owned and moved to the city that year too. Rain had been scarce and crops poor. Jobs were harder to find than blueberries on a blackberry bush. But we sold some things we'd brought with us and managed to survive. At least, Rina and I did."

Talisa glanced at his face, then looked away.

Cory shook himself like an ursell shaking rain from its coat. "What am I doing, burdening you with this? What a waste of a beautiful day."

"I don't mind."

But he seemed determined to be cheerful. "And a waste of our time, after not seeing each other for so many months. Things are going well for you then, aside from being homesick?"

Talisa hesitated. Cory had shared his pain with her. Perhaps she should share the aching hollowness she felt at not being able to create songs, the hurt that stabbed her every time she thought about the trust she'd forfeited. But they were almost at Portby Square. There wasn't time. "Yes," she said, and fished in the basket for Mistress Coyne's shopping list.

"I'll carry your basket," Cory offered.

Talisa smiled inwardly, thinking of the heavy loads she was used to carrying at home. "Thank you," she said gravely, surrendering it.

The square was crowded with shoppers and crammed with stalls stacked with food of every description. They wandered through it, inspecting apples and pears, carefully choosing the ripest squash, debating the merits of the different cheeses, lingering before a tempting display of fruit tarts, exchanging comments, exchanging smiles. The sun felt warm once more. Talisa made no attempt to hurry.

"Freyn's Day to you, Cory. And to you, Mistress."

Talisa looked up from the fish she was examining. A tall young man had stopped beside Cory. He was dramatically handsome and dramatically dressed, in total black except for the crimson cape flung flamboyantly over his shoulders and the scarlet plume in his hat. He swung his hat off, revealing midnight black hair, and gave a sweeping bow.

"Your servant, Mistress. Well met. Cory, I trust you'll introduce me to your friend."

Cory sighed. "Talisa, please meet Andreas Wells. Andreas, this is Talisa Thatcher."

Andreas raised thin, soaring eyebrows. "A famous name. Any relation to Alaric Thatcher?"

"My grandfather."

"Ah." His eyes moved to her hands, verified the number of fingers, then returned to her face. "A pleasure indeed to meet you, Mistress Thatcher. You're keeping impressive company these days, Cory."

Cory looked uncomfortable.

"Are you gracing Freyfall long with your presence, Mistress Thatcher?"

"Two years. I'm here studying music."

Andreas gave a dazzling smile, displaying strong, even white teeth. "I knew we were soulmates. I am proud to be able to claim that I too study music. I am apprenticed under the tutelage of the talented Alain Swanson."

"How *is* Master Swanson?" Cory asked.

"In good health and spirits, thank you. And that reminds me. He sent me with a message for you, Cory. I was so distracted by your fair companion that I almost forgot it." He smiled at Talisa again, a languid smile this time, half closing his eyes and fluttering his long dark lashes. "I'm so glad I ran into you here. It's a long walk to your abode, and half the time you're not there when I arrive."

"You can always leave a message."

"With your brother-in-law? The last time, he almost slammed the door in my face. Even your sister doesn't seem happy to see me."

Cory frowned. "What's Master Swanson's message?"

Andreas lowered his voice. "Perhaps we should withdraw a few paces. I'm sure Mistress Thatcher won't mind."

"Certainly not," Talisa said, hiding a smile. Cory gave her an embarrassed smile and moved a few steps away. Andreas looked around furtively, then spoke into his ear. Cory nodded and the two returned.

"I see you were hesitating over the selection of fish, Mistress Thatcher. May I offer my assistance? As a native of Freyfall, I feel I am an expert in such matters."

"Don't you have other messages to deliver?" Cory asked hopefully.

"Nothing so urgent it can't wait, I assure you."

Cory sighed.

They continued with the shopping, Andreas sticking close to Talisa's side and solicitously offering his hand whenever they encountered an unusually uneven cobblestone. Cory trailed with the basket, looking glum.

Talisa consulted her list. "I have everything I need. Thank you for your help, Master Wells."

"It was my privilege and pleasure. May I escort you home?"

"Thank you, but Cory will do that," Talisa said firmly. She found Andreas amusing, but enough was enough.

He wasn't daunted. "Farewell until our paths cross again then, which I'm sure they soon will. I await that happy moment with bated breath." He gave her another sweeping bow, flashed another brilliant smile, and swaggered away.

She watched him go, a small smile twitching her lips, then turned to Cory. "Shall we go? At least... I'm sorry. I didn't mean to assume you'd accompany me home." Pink stained her cheeks. "I can carry the basket now."

"Of course I'll accompany you. And you're not getting the basket until we arrive at Master Coyne's house," Cory said.

Talisa smiled.

"Are you and Andreas good friends?" she asked as they left Portby Square and made their way down Hallmark Way. It was almost midday, and the street was even busier than it had been earlier. She had to keep close to Cory to avoid being separated from him by the press of the crowd.

"We...know each other." Cory's voice was guarded.

Talisa nodded. She couldn't imagine Cory having much in common with the flamboyant Andreas. "He's certainly dramatic."

Cory snorted. "He likes making a spectacle of himself, if that's what you mean."

She laughed. "He certainly made a show out of passing on a message. You'd have thought it was a conspiracy, the way he acted."

Cory's face flamed.

She stopped and stared at him. A heavy-set man bumped into her, then walked on with a muttered apology.

"Yes. Well, Andreas does a lot of play-acting," Cory said.

She continued to stare at him. He looked away. Another man jostled her as he walked by. This time it was she who mumbled an apology before moving on.

Was there a conspiracy?

Nonsense. The idea was ridiculous. Wasn't it?

Of course it was. Cory was just embarrassed by Andreas's theatrics. He wouldn't be involved in something like that. He *wouldn't*.

They walked down Hallmark Way, then along Gleeman Street, in silence.

Cory cleared his throat. "When... That is, may I see you again?"

Her hesitation was fractional. "Yes. Of course."

"When?"

She considered. "I'm not sure. I'm fairly busy with household chores and practising."

"Do you often go shopping? Perhaps we could meet then."

"No. Mistress Coyne usually goes, or sends Lem or Shep. In fact, this is the first time she's sent me on an errand since –" She stopped.

"Since when?"

She took a deep breath. "Since I spent the money she'd entrusted me with on something else."

Why had she put it that way, so baldly, so negatively, as though she were laying a bare and broken carcass at his feet? Talisa looked down at the cobblestones. A worm was inching its way through the cracks.

"On what?" he asked. There was no shock in his voice, no condemnation.

She took another deep breath. "Mistress Coyne had sent me with three silver coins to pick up a new cloak for Master Coyne. But I saw a woman singing on the street. She had no shoes. I gave her the money."

"Good for you."

Talisa's head flashed up. Cory smiled at her. "Good for you," he repeated.

Relief rushed through her. She was surprised at just how relieved she felt. She smiled back. Then her smile faded.

"The Coynes don't think so. They've lost their faith in me."

He scowled. "They're just like everyone else of their kind. They've never been hungry or cold themselves, so they don't understand. They don't even *try* to understand." He kicked the stones at his feet. "Selfish beasts."

"No! No, they're good people. Kind people."

His scowl deepened. "Doesn't sound very kind to me, treating you like a thief."

"They don't treat me like a thief. It's just that...that some of the warmth and trust between us has gone. And that hurts because they *have* been so kind. And because..." She stopped, hunting for words. Groping, for the first time, to understand just why the Coynes' reactions mattered so much.

"Because?" Cory prompted.

"Because they made me feel...special, somehow. Valuable."

They'd been walking more and more slowly. Now Cory came to a complete halt and stared at her. "Of course you're valuable."

The vehemence in his voice warmed her, but she shook her head. "I'm not. Oh, I know I have a gift for singing. But that's not important, compared to other gifts."

"Like what?"

"Magic."

"What's so special about being able to cast a few spells?"

He couldn't mean that. He was only saying it to make

her feel better. She shook her head again. "It's the most important thing there is. If I could use magic, I could improve Uglessia. Make life better for my people."

Cory started to speak, then stopped. He frowned down at the street. The tip of his boot poked its way between the stones.

Talisa's shoulders slumped. What had she expected him to say? That music *was* as valuable as magic? She wouldn't have believed him if he had said it.

Finally he looked up. "What about the evenings?"

She blinked. "What?"

"Are you free in the evenings, or does your 'kind' master keep you busy then too?"

"No. That is, I have some tasks, but when I'm finished them, my time's my own." It had never occurred to her to go out at night, though Lem and Shep often did. Most evenings, she practised her songs and scales in her room or, earlier in the year, when light had lingered longer, in the garden. Sometimes, when she wasn't too tired after her practice, she read a book from the Coynes' library.

"Could we meet in the evenings then?" Cory looked eager. Then his face fell. "Though I'm not sure what we'd do, except walk and talk. I don't have any money."

"Walking and talking is fine."

He smiled. "Good. Can you meet me tomorrow?"

She hesitated, then shook her head. She wasn't sure why. It just seemed...too soon, somehow. "What about the next night?"

It was his turn to shake his head. "I have something on then. Would the evening after that work?"

"It will be fine." And she really thought it would.

WALKING WITH CORY

IT WASN'T FINE, MEETING CORY TWO NIGHTS later. It wasn't fine at all. At least not with Master and Mistress Coyne. When Talisa told them after dinner that she was going out, they wanted to know where. They wanted to know what she'd be doing.

"I'm just going to walk with a friend."

"It's dark," Master Coyne objected. "Many of the streets around here have no lamps."

"There's a moon," Talisa pointed out. "And stars."

"They don't give much light."

"They're all we have at home, once the sun goes down."

"Who's your friend?" Mistress Coyne asked.

"His name is Cory."

Shep was stuffing a last piece of treacle tart into his mouth. He choked. Lem, who was twiddling with the stem of his glass, let it go and looked at her sharply. "A boy?"

"Yes."

Master and Mistress Coyne exchanged a glance. "What's his last name?" Master Coyne asked.

"I...don't know. I never thought to ask. His sister and brother-in-law are called Berrymore," Talisa added weakly.

The Coynes exchanged another glance. Then their questions began in earnest. How old was this boy? Who were his parents? Where did he live? What did he do?

Talisa answered as best she could. He was about her age. His parents were dead. He lived with his sister and brother-in-law. Where? She wasn't exactly sure. He carved wooden statues.

"A woodcarver," Master Coyne said. "Who is he apprenticed to?"

"He's not."

Master Coyne shook his head. "He'll never get far that way. Who will buy his work if he hasn't gone through the proper stages from apprentice to master?"

"His brother-in-law sells them," Talisa said tightly. *Why* all these questions?

"His brother-in-law has a shop then?" Mistress Coyne asked. Was there a hint of approval in her voice?

"No, a stall."

"Oh."

Lem and Shep looked smug. Obviously a stall wasn't as respectable as a shop.

Master Coyne was frowning. "Do your grandparents know him?"

"No."

Another glance between the Coynes. Then Master Coyne turned back to her. "I'm sorry, Talisa, but we can't let you go out with this unknown boy."

Talisa took a deep breath and let it out slowly. She tried to make her voice calm. "I'm only going for a walk. And I've been responsible for my own actions for some time. I travelled from Uglessia to Freyfall by myself. My father and grandparents trust me to make my own decisions."

"Perhaps customs are different in Uglessia," Master Coyne said. "But you are in Freya now, and here we are responsible for you."

Lem cleared his throat. "If you want to go out, why not come to The Laughing Lute with Shep and me? Musicians gather there to talk and play. I'm sure you'd like it."

"We'd have asked you before, but you always seemed content to stay here," Shep added.

"Thank you," Talisa said politely. She had no desire to go to The Laughing Lute or anywhere else with them, but it would be unkind to say so. "I'll be glad to go some other time. But I've promised Cory I'll walk with him tonight."

"I'm sorry, Talisa," Master Coyne said. "I know a promise is sacred, but we cannot let you leave this house."

"Why not? You've never stopped Shep and Lem from going out." She tried to sound respectful, the way a good apprentice should. She wasn't sure she succeeded.

"That's different."

"Why? They're your apprentices too, and no older than I am."

"But they're boys." He sounded as though that answered everything. Talisa stared down at a piece of lamb fat left on her plate and took another long, slow breath. She raised her head to face him.

"I realize that. I didn't realize that being boys meant they were more trustworthy." She heard the tremor of anger in her voice and stopped. Long slow breaths didn't help, after all. And perhaps she shouldn't speak about being trustworthy, not after she'd given away the three silver coins.

Master Coyne had pushed his chair back from the table and sat, hands folded over his round stomach, looking at her above the spectacles perched on his nose. "Not more trustworthy, but certainly better able to protect themselves." His voice was maddeningly reasonable.

Talisa's hands clenched. "Who do I need protection from? Cory?"

"Perhaps. We know nothing about him, after all. Even you seem to know very little. Not even his last name."

"Why doesn't he come here to introduce himself?" Mistress Coyne asked. "It seems suspicious, his wanting to meet you on the street."

Shep sniggered, then stopped when Talisa glared at him.

She looked back at Master Coyne. "If he comes here and meets you first, may I go for a walk with him?"

He pursed his lips. Talisa held her breath.

"Perhaps. We'll see, after we've had a chance to talk to him and find out what he's like."

PERSUADING CORY to enter the house was as easy as persuading an ursell to enter a cave where a mountain lion had wintered.

He'd left the shadow of the hedge as soon as she stepped outside, and met her in the middle of the street with a broad smile. The smile fled when she told him what she wanted.

"No."

"But Cory –"

"No. It wouldn't do any good anyway. They'd accept me as warmly as they would a bad smell."

"You don't know that."

"Yes I do." His face looked pale in the moonlight. His eyebrows were drawn in a fierce frown.

"Please."

"No."

"So you don't really want to walk with me," Talisa snapped. She had thought it was such a simple thing, to go for a walk with a friend. Such a simple pleasure. But everyone was putting barriers in her path. First the Coynes. Now Cory.

"Of course I do." He sounded hurt.

Talisa gritted her teeth. "Yet you won't do the one thing that will make it possible."

He was silent for a moment. "Maybe there's another way we can meet. You could sneak out of the house some evenings."

"I'll do nothing of the sort! I'm not a sneak! Or a liar. If you don't have the courage to meet some good, honest people, then this is the last time we'll see each other." She swung on her heel and marched towards the house. When she was almost at the door, Cory caught up with her.

"All right. I'll try. It won't work, but I'll try."

The house seemed warm after the cool evening air. Master and Mistress Coyne were comfortably ensconced in their favourite chairs by the fire. Thanks be to all the mountain spirits, Lem and Shep had left a half-hour ago.

"Master Coyne, Mistress Coyne, I'd like to introduce Cory. Cory, please meet Master and Mistress Coyne."

Cory bowed slightly. "Freyn's Evening."

Master Coyne rose. "Glad to see you, lad. Please have a seat." His tone was easy, but his eyes, above his half-moon spectacles, were shrewdly appraising.

Cory glanced around, then perched on the edge of a plum-coloured chair, first dusting off his trousers. Master Coyne reseated himself.

"So you and Talisa want to go walking."

"Yes sir."

"A mite chilly, isn't it?"

"It's not that bad."

"Hmmm." There was a silence. "Talisa says you live with your sister and brother-in-law."

"Yes sir."

"She says their name is Berrymore but she doesn't know yours."

"What?" Cory looked startled. "Oh. It's Updale."

"I see." Another silence. "You're a woodcarver, I understand."

"Yes sir."

"But not apprenticed, she says."

"No sir."

"You taught yourself, then?"

"Yes sir."

Yet another silence. From her chair across from him, Talisa tried to catch Cory's eye. Surely he could say something more than "Yes sir." "No sir."

"And can you make a living by carving wooden statues?"

"No," Cory said shortly.

"No?" Master Coyne raised his eyebrows. Mistress Coyne was studying Cory, her head cocked to one side. "You have other work then?"

"No." After a moment, Cory said, his voice as grudging as though the words were being dragged out of his mouth, "Work's hard to find. I get a few hours, now and then, helping unload boats at the dock."

Master Coyne nodded. "The best thing for you to do, young man, is to apprentice yourself to a master carver. Being an apprentice is hard work, but it's the only way to guarantee your future."

Cory said nothing, only stared at him, jaw set. Talisa looked from him to Master Coyne and back, and winced.

Mistress Coyne spoke for the first time. "It's not that easy to become apprenticed, William. You've said yourself, more times than enough, that there are more promising young people than you and all the other master musicians could possibly take. I'm sure it's the same with master carvers."

"That's true," her husband conceded. "Do you like carving?" He was back at his polite interrogation.

Talisa expected Cory to return to his polite monosyllables. Instead, he considered the question the way her father studied a puzzling spell. "I don't know that I *like* it," he said finally. "When the wood flows the way I want it to, it's the best thing in the world. When it doesn't, and the picture in my mind won't come to life... I almost think I hate it then. But I have to do it."

"Have to?" Master Coyne cocked his head, just like his wife. Two birds inspecting one worm. "Why? To make money?"

Cory smiled wryly. "Little enough money I make with my carvings. No. But when I'm not carving I feel...lost. Empty."

The way I feel, now that my songs have flown away. Talisa looked down at her hands, folded in her lap.

Master Coyne considered Cory thoughtfully for a minute. He glanced at his wife, then back at Cory. "You'll have to show us your carvings sometime. Now I imagine the two of you want to be off."

Talisa sat still for a moment, too surprised to move. Then she jumped to her feet.

"You're not dressed warmly enough for this weather," Mistress Coyne told Cory. "There's a cool wind blowing out there."

"I'm fine, thank you." He had risen too, looking bemused.

She shook her head. "Those clothes are far too thin. You'll have to get warmer ones before winter sets in. For now, you can wear William's old cloak. No arguments," she said firmly as Cory opened his mouth, and left to get the cloak Talisa had forced Master Coyne to wear to his Guild Hall meeting a fortnight ago.

"Thank you," Cory said when Mistress Coyne returned with it. Talisa put on her own cloak, made from warm grey ursell wool, and they escaped into the night.

"Whew," Cory said. "I didn't think they were going to let you come with me."

"You didn't help," Talisa said tartly. "'Yes sir.' 'No sir.' Did you expect to make a good impression that way?"

"I couldn't think of anything else to say," he confessed. "I felt like a hare, afraid to move in any direction in case I darted into the hunter's path. Anyway, it worked. At least, *something* worked."

"Yes," she agreed, calming down. And why was she upset anyway? Surely going for a walk on a chilly night with a boy she scarcely knew wasn't that important.

Freyfall was a transformed city at night. The shops were closed, the stalls deserted, the carts and crowds gone. Candles gleamed in the houses they passed. In the distance, the waterfall shimmered like a silver curtain of light. Their feet clattered over the cobblestones.

"What's it like in Uglessia?" Cory asked.

Talisa looked around and laughed. "Different."

"In what way?"

"We have no cities. No streets, no shops, no crowds. No one lives in grand houses like that one." She gestured to a large house they were passing. It had a marble statue beside the front door and an imposing iron railing. "We live far apart. We must, so the land can support us."

Cory was silent for a moment. "I've heard that you don't have kings or queens. But you must have people who run things."

"No. When decisions have to be made, someone calls a circle and everyone gathers to have a say and vote. No one is more important than anyone else."

He glanced at her. "Not even your family?"

"No," she said firmly, then thought for a moment, a frown digging into her forehead. "Well, maybe. In a way. Because of the magic." The magic she didn't have.

She raised her head. The stars seemed very bright, though not as bright as they'd be at home, where they hung above the mountains looking close enough to touch.

"You said no one lives in grand houses," Cory said. "Does that mean no one is richer than anyone else?"

She smiled, still watching the stars. "No one is rich period. We have no such word in Uglessian. We didn't have a word for money either, until we started selling kala to Freyans, and that's only been for the last forty years. Everyone in Uglessia is poor compared to Freyans. At least, most Freyans," she amended, remembering the singer with bare feet. She shivered. "I guess there are Freyans who are worse off than any Uglessian."

"That's because no one in Freya cares about the poor." Cory's voice was harsh, a harshness matched by the frown Talisa saw on his face when she glanced at him.

"Cory..."

"Mmm?"

"You're all right, aren't you? I mean...I know you don't have much. But with what Bart sells..."

"Oh yes. We're all right." Cory's voice was flat. Talisa winced. Had she made a mistake? At home, no one hesitated to ask a neighbour how his or her usit crop was doing or if a family had enough food to survive the winter. But in Freya, she'd learned, it was impolite to ask people how much money they had.

Perhaps she hadn't offended Cory, though, for he continued. "We have a place to sleep and clothes to wear and food for our bellies. Oh, it's not a great place, and our clothes aren't good, and we never have an abundance of food. Bart had to borrow money to buy a stall and most of the money he makes goes to pay the interest on the loan. But we have enough. At least, Bart and Rina do, and they share it with me."

"You help with your carvings."

"Not much. Not enough, according to Bart."

"But –"

"He's always telling me I'm not producing enough. Then when I do carve something, he says it's all wrong, that he can't sell it."

She thought of the statue she'd seen on the stall counter. "The carving of the old beggar woman...I love it."

"You're the only one. It's sat there for over a month."

She said nothing.

Cory laughed suddenly. "To tell the truth, I'm glad no one's bought it. I like it too much to want it to be sold." The bitterness was gone from his voice. Talisa was glad.

They walked on. The wind picked up. It blew eddies of dust and dead leaves around their legs. Talisa shivered.

"Maybe we should turn back now."

"All right."

They headed back the way they'd come. Talisa wasn't tall for a Uglessian, but taller than most Freyans. She and

Cory were much of a height. Their legs matched, stride for stride.

"Tell me about your family," Cory said.

"What would you like to know?"

"Well, about your great-grandmother Yrwith, for instance. I've heard of her all my life in songs and stories. The Uglessian wizard who shifted the winds and caused the great drought. Is she still alive?"

"No. She died when I was a baby. All I know about her comes from stories too, told by Grandmother and Great-uncle Urwin. And by Father and Aunt Gwynne, a bit."

"What is your father like?"

"He doesn't say much." She thought about him, his silence, his quiet words, his slow, grave smile. "But he thinks a lot. And he's kind."

Cory said nothing for a while. The wind whistled as it rounded houses. A cloud raced towards the moon.

"Do you have any brothers or sisters?"

"One sister, like you. Welwyn. She's two years older than I am."

Cory laughed. "And Rina's two years older than me. Does your sister try to mother you, the way Rina sometimes does with me?"

"Maybe a little, when I was younger. Now we're just friends." Though never equals, Talisa thought. Not in all ways.

"You miss them, don't you?" Cory asked gently.

"Yes."

"I'm glad..." He stopped.

"Glad of what?"

"Glad you decided to stay here and study music even though you miss your family. I'm sorry. That's selfish."

She smiled. "That's all right."

"Talisa..."

"Yes?"

"Will you sing for me?"

She looked at him, surprised, then glanced around them at the dark road, the candlelit homes. "Here? Now?"

"Please. I've been wanting to hear you ever since Midsummer."

She laughed. "All right." She came to a halt and considered. What to sing? One of the songs she'd learned recently?

No. She had seen his carvings, and she wanted to give him a song she had created herself. She glanced around again, and remembered a clear, cool evening much like this one, when she had left her father and sister by the fire and gone outside. Cory wouldn't understand the words, but she hoped he would hear their meaning in her voice.

Wild mountain wind, sing me your song
Sing Midsummer light when the days are so long
Sing Midwinter hopes for the blessing of snow
Help me to learn what the high mountains know.

As she sang, Talisa felt again the love for her land that she had felt that night as she walked with the wind and gazed at the stark beauty of crags and cliffs in the silver light of the stars. Felt, too, the aching longing that had filled her, knowing that when she went back inside, she would be with people she loved, who loved her, but that she would not belong with them, for she could never share their studies, their work, their ability to help.

Wind, dancing wind, keep my heart strong
Help me accept that I cannot belong.

When she finished, Cory was silent. She waited. Then he said, very softly, "Thank you." That was all, but it was enough.

They resumed walking, and turned onto Gleeman Street. They'd soon be at the Coynes'.

"I wish I could go to Uglessia," Cory said.

"Maybe you will, some day. The guards at the tunnel are there to stop Uglessians from invading Freya, not Freyans visiting Uglessia. And we have no guards at our end."

"I don't suppose your people would let me stay there, though."

Talisa stopped, astonished. "Why would you want to stay? Usually it's Uglessians who come to Freya in hopes of a better life, not the other way around."

"Why would I want to? You saw that street singer. You don't imagine she's the only one, do you?"

"No, but —"

"At least in Uglessia you don't have some people dining on cream while others have to beg for a drop of water. You don't have men like the Count of Eastlands who care for nothing, *nothing*, do you hear me, except making a grand splash at court. You don't have soldiers ready to do his bidding and force people off the land where their families have lived for generations, to starve in the streets for all he or they care!"

A cloud hid the moon. All she could see of Cory's face was a pale blur. But she heard the rage that filled his voice. Filled him. She wrapped her arms around herself, shivering.

He stood there a moment, literally shaking with the force of his anger. Then, slowly, she saw it subside. His shoulders slumped. He looked away. "Sorry."

She said nothing. After a moment, they walked on. They reached the Coynes' house and stopped. Neither of them spoke.

Finally Cory said, "Thank you for walking with me. Freyn's Night." He started to walk away.

"Cory!"

He whirled around and took two long strides back. "Yes?"

"The cloak."

"What?"

"You're still wearing Master Coyne's cloak."

"Oh. I'd forgotten. Sorry." He fumbled with the clasp. "Here."

She took it, hesitated, then asked, "When will I see you again?"

"You mean...you still want to?"

She hesitated again. "Yes."

"I thought... I do go on sometimes."

"I noticed," Talisa said wryly.

He laughed shakily. "I'm sorry." He paused, then said, his voice unsure, "May I see you tomorrow night then? Though I'm afraid it will just be another walk."

Talisa considered. The Coynes may have allowed her to go out tonight, but she didn't think they'd approve of her seeing Cory every night. "Shall we say two nights from now? And I like walking."

The cloud had moved away. In the moonlight, she saw the flash of Cory's delighted smile. Then he turned and walked down the street again. This time there was a spring in his step.

THE LAUGHING LUTE

"You're fond of that boy, aren't you?" Mistress Coyne asked.

Talisa glanced up from the plate she was drying. "Cory?" A flush spread over her face. "We're good friends."

Mistress Coyne looked at her sideways. "Hmm." She washed a bowl and handed it to Talisa. The two of them were alone in the kitchen, washing the breakfast dishes. "It might be better if you saw more of other people."

Talisa said nothing.

"It's not that I have anything against Cory, though I *do* wish he didn't act as though he thought William and I were about to pounce."

"He's shy," Talisa said, though she didn't really think he was, at least not with people with whom he felt he had anything in common.

"It's not that I have anything against him," Mistress Coyne repeated. "But you're young, and new here, and there's more to Freyfall than this household and that one boy. He's been taking up too much of your time, these last few weeks."

"I've seen a great deal of the city during our walks."

"Only the streets around here. And Freyfall is more than streets. It's people. You should get out and meet them."

Talisa picked up another bowl and dried it.

"They don't bite, you know."

Talisa flushed again. Did Mistress Coyne think she was frightened of meeting strangers? She, who had come to Freyfall by herself, competed before foreign judges, sung before a foreign queen?

But performing in front of Freyans wasn't the same as being *with* them, Talisa admitted grudgingly. Maybe Cory wasn't the only one who shied away from those who seemed...different. All too often, she felt she had to be so careful of what she said and did. Only with Cory did she feel at home. Their walks had fallen into a rhythm of easy talk and comfortable silence that felt as natural as walking on the mountains with Welwyn.

Sometimes their talk was about nothing more than the cat that made them both jump as it streaked out from behind an empty cart, or the brightness of the harvest moon, or the statue they passed that looked as though its sculptor had started out carving a horse, then changed his mind by the time he got to the head and created a lynx face and ears. Other times, Cory peppered her with questions about Uglessia, or she asked him about life in the hills. The Updale farm became a very real place for her as he spoke about waking up on mornings in early spring and seeing, despite the tattered rags of snow that still clung to the ground, tender buds on the apple tree beside the house. Or about wandering with his sister along the creek at the foot of their hill, stuffing blackberries into their mouths till their lips turned purple. Or sitting by the hearth on winter evenings with a piece of wood and a knife in his hands, teaching himself to carve, while Rina worked on the loom and his parents talked quietly about the harvest just past and their plans for spring planting. Words and snatches of melody sang in her heart then, as they hadn't done since she first arrived in Freyfall.

When she asked him about his life here, though, he usually answered only with a light jest or bitter jibe. Talisa tried not to feel hurt. Perhaps it was for the best. When he did talk about life in Freyfall, the anger in his voice made her shiver.

Mistress Coyne washed the last dish and put it on the counter. "Why don't you go to The Laughing Lute with Lem and Shep? I wouldn't advise a girl to go to a tavern by herself, mind, but you'd be safe enough with them. It's a good place, The Laughing Lute, full of music." She smiled at her memories. "They've asked you often enough, the poor lads."

They had. Talisa sighed. "All right. The next time they ask, I'll accept."

That was sooner than she expected. Mistress Coyne must have dropped a hint in their ears. That very night, Talisa found herself heading for the tavern.

"Maybe we should take a carriage," Shep said.

"I'm used to walking."

"But it's a long way," Lem said.

Talisa suppressed a sigh. The two of them walked to The Laughing Lute all the time. Did they think she was made of rose petals? How would they fare struggling up a Uglessian mountain? "We'll walk," she said firmly.

Halfway there, she wished she *had* accepted a carriage. The two boys insisted she walk between them, then proceeded to talk only to each other, too bashful to speak directly to her. She might have been invisible.

She grinned suddenly, remembering her sister. When they were children, Welwyn would sometimes cast a spell and walk beside her, unseen and unnoticed until overcome by a fit of giggles. Would Lem and Shep jump, the way she used to do, if she started laughing at her new invisible self?

Even before she saw the sign of The Laughing Lute, Talisa heard the noise that erupted from it. A loud shout of laughter greeted them as they entered. She stopped.

The tavern was crowded. Some people sat at long wooden tables, others stood in clusters in the middle of the floor. Some strummed lutes or small harps. All of them were talking, all laughing, all full of boisterous good cheer, or so it seemed to her. There were so *many* of them.

Shep grabbed her elbow. "This way." He started to lead her towards a table in the far corner.

But by then her eyes had adjusted to the bright candlelight. "Look. There's Garth. Let's join him." If she had to be here all evening, at least she wanted to be with someone who would *talk* to her.

Reluctantly, Shep changed course and headed to the table where Garth sat at the end of a long bench that seated a dozen or more. Lem tapped him on the shoulder. Garth turned, then rose to his feet.

"Talisa! And Lem and Shep. Welcome. Is this your first visit to The Lute, Talisa?"

She nodded.

He grinned. "Don't let the noise bother you. It will quiet down once the music starts in earnest. It's a bit early for that yet."

"We have to get Talisa home at a reasonable hour," Lem said.

As though I'm an ursell to be herded to and from pasture, Talisa thought.

Garth nodded and sat down again, squeezing over to make room for them. Talisa sat beside him with Lem on her left. Shep had to sit across from her. He glowered.

"Do you want a glass of wine or ale?" Lem asked.

"Would it be possible to have kala?"

"Of course. I'll get it." Lem jumped to his feet.

Garth shouted introductions. It was hard to catch names above the noise, but she thought a young man who owned a merry face topped by a mop of brown hair was Mel, and a small man with a booming voice was Gilbert. She was pleased to see two other women at the table. One was called Lark. The other's name she missed. She doubted that many of them heard her name either, but they all smiled and nodded.

She wrapped her hands around the mug of kala Lem brought and tried to listen to the conversation. It was hard to hear above the buzz of voices and music in the background, but it was clear that everyone at the table was talking about music and musicians. They laughed at a certain Master Glendale's apprentice, who was so clumsy he'd already broken two pipes, but had such a promising voice that his master was keeping him on anyway. Someone announced that he'd heard there was a vacant position at court for a musician, and was anyone here going to apply?

"Did you hear?" someone else asked. "That rogue Bellmore bought a house in Applegarth with the money he gained from his part in the assassination attempt. He settled his wife there, then took off with a troupe of wandering minstrels."

Garth, who'd been talking quietly to the person on his right, turned his head and listened attentively to this. But then he would. Master Bellmore was his friend Cat's father.

"Has everyone heard Mel's outrageous new song?" called a man at the far end of the bench.

Mel grinned, grabbed a lute from the person next to him, and proceeded to demonstrate just how outrageous his song was. Talisa raised her mug to hide her red cheeks.

She felt eyes on her and looked across the table. Lark was staring at her hands. Talisa lowered her mug slowly.

Lark leaned forward. "You're Uglessian."

Talisa nodded and smiled. The smile felt stiff.

"I didn't quite hear... Did Garth say your name is Talisa?"

She nodded again.

"So you're the Uglessian who was chosen as one of the winners in the competition last summer. I entered the contest too, but it seems I wasn't good enough." Bright blue eyes stabbed Talisa. "I always wondered whether you were chosen because of your voice or because the judges wanted a Uglessian among the winners."

Talisa's hands clenched around the handle of her mug. "I won on merit."

Lark stared at her a moment more, then shrugged dismissively and turned away. Talisa glanced around. No one seemed to have heard their exchange. Mel's song ended with a flourish and was followed by a tumult of laughter and jeers. Glasses were refilled. Talk resumed.

It would be so good to be walking with Cory right now. Even sitting in her small room, practising scales, seemed appealing.

About an hour after they'd arrived, the noise subsided somewhat. There was still talk, but it was expectant now. People glanced around and nudged each other.

A tall man with rust-coloured hair and a broken nose, who looked more like a fighter than a musician, strode to the front of the room. "Very well. If no one else will start us off, I will." He beat a tattoo on the small drum he carried, then swung into a rousing marching song that called men, not to arms, but to drink and good times. His offering was greeted with cheers.

Lem leaned closer. "This is the time anyone who wants to can sing or play," he whispered. Talisa nodded.

During the next hour or so, her tension eased. She listened and clapped with the rest of them. There were traditional songs and those newly composed, comic songs and sad ones, love ballads and marching tunes, lullabies and jigs that made her feet itch to dance. A woman with jet black hair but a deeply lined face played a tune on her flute that made Talisa think of the mountains at home when they were touched by the purple shadows of twilight. Her eyes misted.

There was a brief pause. Then someone called, "What about you, Garth? Do you have a new song for us?"

"That's right," someone else shouted. "A boy who entertains the queen can entertain us."

Garth half rose, smiling, then stopped and looked at Talisa. "What about you, Talisa? Would you like to sing?"

She shrank back and shook her head. She was glad he had spoken quietly.

But not quietly enough. The woman across from her smiled. "So the Uglessian who won a music contest won't perform for us? I wonder why."

This time others heard her words. Shep frowned, but Lem just looked bewildered. Garth started to say something, then stopped.

Talisa stared at Lark. The other woman stared back. Her blue eyes mocked. Challenged.

I don't have to accept your challenge, Talisa thought. *I have nothing to prove to you. To myself. I won the contest on merit alone.*

But somewhere, in the back of her mind, doubt wriggled like a worm on a fishing line. Slowly, she rose. Garth sank back onto the bench.

Talisa walked forward. She didn't look at any of the people she passed, but she was very conscious of their eyes on her. *You've sung before a queen and a roomful of wizards and courtiers,* she reminded herself. *Why should you be frightened now?* But she was, so much so that her knees wobbled and her throat hurt.

She reached the front and turned. She could see their eyes, curious, judging.

She hadn't planned this. She had no idea what to sing.

The silence was going on too long. She must decide. Should she sing a Freyan song?

No. She would sing the song that had won her a performance at the council. Prove Lark wrong. Prove that there was no place for that wriggling worm of doubt. She sang of the friendship between individuals and countries that had been planted forty years ago, and how it had blossomed into life-giving traces of green and blue on the grey Uglessian mountains.

Silence filled the room when she finished. She stood, head up, refusing to look down. She thought she'd sung well, but...

Doubt wriggled again.

Then the applause came, mingled with cries of "Bravo!"

She stumbled on her way back to her table, and was only dimly aware of the beaming smiles and congratulations of her fellow apprentices. But she heard the words of the woman across the table very clearly.

"That was a beautiful song, sung beautifully." The eyes that had looked like blue stones weren't stony now.

Others took Talisa's place. She tried to concentrate on the music, but her mind kept wandering. Then a harsh, discordant sound jerked her to full attention.

The tall, lean man at the front of the room struck his lute again. More discord. Then he began to sing.

She comes.
From the hill she comes
to Freyfall's streets.

For a minute, the lute sang alone, in a minor key.

She comes.
With her young
she comes
seeking work
seeking shelter
seeking bread
that her children
may be fed.

The singer's playing was skilled, his voice trained. His words carried clearly, even when he sang barely above a whisper. His spare, austere face was intent. His dark eyes were focused above the heads of the audience as though he only saw the woman he sang about, the woman who went from house to house and shop to shop looking for work and finding none, who sought refuge in a shed with a leaking roof, only to be driven out, who finally held out her hand to beg for money, for food, for something, *anything,* that would keep her and her children alive.

Talisa closed her eyes. She saw bare feet on cold cobblestones, heard Cory's words. Cory's bitterness.

The music wasn't all discords. There was a haunting melody that ran through it. A lullaby perhaps. A dream. But the harsh notes returned again and again as the nameless woman met indifference and scorn, lost children, lost hope. The song ended as it had started, abruptly, jaggedly. No one clapped. Talisa wanted to but couldn't. She was too disturbed. Too close to tears. The singer lowered his lute and walked quietly back to his place in a corner of the room. After a moment, there was a polite round of applause.

Talisa swallowed. "Who is he?"

"Master Alain Swanson," Garth said. "He's very good, isn't he?"

"Too gloomy for my taste," Shep objected. There were murmurs of agreement.

Swanson. Alain Swanson. Where had she heard that name before?

Lem stood up. "Time to go. We promised the Coynes we'd get Talisa home early."

Talisa grimaced, again feeling like an ursell herded here and there, but rose. As she did so, the door opened, letting in a draft of cool night air and a young man dressed all in black except for a crimson cape and a scarlet-plumed hat. Talisa recognized him immediately. Andreas Wells. She smiled, remembering that morning in Portby Square, remembering the way Andreas had drawn Cory aside to deliver a message from...

From Master Swanson. That's where she'd heard the name before. Andreas was apprenticed to him.

Andreas looked around, then hurried towards the table where Master Swanson sat.

Someone was singing a rollicking song intended, no doubt, to lighten the sombre mood that had fallen after the last performance. Talisa fastened her cloak, her eyes still following Andreas. She saw him stop at the table, bend and say something to the musician. Alain Swanson rose abruptly. He and Andreas headed for the door.

They passed close by Talisa. Andreas's eyes brushed past her, unseeing. His face was the colour of flour.

She watched them leave, her eyes wide.

FIRE!

TALISA WOKE THE NEXT MORNING TO THE wailing of wind and drumming of rain on the roof. She went to the window and looked out. Up till then, the garden had retained some last, defiant remnants of colour. Now the wind and rain battered at those remnants as though hammering nails into summer's coffin. Talisa felt as grey and dismal as the day itself.

Garth arrived at his usual time with water dripping down his collar and his dark hair plastered to his head.

"You're soaked to the skin!" Mistress Coyne exclaimed, and hustled him into some of Lem's clothes. They were too big, but they were warm.

Dampness invaded the house. Even the fires in the hearths couldn't drive it away. It seemed to seep into Talisa's mind and bones. Her fingers stumbled so much on the harp strings that Master Coyne finally lost patience and set her to work copying sheets of music.

It would have been unreasonable to expect Cory to arrive, even though he had said he would, two evenings back. By nightfall, the wind had died, but the rain was still an unbroken curtain of water. But as Talisa stood staring out the window into the darkness, she couldn't help wishing he would. She'd been imprisoned by the weather all day. Any excuse for an outing, however brief, would be welcome. And...

And she wanted to ask him about last night. Oh, there was no reason to think Andreas's white face and Master Swanson's abrupt departure had anything to do with him. All the same...

"Come to the fire, child. You're shivering," Mistress Coyne said.

Reluctantly, Talisa left the window and hitched a chair close to the fireplace. The others were already huddled around it.

"Did you enjoy your evening at The Laughing Lute?" Master Coyne asked.

"Yes, thank you. There was fine music."

"Including yours, I hear." He beamed at her.

She blushed. "Thank you." She hesitated, then said slowly, "One of the musicians who was there, a Master Swanson... I was wondering if you knew him."

He raised his eyebrows. "Alain Swanson was there, was he? Yes, I know him."

She waited, but he said nothing more. "His singing and playing were..." She hunted for the right word. "Powerful."

"Oh, he's a fine musician, is Alain Swanson."

"But?" she prompted.

"But he threw it all away. Walked out of the Guild a year or more ago, saying we were all... Well, I won't repeat what he said. He could have gone far, with his talent – and he has talent, of that there's no doubt, not only in singing and playing but in making songs too. But he turned his back on it as though it didn't matter." He frowned. "I hate waste."

Talisa was silent a minute, looking into the fire. A twig snapped. "The song he sang last night was about a woman who couldn't find work or food for herself and her children."

"That sounds like something he'd sing, all right."

She was still gazing into the flames. "The woman in the song came from the hills. She and her family had been thrown off their land."

Master Coyne sighed. "They and others, I'm afraid. There's not been enough rain, these last few years. At least not at the right times." He shot a baleful glance at the rain-soaked world beyond the window. "The landlords didn't have much choice. They'll get far more profit grazing sheep than from the rents their tenants were able to pay them."

"They say there'd be more rain if –" Lem stopped abruptly.

Talisa looked at him. "If Freya didn't send some of its rain to Uglessia?" she asked softly.

His face went the colour of a brick wall.

"We're glad to send you some of our rain," Shep said gallantly.

Talisa found that her fingers had curled into fists.

There was an uncomfortable silence. Master Coyne cleared his throat. "Yes. Well. Alain Swanson's songs may be powerful, but no one's likely to hire him to sing them at a dinner party. I don't know how he supports himself. And to think he could have had it all – a fine house, the respect of his fellow musicians, apprentices –"

"But he does have an apprentice," Talisa interrupted.

"He does?" Master Coyne raised surprised eyebrows. Then he peered at Talisa. "How do you know that?"

"I've met him. The apprentice, I mean. Cory knows him."

Lem and Shep exchanged knowing glances. Master Coyne frowned. "I'm not sure I like the sound of that."

Mistress Coyne gave her husband a sharp look. "There's nothing wrong with Cory knowing the apprentice, William. It doesn't mean he has anything to do with Master Swanson. And speaking of Cory..." She turned to Talisa. "Please ask him to come to dinner the next time you see him. We'd like to have him, wouldn't we, William?"

He nodded. "And tell him to bring some of his carvings with him."

BY THE NEXT DAY, the rain had stopped and a pale sun shone in the watery sky. It was the apprentices' regular day off so there were no music lessons, but household tasks still needed to be done. After breakfast, Mistress Coyne handed Talisa a basket and a shopping list, and she set off for Portby Square, breathing in the cool, rain-washed air.

The square was even busier than usual as shoppers emerged after being kept indoors the day before. But they were doing more than just shop, Talisa saw. People clustered in groups and congregated around stalls, talking busily. Were they starved for gossip after a day's absence, or had something happened?

She didn't have to wonder long. Even before she reached the first stall, a man hailed her. "Have you heard the news, Mistress?"

"No. What news?"

"The soldiers' barracks were burned to the ground."

"Burned? Was anyone hurt?"

He nodded solemnly. "As many as ten soldiers were killed. Burned to a crisp, they say. Terrible, isn't it?" His eyes shone with excitement.

Talisa swallowed. "Yes." How old had they been, those soldiers? Had they had families?

He drew closer and lowered his voice, as though sharing a secret. "I heard the fire was deliberately set."

"What?" She stared at him. "But why? Who would —" She stopped. Fear clutched her stomach. Would these people jump to the conclusion that Uglessians were responsible, as the crowd in Fallmart Square on Midsummer had done? Instinctively, she thrust her left hand into her pocket. Her right hand, holding the handle of the basket, tried to hide itself in the folds of her skirt.

He shook his head. "No one knows why. Or who."

"It was a band of ruffians," someone said. Talisa turned her head and saw a plump woman carrying a basket laden with bread, tarts, eggs, cheese, and raw fish. Talisa moved back a couple of steps to get further from the smell of the fish. "My cousin Lena heard there were twenty or thirty of them."

The man who'd been speaking to Talisa snorted. "Rumours. Did anyone see them?"

"No but –"

"Probably the same bunch as tried to kill Queen Elira last summer," another man broke in.

"But they caught all of them," the first man protested.

"As for that, who can say for sure?" the other said darkly.

At least no one was blaming Uglessians – at least not yet. Talisa breathed more easily but kept her hands hidden.

A small, elderly woman had joined the crowd around the stall. The man who had informed Talisa of the tragedy turned to her, big with news. She listened, her eyes widening in shock.

"But why would anyone do something like that? Such a terrible thing. Why, my grandson's a soldier. He's in Freybourg now, thank Freyn, but he might just as easily have been here and been burned to death. And the others, the ones who were killed... Why?"

The stall owner, a lean, grizzled man, spoke up. "People will do anything if they're angry enough."

"That's what I said," the plump woman insisted. "A band of ruffians."

The stall owner shook his head. "Not ruffians. Ordinary folk who came here from the country, looking for work and finding none. Nor homes, a lot of them."

A cold finger ran down Talisa's spine. "But they'd have no reason to burn the barracks," she said before she thought. She shouldn't have spoken. Shouldn't have called attention to herself. Her right hand wriggled deeper into the folds of her skirt.

The stall owner shrugged.

"You think it was street people then?" the first man asked him.

"Could have been."

"It was a band of ruffians. Stands to reason," the plump woman asserted.

A black-bearded man joined them in time to hear this. "Whoever it was, they'll soon be caught. There are enough soldiers around today to form a small army. Yesterday too, I gather, though there were few people out to see them."

"I thought the fire was last night," someone said.

The newcomer looked amused. "Any fire last night would have been doused by the rain before it could do any damage. No, it was set the night before last."

The night before last. The night she'd been at The Laughing Lute. The night Andreas had looked as white and shattered as a broken eggshell.

The speculation continued, but Talisa didn't want to hear more. She purchased what she needed from that stall and continued on her rounds. Amidst all the excitement her progress was slow, and it was almost noon by the time she got back to the Coynes' house.

"That took you long enough," Mistress Coyne said as Talisa deposited the basket on the kitchen table. "I've been waiting for those onions to add to the soup."

Talisa started to explain.

"Wait," Mistress Coyne said when she'd finished her first two sentences. "I'll call William. He should hear this too."

Master Coyne listened, frowning. "Not good. Not good at all. I'd better go and find out what really happened."

"Lem and Shep are out. They'll return with news," Mistress Coyne protested.

"Probably just more gossip. No, I need solid facts."

"And you'll find them at the Guild Hall, I suppose." Mistress Coyne sighed. "Well, at least have some lunch first. The soup will be ready in a few minutes."

Talisa spent the afternoon in the garden, trying to repair the damage the storm had done, but with little success. At least the work gave her something to do rather than pace the floor, waiting, worrying. Just before dinner, Shep and Lem burst into the house.

"You'd better stay close, Talisa," Lem said. "I heard some people say it must be Uglessians who set the fire."

It was what she'd expected. And she was safe inside this house. So why the wave of panic that made it hard to breathe? She clenched her hands and willed it to subside. After a moment, it did. Slightly.

Master Coyne returned as they were sitting down to eat. He looked grim.

"What's the news, William?"

He shook his head. "Later, Lizbet. It can wait till I've had my dinner."

Shep and Lem groaned in unison.

There was little talk over dinner. Talisa tried to eat her stew, but each piece of meat seemed to take so many bites. Her mouth was dry.

Finally, Master Coyne pushed back his chair with a sigh of satisfaction.

"Well?" his wife demanded.

"It seems the whole barracks wasn't burned after all, only an unused wing at the back."

"Then no one was hurt?"

"No one *should* have been hurt. Unfortunately, two soldiers on guard duty heard a suspicious noise and went to investigate. One was killed instantly. The other was badly hurt. The best healers are with him but... Well, they don't expect he'll survive."

They were all silent.

"Have they caught the ones who did it?" Shep asked.

"Not yet. If they suspect anyone, the news hadn't reached the Guild Hall. I did hear, though, that they think whoever did it might strike again. They've called in extra troops, though not from Freybourg, in case the firebrands plan to attack the queen and court next. They're taking this very seriously indeed."

Talisa pushed some meat and potatoes around with her fork. "If it was an unused wing that was burned, maybe the person or people who set the fire didn't mean to hurt anyone."

"Maybe not. But they did hurt them, didn't they?"

She didn't answer. After a moment, she put her fork down. She couldn't finish the stew.

Lem cleared his throat. "We think Talisa should stay indoors for a while. Some people think Uglessians were responsible."

"What? I didn't hear that particular piece of gossip."

"We heard it twice. Didn't we, Shep?"

Shep nodded.

Master Coyne snorted. "Nonsense. What a ridiculous idea." He thought for a moment and sighed. "Still, with tension high and rumours flying, maybe you're right. You'd best stay home, Talisa, or only go out if one of us is with you." He looked at her face, then reached over and patted her hand. "Don't look so unhappy, my dear. I'm sure this will be cleared up in a few days and the guilty parties caught and hanged." He smiled kindly.

She nodded and tried to smile in response, but his words brought no comfort. No comfort at all.

FOUR CARVINGS
AND A QUESTION

CORY DID NOT COME THAT NIGHT. NOR THE next. Nor the next. Talisa tried not to pace too long at night. Her sleep was uneasy.

But then, that might have been because she got little exercise. She felt like a captive, allowed out only briefly, and then only when Lem or Shep was available to act as solicitous guards. She tried not to snap at them when they steered her to the other side of the street or stepped in front of her whenever they saw anyone approaching.

The boys weren't available often. They were out every free moment, soaking up the news. The city seethed with rumours, they reported. Soldiers were everywhere.

"Don't worry," Garth said on the fourth day. "Even if the culprits aren't caught, the excitement will soon die down. It always does, in Freyfall."

Talisa smiled at him.

"But the culprits *will* be caught," Master Coyne said. "I have faith in the army."

Her smile faded.

Cory came that night. Master Coyne answered his light tap on the door.

"Come in, come in. We haven't seen you for some time."

"No. I... Can Talisa come for a short walk with me?" Cory's eyes swept the room and found Talisa. She rose.

Master Coyne shook his head. "I'm afraid not."

"But I won't keep her long. And it's a fine night."

"It is," Master Coyne agreed. "But it's not the weather I'm worried about. It's all this turmoil. Here. Come in and sit down."

Cory edged inside and perched on the plum chair. Master Coyne sat opposite him.

"We don't dare let Talisa go out until this uproar settles down."

Cory stared at him. "But why –"

"She's Uglessian," Master Coyne explained.

"Yes, I know. But... This doesn't have anything to do with Uglessians."

Master Coyne beamed at him. "You know that. I know that. But apparently some people don't. I'm sure you don't want to put her in danger."

"Of course not!" Cory sounded horrified.

Talisa's hands clenched at her sides. "I go out for walks with Shep and Lem."

"That's different, dear," Mistress Coyne said. She was knitting a rust-coloured sweater by the fire.

"Why?" Talisa hoped she didn't sound as upset as she felt.

"You go out with them during the day. And they look more...well, more respectable. No offence meant," she told Cory.

He was gazing down at his hands. "None taken," he mumbled.

Talisa glanced from face to face. She could tell there was no point in arguing. But she *had* to talk to Cory. She opened her mouth, but Mistress Coyne spoke first.

"The two of you will have a chance to see each other soon. William and I would like to have you here for dinner tomorrow, Master Updale."

He was still looking at his hands. "Well..."

"Please," Talisa said. She put all the force she could into the word.

He glanced up then. For a long moment, they looked at each other. "All right," he said finally. "Thank you."

"Good. Come at six then."

"And bring some of your carvings with you," Master Coyne added.

LEM AND SHEP WERE OUT the next night, though usually they didn't leave till after dinner. Talisa suspected that Mistress Coyne, always eager for peace in her household, had arranged it that way. Cory and the two apprentices had met once, and all three of them had bristled the way ursells did when one with a strange smell was introduced into the flock.

Cory arrived promptly at six, with his hair not only combed but freshly cut. He wore a blue shirt with yellow flowers woven into it. Mistress Coyne exclaimed over it.

He looked pleased. "Thank you."

"Did Rina make it?" Talisa asked.

"Yes. Normally we'd sell it, but she insisted I wear it tonight."

"Cory's sister is a weaver," Talisa told the Coynes.

"So your sister is an artist too, is she?" Master Coyne eyed the bag Cory held. "And did you bring your carvings to show us?"

"Later, William. Dinner's ready."

Despite the Coynes' best efforts, dinner was strained. Cory was polite, almost excessively so, but his answers were short and he volunteered nothing. He seemed to have trouble concentrating. Twice he dropped his fork. Talisa kept glancing at him. The skin around his eyes was stretched and smudged with tiredness, and the eyes themselves were desperately weary.

She needed to talk to him. Alone. How could she get him by himself? She was so busy puzzling over this question that she missed what Master Coyne said to her and had to ask him to repeat it.

Finally the meal ended. Talisa and Mistress Coyne carried the dishes to the kitchen, then returned to the parlour.

"Let's see these carvings," Master Coyne said.

"William!" Mistress Coyne scolded. "Please forgive him, Master Updale. He's obsessed with fine things, whether they're songs, paintings, or statues."

Cory laughed. For the first time that evening, he looked at ease. "I'll be glad to show you my work. For a price."

"And what price might that be?" There was a faint touch of disapproval in the man's voice.

"Talisa tells me you're the best musician she's ever heard. I'll show you my carvings if you'll play for me."

Master Coyne chuckled. "A fair bargain."

Cory pulled four wooden statues from his bag and placed them on a small table beside the musician. Talisa leaned forward to see better.

Master Coyne picked up a carving of a small dog and turned it this way and that, examining it thoughtfully. The dog was sitting on its haunches, ears pricked, tail raised, head cocked. It looked ready to spring up at any moment to catch a stick or lick its owner's face. Had Cory had a dog like this once? Talisa glanced at him. His face was soft. With memories? Memories of life on the farm?

"Hmmm." Master Coyne put it down and picked up the next one. The boy in it was sitting too, or squatting, to be precise, his head down, his eyes on the ground. Talisa smiled. She had seen small children look like that, absorbed in some rock or insect. Then she caught her breath. The boy's face was pinched, his eyes enormous. The arms resting on his knees were stick-thin.

Master Coyne inspected the carving for some time before setting it aside. His wife picked it up. "Oh," she said, her voice hushed.

The seagull in the third carving seemed to shout with strength and joy and effortless free flight. The grain of the wood Cory had used made it look as though the sun shone on its outstretched wings.

The last statue... Talisa gasped.

Cory glanced at her. "Sorry. I should have asked permission."

He wasn't really sorry, she thought. There may have been a trace of wariness in his eyes, but his mouth tilted upwards.

Master Coyne looked at it, eyebrows raised, then handed it to her. "I think you deserve first inspection."

Her hands shook as she accepted it. "Cory..."

It was her, but not her. Oh, the features were right. But there was strength in the statue, and a sweet gravity, that she didn't possess.

"It's a perfect likeness," Mistress Coyne exclaimed.

Talisa shook her head but couldn't stop the smile tugging at her lips.

"No?" Master Coyne held out his hand. She gave the carving to him and watched him turn it around and around before he put it down.

"May I borrow one of these for a week or so?" he asked. Cory looked startled, then frowned. 'Oh, not the one of Talisa. I imagine you want to keep that."

Cory hesitated. "All right," he said finally.

"Good." Master Coyne examined the statues again, then chose the one of the small boy. He rose. "Now I believe you wanted some music."

It seemed to Talisa that he played especially well that night, precisely, perfectly, with purity and passion. But perhaps she just felt that way because Cory was there. Because the image he'd made of her sang in her heart.

"Thank you," Cory said quietly when the music ended.

Master Coyne bowed. "You are most welcome."

Cory had his cloak on and was almost at the door before Talisa remembered. She had to talk to him. How could she have forgotten?

"I'll go with you to the end of the block." She grabbed her cloak and was out the door before anyone could protest.

They walked for a few steps in silence. Talisa looked up at the clear sky. Tonight, the stars seemed close, almost as close as they did at home.

Cory's gaze followed hers. "If they could sing, they would sound like his music," he said softly.

"Yes."

The night was very still, very peaceful. She wished she could walk through it with Cory, sharing silence, sharing talk about music, and carvings, and stars. But a question burned in her mind just as, six nights earlier, fire had burned in the barracks.

"Cory..."

"Yes?"

"I want... That is, I *have* to ask you something."

"What?" Was there a hint of wariness in his voice?

"Did you..." She stopped. How could she ask this? How could she even *think* it? The idea was absurd. Insulting. But she had to know. She took a deep breath.

"Did you have anything to do with the fire?"

As soon as the words were out, she wanted to take them back. She wanted to explain about Andreas and Master Swanson and the stall keeper's comments. Wanted to apologize. But the silence went on, and on, and on. It constricted her voice.

"No."

Their shoes clattered on the cobblestones. Somewhere, a dog howled.

No. The word echoed over and over in Talisa's head. There had been no anger in his voice. No shock. No hurt. Shouldn't he be angry? Wouldn't he be shocked and hurt if he hadn't done it? If he were innocent?

He stopped. "Do you believe me?"

She stopped too. "I...don't know." Her voice was little more than a whisper.

He sighed. His shoulders sagged. "Yes. Well. Last night, I was going to say maybe we shouldn't see each other again. Funny. I'd forgotten that tonight. I guess...I guess this is it then."

She wanted to say something. She tried to say something. She couldn't.

"Goodbye, Talisa."

She watched him walk down the street. Round the corner. Then he was gone.

RINA

"YOUR YOUNG MAN HASN'T BEEN HERE FOR some time now."

"He's not my young man."

"Hmmm." Master Coyne peered at her from above his spectacles. "Do you know when he's coming next?"

"No."

"He didn't say, the last time he was here?"

Talisa bent her head and inspected her cup, though she knew there was no kala left in it. "No."

"He used to come every second or third night, but I haven't seen him for ten days. We didn't frighten him off, did we?"

Mistress Coyne frowned at her husband. "Leave it be, William." She'd been giving Talisa worried looks lately, though Talisa didn't think she'd let her cheerful mask slip. Maybe she'd been *too* cheerful.

"But I need to see him. I still have his carving."

Talisa raised her head. "Oh." She'd forgotten about the carving. "I know where his brother-in-law has his stall," she said slowly. "I could go there and return it." There was nothing to stop her. It was her free day. Lem and Shep were already out, bundling themselves into their winter cloaks as soon as they'd finished their last spoonfuls of porridge. And she was allowed out now. The arsonists had not been found and soldiers still patrolled the streets but, as Garth had predicted, the buzz of excitement had subsided into an everyday busy hum.

She could ask Bart how Cory was. She could ask him to tell Cory that...

That what? That she was sorry? That she believed him? That she wanted to see him?

But *did* she believe him? And if she didn't...

The fire had killed two men. The second soldier had died of his injuries.

He'd said he 'd had nothing to do with the fire.

Yes. But...

No! She would not go over this again. How many sleepless hours had she spent, thrashing the question this way and that? Cory deserved to have his statue back. She would take it to Bart. That was all.

Master Coyne had said something. "I'm sorry. Would you repeat that?"

"I want to speak to the boy. I have some news for him."

"News?"

He nodded. "I took his carving to an acquaintance of mine, a certain master woodcarver named Mathew Fletcher.

He was taken with the figure, so much so that he wants to meet the lad who made it."

"Mathew Fletcher!" exclaimed Mistress Coyne. "He's the best carver in all Freyfall."

"So he is." The musician looked like a cat licking its whiskers after lapping a whole bowl of cream.

"And he wants to meet Cory? Why?"

Master Coyne practically purred. "He wants to talk to him. Something about an apprenticeship, I believe."

Talisa gasped. Mistress Coyne gaped at him. "An apprenticeship?"

"It's not done this way, not usually. Not for an unknown boy. But Mathew thinks this Updale lad has exceptional talent. I thought he might." Master Coyne turned to Talisa. "So you see why it's so important that Cory hears this news. As I told him, the only way he'll succeed is to apprentice himself to a master. It's not definite that Mathew will accept him, of course, but it would be a shame to miss this opportunity."

She nodded. "I'll ask Bart to tell Cory."

"And say he should come here first. Best I introduce him."

Come here first. She would see him then. Her fingers shook slightly as she picked up a bowl. "I'll wash the dishes, then go."

Mistress Coyne waved her aside. "Don't worry yourself about that. I'll see to the dishes. You'd better be on your way. And be sure you wrap up warmly. It's a miserable day."

It was. Despite her warmest dress and her cloak made of heavy grey ursell wool, Talisa shivered as dense wet mist dug into her bones. She walked quickly, her left hand curled protectively around the small statue resting in her pocket.

The stalls along Weavers Street were practically deserted. People hurried by, huddled into their cloaks, or scurried into the warmth of shops. Bart was shouting the virtues of his wares bravely, but Talisa thought he looked grim. His face brightened as she approached.

"Mistress Thatcher! It's good to see you."

She smiled. "Thank you. How are you doing?"

He waved his hand at his counter, piled high with clothes. "As you can see."

"It's early yet. Perhaps later..."

He snorted and glanced at the sky. "It will be damp and dismal all day. Shoppers don't stop in weather like this. I sometimes wonder why I bother opening up."

Talisa noticed that there were no wooden figures on the stall. "Did someone buy the statue of the old woman?"

"Finally. Though it fetched little enough."

She hoped the person who had bought it loved it as much as she did. "It's about Cory's carvings that I've come."

Bart frowned and started to say something, but she hurried on as she pulled the figure of the small boy out of her pocket. "Master Coyne asked to see some of Cory's work and borrowed this one. He showed it to a woodcarver named Master Fletcher, who thought it was so good he wants to meet Cory and possibly take him as his apprentice. Master Coyne said that if Cory will come to see him, he'll introduce him to Master Fletcher. Will you tell Cory that? And give him this?" She held out the statue.

He didn't take it. "I can't."

She stared at him. "Why not?"

"He doesn't live with us any more."

"Oh." Her hand dropped. "Where does he live?"

"I have no idea. And, quite honestly, I don't care." Bart's voice was hard. So was his face.

She swallowed. "When did he go?"

"A week or more ago."

Shortly after he said goodbye to me. Not long after the fire.

"Why did..." She stopped. It was none of her business. And she wasn't sure she wanted to know. She shivered.

"I don't know. He said he was going. He didn't bother to tell us where. Or why." Bart jammed his fists into his pockets.

They were silent. Passersby hurried past. No one stopped. Talisa looked down at the carving in her hand and held it out again. "Here. If you can't give this to Cory now, at least you can keep it for him. Or sell it."

Bart glanced at the wooden figure. His hand reached out and touched the boy's shoulder gently. But he shook his head. "No."

"But –"

"No."

There was nothing more she could do. She felt as helpless as she had when a neighbour at home had asked her to use a spell to find a missing ursell. He hadn't understood when she'd refused, not believing that a member of her family couldn't work magic.

She wouldn't give up. Not yet. "Does Rina know where Cory might have gone?"

He said nothing, just looked at her. She raised her chin. "It's very important that he gets the message and meets Master Fletcher. It might make all the difference in the world to him."

"It might," Bart agreed. "Unfortunately, Rina has no more idea of where he is than I do."

Her shoulders slumped. There really *was* nothing she could do. "I see. Well, thank you. I'd best be on my way. It was good seeing you."

"Wait," he said. He was frowning, but it was a thoughtful frown, not an angry one. "Rina... She's not been herself lately. A visit from you might cheer her up. She's talked so much about you since Midsummer. If you have time to visit her... If you'd like to, that is."

"I have time, and I'd love to," Talisa said promptly. "I'm afraid I'm not sure how to get there though. If you could give me directions..."

He shook his head. "You'd never find it. The streets are too twisting around our place. Maybe not overly safe for a young woman on her own either. No, I'll close up for a while and go with you. I might as well, for all the business I'm getting."

A moment later, the shutters were down and locked and they were on their way.

THE BUILDING WAS EVEN SHABBIER than she remembered, the hall dustier, the smell of mould stronger. She followed Bart up the cracked stairs, wrinkling her nose.

Bart opened his door. Over his shoulder, Talisa saw Rina sitting in front of her loom. She wasn't weaving though, simply staring into space.

"I brought a guest," Bart announced.

Rina glanced around, then jumped to her feet. "Talisa! How good to see you. Where did Bart find you? I'm so glad he brought you here. How have you been? Do you like living in Freyfall? Here, sit down. I'll make some kala. We still have some left over from Midsummer, waiting for a special occasion." She darted around, pulling out a chair, setting a pot of water over the hearth, chattering away, her cheeks flushed, her eyes bright. Bart watched her, smiling, for a minute or two, then announced that he should return to the stall.

Rina looked up. "Why not stay for some kala now that you're here?"

"No time."

"How's business?"

"About as you'd expect on a day like this."

"But you still think you should go back? Can't you rest for once?"

He shook his head. "There may be some customers yet."

She sighed but raised no more objections, simply bringing two cups to the table and sinking into a chair.

Talisa sipped her drink as the sound of Bart's footsteps clattered down the stairs, then faded away. She studied Rina. Now that the young woman was still, her face had sagged into lines of weariness. Her eyes, so like Cory's, looked smudged.

As though feeling Talisa's gaze, Rina looked up and smiled. "So how are you? How are your studies coming? Cory said –" She stopped.

"I'm fine," Talisa said slowly. She paused, then asked, "Rina, do you know where Cory is?" She had not meant to ask. Bart had told her Rina did not know. But some stubborn spark of hope made her try anyway.

Rina's hands clasped and unclasped in her lap. "No."

"No idea at all? Not even a guess?"

Rina shook her head.

It had been foolish to ask. Foolish to hope. Talisa looked down at the table. There was a crack in it. She remembered tracing it with her finger the first time she'd come here.

Rina reached over and touched her hand. "I'm sorry," she said softly. "Do you care for Cory then? I've been wondering."

Talisa glanced up sharply. "No! At least... That's not why I need to find him. He has a chance to be apprenticed to a master carver. If I can get a message to him..."

Rina said nothing, just watched her steadily. Cory had watched her that way, more than once. Why did Rina's eyes have to be so like his? So large, so brown, so warm? Talisa gazed down at the crack again, remembered again the night she had come here with Cory. Cory...

"Yes," she whispered. "I do care."

"I'm glad," Rina said simply.

Talisa looked up and swallowed.

"He cares about you so much."

"Does he?" Talisa blinked back tears.

"Oh yes. He was so filled with joy every time he went to meet you. And that carving he made of you... Did you see it?"

Talisa nodded.

A small smile crept into Rina's eyes. "He offered his other statues to Bart – a gull, a dog, some street urchins – but not that one."

Talisa thought of the stall counter, bare of wooden figures. "Bart didn't take them?"

The smile left Rina's eyes. "Bart was far too angry at that point to take anything Cory offered."

"Is that why Cory left? Because he and Bart had a fight?"

"No. The fight came after Cory said he was leaving, not before. Bart kept asking why he was going, and where, and Cory just kept saying it was best he leave and best he didn't tell us why or where. That made Bart even angrier." She looked down at her cup. "It's been so hard keeping peace between them, this past year and more, what with Bart going on and on at Cory, and Cory getting angry and shouting back at Bart. He didn't shout this time, though."

Talisa frowned. "Why was Bart so upset about Cory leaving, since they don't get along?"

Rina tilted her cup this way and that, swirling the kala. "Partly for my sake, I think. But not just that. We grew up together, you see. The Berrymores' farm was next to ours. We were always in each other's kitchens. We tended our sheep together, and helped each other get the seeds in and the harvest off. Bart always treated Cory like a younger brother. He went on at Cory not because he didn't care for him but because he *did*. He was afraid –" She broke off.

Talisa gripped the edge of the table. "Afraid of what?"

Rina said nothing.

"Rina..." Talisa stopped. Took a deep breath. Let it out slowly. "Rina, is Cory in danger?"

There was a fractional pause. "Of course not. Why would he be?"

"Because of the fire."

Rina's fingers were clenched so tightly around the handle of her cup that they looked white. "What fire?"

"The fire in the barracks." Talisa looked away from Rina, then back. "I'm sorry. I know I have no right to suspect anything. And he did deny it. But... He seems so bitter about your eviction from the farm and about the poverty around him. And there were other things. Little things, I know, but... And now he's disappeared, so soon after the fire."

She waited for Rina to speak. To explain. To protest. Surely Rina would. Surely Rina would have good reasons why Cory couldn't have been involved with the arson.

She waited a long time. Finally Rina said, in a great, gasping breath, "I don't know! Oh Talisa, I don't know!" The sobs came then, loud, wrenching sobs that shook her whole body.

Talisa closed her eyes. She shouldn't have spoken. She hated herself for speaking. She hated Rina for not giving her the reassurance she hungered for.

No. She didn't. But she couldn't wrap her arms around her, the way she wanted to. If she did, something inside her would shatter and she would start shaking too.

At last Rina's tears subsided. She wiped her hand across a tear-stained face. "I'm sorry."

Talisa shook her head. "It's my fault."

"No. What a way to treat a guest. Drowning you in my tears. You must think... But I've been so frightened. And I can't talk about it to Bart. He just gets angry. I haven't been sleeping well," she said apologetically.

Talisa nodded.

Rina stood up, a bit clumsily, and found a handkerchief. She blew her nose.

"I don't know," she said, her back to Talisa. "Cory talked a lot about the need to stop landlords from evicting their tenants, the need to make Queen Elira and her court see how desperately things needed to change. He would go on and on about it, till Bart would snap that there was nothing he or anyone else could do, and that such talk would only get him into trouble. I don't know if it was more than just talk. I do know Cory met with others who felt the same way. He spent more and more time with them. He even neglected his carving. That enraged Bart too."

She turned. "I don't know," she repeated. "I didn't think Cory would do anything *wrong*. Anything violent." Tears started to flow again. She wiped them away angrily.

"He said he had no part in it," Talisa said quietly.

A smile flickered through Rina's tears, like sun through rain. Then it disappeared. "But you don't believe him."

Talisa hesitated. "I'm...not sure," she said finally. Rina deserved the truth. Anyway, she wouldn't believe her if she said she was sure.

Rina rubbed the heels of her hands across her eyes. "If he did... If he had anything to do with the fire, it's only because he thought no one would be hurt."

"Yes."

They were both silent. A stray beam of sunlight broke through the grey mist and fell onto the table. Rina glanced out the window. "It's close to noon. You'll stay and have a bite to eat, won't you?"

"I don't want to be a bother."

"You won't be." Rina took a loaf of bread from a shelf. "I don't often have anyone to talk to during the day. Bart's too busy. He tries so hard to make enough for us to live on, especially now."

"Why especially now?"

Rina blushed. "I'm having a baby."

Talisa jumped to her feet and hugged her. "That's wonderful! When?"

"Late spring. It's early days still. You're the only one I've told, except Bart, of course. I was going to tell Cory, but that was the night he left." She blinked back tears. Talisa felt a sudden flash of anger at Cory.

Rina set two plates of bread, cheese, and onions on the table and sat down. "Tell me about this woodcarver who's interested in taking Cory as an apprentice."

Talisa told her as much as she knew.

"Oh," Rina said when she finished. "That would be perfect for Cory."

Talisa nodded. "So you see why it's so important that I let him know about this." *If it's not too late,* a voice said loudly in her head. *If he's not entangled in fire and death and all their consequences.* She was sure the same thoughts ran through Rina's mind. She cleared her throat. "Are you sure you have no idea where he may have gone? You said he met with others who shared his ideas. Do you know who they are? Where they live?"

"No. He never said and I never asked. I guess I didn't want to know. The person I remember best is a handsome young man with dark hair who sometimes came with messages. But I have no idea what his name is."

Talisa almost choked on the piece of bread she was chewing. Andreas Wells! Of course! Why hadn't she thought of him?

She stayed for some time. They talked about weaving and music and Rina's hopes for her baby, but Talisa thought both their minds were on Cory. Around mid-afternoon, she rose.

"I really must go."

Rina stood up. "I'll come with you. No," she said firmly as Talisa started to protest. "I insist. The walk will be good for me, and I'll only go as far as Weavers Street. Bart and I can come home together when he closes the stall."

As they left the room, the door opposite opened and a man came out. Behind him, a baby was wailing. He staggered past them and down the stairs. Even after he'd gone, Talisa could smell the wine fumes from his breath.

Rina said nothing till they were halfway down the street. Then she turned to Talisa, her hands clenched, her eyes bright with unshed tears. "I do not want to raise my child here. Not in this building. Not in this neighbourhood. Not in this city."

Talisa touched her arm. "Rina..."

Rina's shoulders slumped. "I know. I have no choice. There's never any choice when you're poor." She turned and walked on. Talisa walked beside her. If only there was something she could do to help.

Well, maybe there was. If finding Cory would help. Because she was determined to find him. And she thought she knew where to start looking.

SEARCHING FOR CORY

How was she to find Andreas and Master Swanson? Talisa brooded about it that night as she lay in bed, unable to sleep. At least it was better than thinking about Rina's tear-soaked face, about Rina's words, about Cory... Talisa twisted over and lay face down.

Master Coyne might know where the musician lived. How could she bring up the subject without making her interest too obvious?

The next night at dinner, she asked about various people who'd performed at The Laughing Lute the night she was there: the drummer who'd started them off, the flutist with the long dark hair and worn face, Mel. Master Coyne had a wealth of information about the first two, but shook his head over Mel.

Lem grinned. "He's young and loves to make up funny songs. Not always very respectable ones. You might ask Garth about him. They seem to be friends."

148

Talisa nodded, her eyes on her plate. "And that man who sang about the woman from the hills. Alain Swanson. Does anyone know where he lives?" She raised a piece of salmon to her mouth and chewed.

Master Coyne snorted. "Probably in some hole in the wall. It's all he could afford, with the money he doesn't make from his music. I'm more interested in the where-abouts of that young friend of yours. Still no word of him?"

"No."

"A pity. Mathew Fletcher won't wait forever."

Lem and Shep smirked. They weren't making any effort to hide their pleasure at Cory's absence. Talisa forced herself to smile at them. "Are you going to The Laughing Lute tonight? I'd love to join you if you are."

"No. No, I'm sorry," Shep stammered.

"We could change our plans," Lem offered. "At least, *I* could."

Shep glared at him. "So could I."

"No need of that," Mistress Coyne said. "It's been ages since we've been there. We could go and take Talisa with us. Couldn't we, William?"

"Eh? What's that, my dear?" Master Coyne peered at her.

"We could go to The Laughing Lute with Talisa."

"But it's a chilly night," he protested.

"So? There are cloaks."

"And it's a long walk."

"There are carriages."

"But —"

"Really, William. I sometimes think you wouldn't budge from this house if it weren't for your performances and Guild meetings."

He threw up his hands. "Very well, very well. Have it your way, Lizbet."

"Good. We can enjoy the music and the boys won't have to change their plans."

The boys didn't look happy about not changing their plans. Talisa hid a smile. But later, jolting over the cobblestones in the carriage, she chewed her lip. It would be easier to have a quiet word with Master Swanson if she were with Lem and Shep. Mistress Coyne's eyes were too sharp.

She needn't have worried. Alain Swanson wasn't there. Nor was Andreas. Talisa kept glancing up every time the door opened, but they never appeared. It had been foolish to hope.

The evening wasn't a total waste. The music was good, very good, and Master Coyne's the best of all. He was called on time and again, and practically had to be dragged from the tavern. The three of them sang in the carriage all the way home.

The next morning, Talisa and Garth were set to copying music while Shep and Lem had a lesson on the pipes. Talisa glanced sideways at Garth, who was concentrating on drawing a treble clef.

"Do you remember hearing Alain Swanson, the night we were both at The Laughing Lute?" she asked.

"Yes, of course," he said promptly.

Talisa tucked a strand of red hair behind her ear and reached over to dip her pen in the inkwell. "Do you know anything about him?"

Garth looked up. "Not much. He keeps himself apart from the rest of us. I heard that it was once thought that he had a promising future, but that he lost it over some dispute with the Guild. That's just a rumour, of course," he added, and returned his attention to the notes he was copying.

Talisa drew in a chord. "Does he often play at The Laughing Lute? Or anywhere else?"

"I've never seen him anywhere else, only sometimes at The Lute. Not often enough," he said regretfully.

"Do you know where he lives?" She tried to make her voice casual.

"I've no idea."

Her pen stopped for an instant and left a blotch. She reached for a piece of linen to blot it.

"Is something wrong, Talisa?" She felt Garth's eyes on her face.

"Wrong? No, of course not. Why do you ask?"

"No reason. I just... Sorry." He bent over his sheet of paper.

Talisa pressed the linen to the ink spot, then removed it and dipped her pen again.

No one seemed to know where Alain Swanson lived. If she couldn't find him, how was she to find Cory?

If she were a wizard, she could use a spell. But she wasn't. An old, familiar ache twisted in her stomach.

She wasn't a wizard. But Garth was. She sucked in her breath and stared at the notes dancing up and down along the page.

Did she dare ask Garth to cast a finding spell for her? What would she say if he asked her why she wanted to locate Master Swanson? The truth? That she thought the musician might know where Cory was? But what if Garth then wanted to know how come Cory and Master Swanson knew each other? She thought about secret messages, and fires, and shuddered.

Perhaps she should simply ask Garth to cast a spell to find Cory.

But Garth and Cory had never met. She might not be a wizard, but she had lived with them all her life. She knew it was far easier to locate someone you'd met, if only briefly, than someone you'd never even seen.

If she didn't ask Garth for his help, what else could she do? Nothing.

She glanced at Garth again. "Garth..."

He looked up. "Yes?"

"Will you make a finding spell for me?" She spoke softly, though there was little need. Shep was practising the pipes while Lem and Master Coyne listened critically. Shep was a skilled harpist, but he hadn't learned the art of playing the pipes yet. He seemed to think that loudness could hide his lack of expertise.

Garth's eyebrows shot up. "A finding spell?"

"Yes. I want to find Master Swanson." Talisa waited tensely for Garth to ask why, but he didn't. He shook his head. "I'm not the person to ask."

"I know you don't like magic, but –"

"Oh, it's not that I *dislike* it. It's just that I like music more. But a finding spell?" He grinned suddenly, his intent, serious face turning into that of a mischievous imp. "The last time I tried one, I transformed a girl into a cat."

Talisa smiled. "So you did. I'd forgotten."

"So you see, it might not be safe."

"I'll stay well clear of you," she promised. She paused. "Will you do it?"

He hesitated. She held her breath.

"All right. Don't hope for too much, though. It's not just my past history with this spell. It's also that I don't really know the man, and I have nothing that belongs to him. But I certainly remember his songs. Maybe through them..." Garth looked thoughtful. "I'll cast the spell tonight and let you know tomorrow if it worked."

Sleep was harder than ever to capture that night. Questions kept running through Talisa's head long after all the candles in the house had been extinguished.. Would Garth be able to locate Master Swanson and his apprentice? If he did, would they know where Cory was? And if so...

Did she want to see him?

Yes. No. She didn't know. If he'd had anything to do with the fire...

She could leave a message for him about Master Fletcher. She didn't have to see him.

Yes, but...

She woke the next morning with tiredness attached to her like a layer of dirt that couldn't be washed away with cold water. Garth never appeared till after breakfast and morning chores were done. They seemed to go on forever that day. But at last he arrived. The first thing he did was look at Talisa and nod. Her heart started to thump.

It wasn't until afternoon that she had a chance to speak to him privately. Master Coyne had asked Garth to give her a lesson on the harp while he tried to get Shep and Lem to produce something that sounded like music on the pipes.

"Where does he live?" Talisa asked.

"I can't really say."

Her fingers stumbled on the strings. "What? I thought –"

"Oh, the spell worked. The trouble is, I don't know the part of Freyfall he lives in. I can't tell you the name of his street or even how to get there. Here. Move your hands like this."

She did.

"I wish I had six fingers," Garth said, watching her hands. "They work so much better on stringed instruments."

Talisa ignored this comment. "Are you sure you didn't see any street names?"

He nodded.

She stopped playing. Master Coyne turned around and looked at them, eyebrows raised. Hastily, she started playing again. Garth leaned closer, as though inspecting the position of her fingers on the strings.

"Don't look so unhappy. I'm fairly sure – well, I *think* – I can find Master Swanson's house if I walk around the area. I thought we could go there on our first free day."

That was three days away. Talisa said nothing, but Garth must have seen something in her face.

"Or sooner. We could go tonight if you like."

Tonight! Her hands on the harp strings produced a sound that made her wince. Master Coyne glanced at her again. She flushed and tried to concentrate.

"The Coynes will want to know where I'm going, and why," she murmured.

Garth considered this. "I could say I'm going to The Pelican's Nest and ask you to join me. You've never been there, have you?"

"No."

"Good. The Coynes can't refuse you the opportunity to hear the music there." He paused, then said softly, "I don't know what this is all about or why it's so important, but don't worry. Our plan should work."

IT ALMOST FAILED. Master and Mistress Coyne agreed readily enough, but when Lem and Shep heard that Talisa was going to The Pelican's Nest with Garth, they immediately said they'd come too. Talisa scrambled for a polite way to discourage them, but came up with nothing.

"What was that?" Mistress Coyne asked. "Plans to go out? I'm afraid I need you to move the furniture in the parlour and dining room tonight so Mistress Glover and I can give the floors a good scrubbing and waxing first thing tomorrow."

Shep and Lem looked glum. Talisa breathed a sigh of relief.

Garth called for her soon after supper and they set off in the clear, cool night. There'll be frost come morning, Talisa thought, and shivered.

"Cold?"

"Mmm." After a moment she said, more to herself than to him, "I wish I hadn't had to lie to the Coynes."

"We could stop at The Pelican's Nest on our way," Garth suggested. "Then it wouldn't be a total lie."

He sounded far too eager. Just how difficult would it be to get him to leave once the music started? "No, thank you."

The way soon grew unfamiliar. Talisa gazed at the landmarks they passed, trying to memorize them. Garth strode along confidently at first, but as the streets narrowed and the houses became poorer, his steps faltered. He peered about anxiously and retraced their route a couple of times. Talisa was glad the stars were out. There were no lamps on these roads, and many of the decaying buildings had no candlelight reflected in their windows. The buildings themselves cast long shadows across their path. Several times, she stumbled over unseen garbage.

"This is one of the oldest parts of the city," Garth explained. His voice sounded loud in the silence. "The roads follow ancient cow paths."

She could believe it. The streets seemed to wind in and out of each other like threads woven by some mad artist.

"This isn't going to work," Garth muttered, coming to a halt in an ill-smelling cul-de-sac. They were somewhere near the river. Talisa could hear it and feel its cool breath.

"You don't think you can find it?" She tried to keep her dismay out of her voice.

He shook his head. "Every time I think I'm on the right track, I get turned around. I'm sorry, Talisa."

She swallowed. "It's not your fault."

"Yes it is. If I were a better wizard, I would have made a spell that worked."

If she were *any* sort of wizard, she could have made a spell herself. If she were her sister, she would have found Cory by now. She remembered her neighbour's strayed ursell again. Welwyn had tracked it down even though there were no visible hoofprints to be seen. The animal had gone far. At one point, Welwyn had thought she'd lost it. She hadn't given up though. She'd...

"Garth, could you make a new finding spell? Now that we're closer."

He stared at her, his face a pale oval in the moonlight. Then he slapped his thigh. "Of course! Why didn't I think of that?"

He shut his eyes and muttered some words. As always when she was close to a spell, Talisa could almost *see* power trembling in the air.

She waited. Minutes ticked by. If only she could help. If only...

No. This was no time to let her old feelings of frustration and helplessness overwhelm her. She took a deep breath and let it out slowly. And waited.

A man came out of one of the buildings. He gave them a curious glance as he passed. No wonder. They must be a strange sight, two people standing motionless in the middle of the street.

Garth opened his eyes.

"Did you find...?"

He nodded. "It's not far. I can't say I know where it is

exactly, but I know the direction to go, and I think I can spot it when we get nearer."

She followed him out of the cul-de-sac, down a winding road, then another. They met no one else, and none of the buildings they passed betrayed any lights. Most of them looked old. And decrepit. And deserted. The sound of rushing water was louder now. The river must be very close.

Then Garth stopped in front of a lean, two-storeyed house that looked as derelict and deserted as its neighbours. "Here."

The House by the River

TALISA STARED AT THE BUILDING. IT SEEMED to stare back with dark, vacant eyes. "Are you sure this is the right place?"

"Yes. At least, I *think* so," Garth said uncertainly. He peered into the darkness. "Look. There's a light."

There was. A frail light shone at the back of the house. So someone was home. Andreas? Master Swanson? If the latter, how would he react when a perfect stranger asked him if he knew where Cory was?

Well, there was only one way to find out. She squared her shoulders and started towards the building.

"Talisa, wait," Garth said. He was frowning, his eyes shifting from the house to the street and back. "This isn't a very good place to be. Especially at night. Maybe we should go back."

She shook her head.

He sighed and moved forward.

"No. Wait here. I won't be long."

"I can't let you go in by yourself," he protested.

"I won't go inside. I just want to ask a simple question."

"But —"

"Please."

He stopped. Talisa felt a wave of affection wash over her. Even now he wasn't asking any awkward questions.

The door, made of unpainted, unvarnished poplar, was thin and cracked. She hesitated, then raised her hand and knocked firmly. Waited. Knocked again.

The door opened. "Yes?"

There was no light in this part of the house. The man facing her was nothing but a shadow.

"Master Swanson?"

"Yes. What can I do for you?" His speaking voice was lower than his singing voice, and soft.

"I...I want to ask you a question."

He waited, dark, unhelpful. Now that she was standing still, the cool air bit into her. She wrapped her arms around herself.

"I... Do you know where Cory is?"

"I'm acquainted with several Corys," he said promptly. "Which one?"

Fool. This is Freya. You need two names. "Cory Updale."

"Updale...Updale. No, I'm afraid I know no one of that name."

She stared at him, but could only make out his outline. "But you must!"

"I must? Why must I?" Mockery edged his tone.

She flushed. "Andreas said —"

"Ah, Andreas. Yes, Andreas says many things, most of them untrue. Not that he means badly. He just likes making up stories. Perhaps it's Andreas who knows this...Updale, was it? Unfortunately, Andreas is no longer with me. He found that living with a master who was — less than affluent, shall we say? — was harder than he'd foreseen. He took off for more promising pastures. Now, if you'll excuse me..." He reached for the door.

"No. Wait. Please." Disappointment, as bitter as wormwood, clogged her throat. She cleared it. "Can you tell me where Andreas is now?"

"I have no idea. He didn't grace me with that information."

It was all for nothing. Her hope. Garth's spell. Their walk through the narrow, deserted streets. Master Swanson not only didn't know where Cory was, he didn't even *know* him. And Andreas, charming, dramatic Andreas, who liked making up stories, had vanished as completely as Cory had. For a moment, the darkness in front of her, with its darker shadow, blurred. She blinked back tears.

"Thank you." She half turned to go.

Wait. Andreas might like telling stories, but Cory didn't. And Cory had asked about Master Swanson. Which meant he knew him.

Why had the musician lied?

It didn't matter. What mattered was that if he'd lied about one thing, he might have lied about another.

She turned back, opened her mouth, and yelled, "Andreas!"

The man in the doorway said something, she wasn't sure what. She ignored him. Behind her, she felt, rather than heard, Garth move forward. She ignored him too. She called again, "Andreas!"

A light appeared in the blackness. A candle, held in the hand of a tall young man. A man she knew.

"Who –?"

"Andreas, do you remember me? Talisa Thatcher? I met you one morning in Portby Square. Cory introduced us. You gave him a message from Master Swanson."

The flame of the candle reflected off Andreas's dazzling white teeth. "Of course I remember you. How could I forget? Every moment of that enchanted encounter is etched forever in my memory. But I didn't expect to see you here. What brings you to our humble abode?"

"Andreas –" Master Swanson started to say.

Talisa interrupted. "I'm here to find Cory."

Master Swanson reached out a hand to stop his apprentice, who was now standing beside him, but he was too late.

"How did you know he was here?" Andreas asked in simple wonder.

She stared at him. Something leaped inside her. Excitement? Relief? Fear? She didn't know.

After a moment, Master Swanson said, "You'd better come inside." His gaze slid across her shoulder. "Both of you."

"I don't think..." Garth began, but Talisa was already following the light of the candle. She heard a muttered curse behind her, then Garth's footsteps.

The room they entered was small and bare, lit only by a stubby candle squatting on the table and its twin in Andreas's hand. In their light, Talisa saw cracks in the ceiling and paint peeling from the walls. There was no fire in the hearth. She shivered. It was almost as cold indoors as out. But at least the room was clean except for the unwashed plates on the table. Three plates, Talisa noted.

"Please sit down." Master Swanson waved to a couple of chairs by the table.

She remained standing. "Cory is here?"

"It would be pointless to deny it now," Master Swanson said dryly.

Andreas flushed. "I thought she knew. Anyway, Cory wouldn't mind her knowing he's here."

"Mmm." Master Swanson didn't sound convinced. He regarded Talisa. "I heard you sing at The Laughing Lute. You have a lovely voice. It's pure and effortless, with undertones that move the heart." He said this, not as one giving a compliment, but as simply as someone would state that it was a clear day.

"Thank you," she stammered. "I... Your song... It was very powerful. But where –?"

"And you?" he asked Garth. "Who are you?"

"Garth Spellman." Garth was eyeing the musician warily.

"Ah." Master Swanson smiled. "A name to be reckoned with. I've been wanting to meet you."

Garth blinked. "You have? Why? And why did you say a name to be reckoned with? Because of Grandfather?"

"Konrad Spellman is indeed a wizard of renown, but no. I wanted to meet the person who composed 'The Helping Hand.' We have much in common."

Garth blinked again. "We do?"

"I too write about those who live on the streets. What inspired your song?"

"Well, I was with Cat —"

"Excuse me," Talisa interrupted. "I'm sorry, but where is Cory?"

Master Swanson sighed. "Upstairs."

She drew in her breath.

"Would you like to see him?"

Her stomach lurched. *Did* she want to see Cory?

She could give Master Swanson her message. Leave.

If she did that, she would always live with unanswered questions, doubts, the ache of not knowing.

"Yes, please," she whispered.

Master Swanson turned to his apprentice. "Andreas, show Mistress Thatcher the way, then rejoin Master Spellman and me. Please sit down," he said to Garth.

Garth glanced uncertainly at Talisa. She nodded and followed Andreas, who was heading towards a door at the end of the room. He opened it and she saw a flight of narrow, uneven stairs.

She climbed carefully, her heart thumping. What would she say to Cory? What would he say to her?

Andreas tapped lightly on a door at the top of the stairs. There was no response. He knocked more loudly. After a moment, a sleepy voice called, "Who's there?"

The apprentice gave Talisa a conspiratorial smile. "Andreas."

"Go away. I'm sleeping."

"No, you're not. And it's important." Andreas was practically purring with pleasure.

There was silence. Then the door swung open. Instinctively, Talisa stepped into the darkness beyond the candle's glow.

"What is it?" Cory's hair was ruffled by sleep, his eyes smudged with fatigue, but his face was alert, his voice sharp.

"Someone came to the house tonight."

Was it her imagination, or did Cory go a shade paler? "And?"

Andreas's voice sank to a murmur. "This person was looking for you."

This time there could be no doubt about Cory's reaction. His body went rigid. Colour drained from his face. His gaze left Andreas and roamed the darkness. Talisa thought of a rock lizard she'd once seen, crouched low to the ground, its eyes flickering here and there, searching for danger, searching for escape. Cory's eyes found her.

Joy flared across his face, like sudden, brilliant sunshine. It only lasted a moment, but it was enough. She stepped forward.

"Hello, Cory."

"Talisa! What are you doing here? How –"

"I'll be glad to tell you. May I come in?"

"What? Oh. Of course." He took a couple of backwards steps and she followed him into the room.

"I'll light your candle, shall I?" Andreas asked. There was a thin little candle on a low chest in the corner. After he'd lit it, Talisa saw a room even smaller and barer than the one below. A sloping ceiling hung above two blankets and a bundle of clothes on the slivery wood floor. One sway-backed chair stood below a small window.

"Please have a chair, Mistress Thatcher," Andreas said. She sat.

"You shouldn't be here," Cory said.

Andreas shook his head. "What a way to greet a beautiful lady who's come so far searching for you. I assure you, Mistress Thatcher, that *I* am delighted to see you. Every minute of our, alas, too brief meeting has etched itself into my mind and heart." He gave her a charming smile.

"You're too kind," she murmured. She should encourage Andreas to leave. She needed to talk to Cory. But it was easier to exchange trivialities with Andreas than to face...

Face the truth.

"I state the simple facts. I only wish that I could think that you remember me half as well as I remember you and that, in your anxiety to find Cory, you also harboured, in a tiny corner of your heart, a desire to see me as well. Not that I wish to come between you or alter the course of true love, of course." He shot a sideways glance at Cory, whose face had gone the fiery red of the setting sun.

Talisa's face was just as hot. "I came with a message for Cory. An important one. That's all." Her voice sounded stiff in her own ears.

"A message?" Andreas looked interested.

She said nothing. He waited a minute, then sighed. "Well, I shall leave you to deliver it. I will see you before you leave, Mistress Thatcher, and in the meantime I will be thinking of how your presence adorns our house." A moment later, his footsteps could be heard thudding down the stairs. She and Cory were alone in the spartan, ill-lit room. He was leaning against the wall. The candle cast strange shadows on his face.

"I'm sorry," he said. His voice was low.

"Sorry?"

"For what he said. I didn't... I never gave him any reason to think..." He stopped.

"No, of course not." She looked down at her hands.

Silence stretched between them.

"What is your message?" he asked at last.

She looked up. "It's from Master Coyne."

His eyebrows shot up. "Master Coyne?"

"Yes. He took your statue, the one you'd left with him, to a carver named Mathew Fletcher. Master Fletcher wants to meet you and explore the possibility of your becoming his apprentice."

He was staring at her as if she were speaking some unfamiliar language.

"Mathew Fletcher is one of the best carvers in Freyfall," she added.

"I know he is. I've seen some of his work. But... He can't want *me* as his apprentice."

She leaned forward. "Why not?"

"Because he's the best. He can't be interested in me. I'm

not... I'm nothing. I've never even had a lesson."

She smiled at him. "He must think you're more than nothing."

"But..." He looked wildly around the room, then rubbed a hand across his eyes.

"You're awake," she assured him.

"I wasn't sure. First you appear. Now this. Dreams..." His voice ached with longing.

Her throat hurt. "It's not a dream."

He gazed at her. She gazed back. Slowly, tension left his body. The strain that had sharpened his face into angular lines eased, to be replaced by dawning wonder.

"To be Master Fletcher's apprentice... To work at what I love... I could learn so much." His fingers moved, as though feeling the wood they would carve.

Then his hands fell. He stared down at the floor. "But I can't."

Talisa caught her breath. "Why can't you?"

He was silent.

"Why can't you?" she repeated.

"Because I couldn't fit it in. I don't have time."

"Don't have time? But Cory, this is important. This is your *life*."

He said nothing for a minute. "It's important, yes. But it's not as important as...well, other things."

"What other things?"

He met her eyes steadily. "Changing Freya. Making sure no more tenants are thrown off their land. Making life better for the poor in Freyfall."

For a moment, the image of the singer with bare feet stopped her from speaking. She shook it off. "Cory, you can't waste this opportunity. You can't waste your talent."

His face was set. "What does my talent, whatever it's worth, matter compared to the lives of those who have nothing?"

"It *does* matter. How can you say it doesn't?" She was trembling with the force of her conviction.

He laughed.

She jumped to her feet. "This is not funny."

"But it is."

"It is *not*. How can you –"

He held up his hand. "Don't you remember what you said to me once?"

She stared at him.

"I can't recall your exact words, but they were something to the effect that your gift for music was meaningless compared to your lack of ability in magic. You wanted to be a wizard like the rest of your family so you could help Uglessia."

"Oh." She sank back into her chair. "That's different."

He'd stopped laughing. "Is it?"

Of course it was. Wasn't it?

His shoulders slumped. He went over and sat on his blankets. "I don't know why we're arguing about this. The opportunity comes too late anyway."

The words hung in the air like ominous black clouds. Talisa closed her eyes. She'd been trying to escape this question. Now she had to ask it.

She opened her eyes. "Cory," she said, then stopped. She took a deep breath and started again, speaking slowly, carefully, as though picking her way along a crumbling cliff edge. "Cory, I know you're angry at the way your family and others were treated. I know you want to change things, make them better. But *how?*"

He was silent.

She wet her lips. "You told me you had nothing to do with the burning of the barracks. I want to believe you."

"But you don't," he said flatly.

"I'm just...not sure."

They were both silent. She found she couldn't look at him. She gazed at the candle instead, flickering on the small chest like the ghost of old dreams.

"But you came here tonight," he said finally. "Why?"

She still couldn't look at him. "To bring you a message."

"Even though you thought I might have played a role in the burning of the barracks?"

What could she say to that? She kept her eyes on the candle. Wax was dripping down it onto the chest. It would be hard to get it off.

Her silence had gone on too long. She turned to face him. "Cory..."

But he wasn't paying attention. His head was cocked. Listening.

Then she heard it too. Feet. Clattering on the cobblestones. Many feet. Coming closer. Closer.

She sprang to her feet. "What is it?"

He held up his hand for silence, but there was no need. Even if she'd cried out loudly, she couldn't have drowned the stamping feet. The pounding on the door. The shouted command.

"Open in the Queen's name."

FLIGHT

BLOOD LEECHED FROM CORY'S FACE. HE looked around wildly, searching for a place to hide in this bare cupboard of a room. Talisa's breath caught painfully in her throat.

Feet leaped up the stairs. A moment later, the door was flung open. "Quick," Garth gasped. His eyes were huge. "Master Swanson says he'll delay them as long as he can. We're to leave by the back door."

Cory didn't pause to ask Garth who he was. He grabbed the bundle that had served as his pillow and dashed for the stairs. Talisa followed. The three of them raced down the dark, uneven steps more quickly than she would have thought possible. Certainly faster than was safe.

The pounding was very loud now. So were the shouts. Above them, she heard Master Swanson's voice, sharp with annoyance. "Who's creating such a racket? What do you want?"

"We're soldiers of the Queen. Open in her name."

A fractional pause. "How do I know you're who you say you are, not some ruffians out to rob an honest man?"

Andreas was standing by the back door. He inched it open, a finger to his lips. Talisa thought she caught a gleam of excited pleasure in his eyes.

Then they were outside, in the wild grass and weeds that fringed the river. From the street, she heard someone call, "This is Captain Waterford speaking. Open up immediately or it will be the worse for you."

She couldn't catch Master Swanson's response, but a minute later the captain roared, "What do you mean, prove it? Look out your window, man, and you'll see that we're soldiers."

It hadn't rained in over two weeks. Every move she made through the brittle waist-high grass rustled and crackled. Surely they would hear, even above the clamour of heated words and banging fists. She tried to hold her skirt tight to her body. It didn't help.

A twig snapped behind her. She turned her head sharply. It was Garth. His mouth opened and closed in what was probably a soundless "Sorry." She nodded and looked ahead again.

In front of her, Cory was hunched forward, face down. Why...?

Of course. If anyone glanced their way, the first thing they'd notice was the pale oval of their faces.

Would the captain think to send one of his men to the riverbank behind the house? He might. She risked a quick glance upwards. The moon was behind a cloud, but the stars were bright. She pulled the hood of her cloak over her red hair and bent forward. *Garth, follow my example. Please.* They were all in dark clothes. That should help. *Please. Spirits of the mountains, please.*

Her heart seemed to pound as loudly as the fists battering Master Swanson's door.

A prickle caught in her ankle. She wrenched it away, wincing as the thorns bit her fingers.

Move. Move faster. We must hurry.

It was so hard, bent over like this. Hard to walk quickly. Impossible to walk silently.

She stumbled. Almost fell.

The banging and shouting stopped. Had Master Swanson finally let them in, or had the soldiers realized their prey wasn't in the house after all? She longed to raise her head and look behind her, but forced herself to hunch even closer to the ground.

No sound of pursuit. Only the panting of their breaths, the rustling of their clothes, the occasional snapping of a twig, the swishing and swirling of the river to their left, the rush of the waterfall further away.

How long did they have before pursuit came? Before the soldiers searched the house and found that their quarry had escaped them? Or perhaps Master Swanson would be able to persuade them that the person they sought never had been there. After all, he had almost convinced her he didn't even know Cory.

Please. Please.

Her back ached as though she were an arthritic old woman. More burrs and prickles stuck in her skirt, her cloak. Her hands were scratched and bleeding from pushing aside thorns.

It seemed lighter. The moon must have slipped out from behind the cloud. The buildings on their right cast protective shadows, but the shadows didn't stretch far enough. Anyone could see their hunched forms bobbing up and down through the rough grass. She held her breath. Listened.

No yells. No running feet.

Not yet anyway. They went on.

She had no idea where they were, or in what direction they were going, only that they were walking – if walking it could be called – beside the river, and that the roar of the waterfall was growing louder. Finally, Cory veered to the right, away from the embankment. She looked up and saw a deserted road lined with dark, shuttered buildings. She straightened painfully as her feet touched cobblestones.

Garth came up beside her. "Do you know where we are?" he asked. His voice was barely above a whisper, but it sounded loud. He brushed a damp strand of hair away from his eyes and glanced about.

Cory nodded. "Not far from the main wharves. There's only warehouses here. No people at this time of day." He was shaking.

"You need a cloak," Talisa said sharply. He was sweating from fear and exertion, like all of them, but his bare arms were covered with goosebumps. A cool wind blew off the river.

He nodded and fumbled with his bundle. A moment later, he shook his cloak free. The other clothes fell to the ground. He stooped to pick them up.

"I'll do that. You put on the cloak." Talisa gathered the clothes and tied them in a new bundle. Cory accepted it wordlessly.

"Now what?" Garth asked.

"I...I don't know."

Talisa frowned. Cory sounded so...dazed. Lost. And the look on his face... "We need to find a place to sit and talk. Somewhere quiet. And warm." The night was too cold, and Cory had been out in it too long with thin clothes and no cloak.

"The soldiers..."

"No one's following us," Garth said.

After a moment, Cory said, "There's a tavern not far from here. It's never crowded."

The building he led them to was small and dingy, with a lingering smell of stale beer and unwashed bodies. But it was warm, and certainly not busy. Aside from two men at a corner table, the tavern keeper was the only one present.

Cory stopped in the doorway. "I'm sorry. This isn't –"

"It's fine," Talisa said firmly, and led the way to a table in the opposite corner from the two customers.

"I'll get some kala," Garth offered. Talisa watched him walk to the counter and bring back three mugs. She wrapped her hands around one gratefully.

Cory blinked at Garth as the other boy sat down. "I don't even know who you are."

Garth's mouth quirked upwards. "Despite fleeing through the night with me. It's quite a way to get acquainted. My name is Garth Spellman. I'm a fellow apprentice of Talisa's. I know you must be Cory Updale."

"Yes." Cory took a deep breath and shook his head, as though trying to shake reality back into it. "I'm sorry. I didn't mean to get you involved in this." He looked at Talisa. "Either of you."

"I don't even know what we're involved *in*," Garth said.

Cory blinked again.

"Drink your kala," Talisa said softly.

Obediently, he did. She took a sip of her own drink. It warmed her and seemed to push the dark night further away.

Cory put his empty mug down with a deep sigh and sat looking at it. Then he raised his head. "I'll try to explain."

Talisa gripped her mug tightly. She wasn't sure she was ready for this. And Garth... How would he react? She opened her mouth, but Cory was already speaking.

"I think the soldiers came to Alain's house looking for me. Because of the fire."

A cold hand twisted her stomach.

"Fire? What–?" Garth stopped.

"The fire in the barracks. I think they believe I set it."

Garth swallowed. "But you didn't. Did you?"

Cory was silent. Talisa couldn't breathe.

"No," he said finally. Talisa's breath rushed out. He glanced at her and smiled faintly.

Then his smile faded. "But I know who did. And I was there that night. Someone saw me."

"And told the army." Garth nodded. "But couldn't you clear the matter up? If you know who did it..."

"No!" Cory's hands clenched into fists. He stopped, then opened his fingers and lowered his voice. "I will not tell them who did it."

"But –"

"No."

"Are they friends?" Garth asked after a moment.

"In a way." Cory was silent, looking down at his mug again. One of the men in the corner staggered to the counter and demanded another jug of wine. Cory waited till he returned to his table, then glanced at Talisa. "Some of this you know already."

He looked back at Garth. "My family was thrown off our farm, as were all our neighbours, when the Count of Eastlands decided he could make more money by grazing sheep on the land than allowing his tenants to rent it. We came to Freyfall looking for work, but there were far too many people seeking jobs for the few to be had."

Garth nodded. "That's what Cat found when she came here searching for her father."

Cory was quiet a moment, then took a deep breath. "My parents died that first year. The healer said it was the summer fever, but I think it was more from lack of hope." Talisa wondered how much it cost him to keep his voice steady. "We were lucky, though. My sister has a gift for weaving, and Bart – my brother-in-law – borrowed money to buy a stall. We make little enough, what with having to pay the interest on the loan, but we get by."

He gazed down at the table, moving his mug in aimless circles. When he spoke again, his voice was low, as it had been all along, but there was passion in it now. "But that doesn't make it any better, what was done to us and so many others. It was *wrong,* and I said so. Most people didn't. They thought they'd just get in trouble for saying anything, and that there was nothing they could do anyway. But gradually I found others who felt as I did – that we had to *do* something. We didn't know what, but we were sure something had to change. We spent a lot of time talking – rather wildly, I admit." He smiled wryly and fell silent again.

Talisa studied his face. He was speaking more openly tonight than he had ever done, and before a stranger at that. Why? Shock? Perhaps. And perhaps it felt natural to share secrets with people who had fled through the night with you.

"Then I met Alain Swanson. He's not like the rest of us. He has a plan. He thinks if enough people – both ordinary folk and those with power – *see* the suffering around them, the situation will improve. Oh, we won't get our land back. I know that. But maybe laws could be altered so it would never happen again. And something could be done to help those who have no work, and no homes, and precious little food."

His voice shook. He leaned forward, eyes bright. "Alain's given up everything – his position in the Guild, his reputation, a life of ease. At first he thought his songs could make people understand that things have to change. Then he realized they couldn't. So he decided that if he could gather together enough people – those living on the streets or starving in hovels or just barely making do, like me and Rina and Bart – then together we could open people's eyes."

"But what would you do?" Talisa asked.

"March to the capital and ask to speak to Queen Elira. Oh, it's a long chance, I know, but at least it's a *chance*. For the last six months, I've been working with Alain, going around talking to people, trying to convince them to join us."

The candle on their table wavered as the door opened, letting in the cool night wind. Their heads jerked around. But it was only one of the drinkers leaving. They'd been too absorbed to notice him stand up and head for the door. The other man remained slumped over his wine.

"Did you convince them?" Garth asked.

Cory's eyes stayed on the door. "What? Oh." He looked back at Garth and Talisa. "It's been hard. Some think it's worth trying, but others have given up. And there are some who are too angry to take part. They hold onto their bitterness like drowning men grasp a rope that could pull them to shore. They want to use...other means."

Talisa's heart was thumping hard again. She swallowed. "Like setting fires?"

He nodded and rubbed his forehead. "I'd heard them talking about making a gesture. Showing the army it couldn't get away with helping Eastlands evict us. But I thought it was just talk, the way it was when they said someone should kill the queen when she came to Freyfall for the council."

Talisa's eyes widened. So that's why Cory had turned green when she convinced him it was Freyans, not Uglessians, who'd been involved in the assassination attempt.

"But this time it wasn't just talk," Garth said quietly.

"No."

Cory traced a wet streak left by his mug. When he spoke again, his voice was very low. Talisa had to strain to hear him. "The wife of one of the men came to me and asked me to stop them. I'd been in their room often enough, and I guess.. Well, I guess she didn't know who else to turn to. I went after them. I thought...I hoped I'd get there before...well, before. But when I was several blocks away, I saw flames, and when I went closer..." He stopped.

"Why did you go closer when you knew it was too late?" Garth asked.

Cory glanced up. From the look on his face, Talisa thought he was almost surprised to see Garth, not flames lighting the night sky. "I thought maybe I should warn the soldiers. Maybe..." He stopped again.

Talisa felt something inside her, a last lingering doubt, a last lingering fear, lift like fog dissolved by the warming sun.

He closed his eyes. "There was no need. By the time I arrived, soldiers were crowding out of the doors and jostling each other in the street. Only...only not all of them. Inside, someone was screaming."

She covered his right hand, clenched on the table, with her own. After a minute, he opened his eyes and looked at her. "I ran. I don't know whether I was running from the soldiers or the screams. I just...ran. Only, as I ran, I bumped into someone hurrying towards the excitement. I don't know who he was. I don't even know what he looked like. I was too... I didn't really see him. But he saw me. And I think he recognized me."

"That's not likely," Talisa protested. "If you didn't even really see him, why do you think he knows you?" Hope stirred in her. Perhaps the soldiers weren't after Cory. Perhaps they had come to Master Swanson's because they had learned about his plan.

"He said something. I'm not sure what it was, but it might have been 'Updale.' I tried to tell myself it wasn't, but the more I thought about it... And there are enough people who've heard me talk about the injustice of what was done to us that he'd be sure to connect me with the fire, when he saw me running from it. I'm surprised it took them this long to find me. Maybe he didn't make the connection right away. Or maybe he doesn't like the authorities any better than a lot of us do."

Hope died.

"I met Andreas on my way home and told him. For once, even he couldn't enjoy the drama of it all." Cory tried to smile. Then he shook his head. "I shouldn't have said that. He was very worried that this might affect Alain's plans, but he was concerned for me too. He urged me to take refuge in their house. I didn't take him up on the offer immediately, but I did after I'd thought for a while. Now I've put him and Alain in danger." There was something close to despair in his voice.

"They'll be all right," Talisa said. She hoped she was right.

He said nothing.

Garth cleared his throat. "What will you do now?"

"Do?"

"You can't go back to Master Swanson's. Where will you go?"

"I don't... I haven't thought." Cory looked down at the table. "If I could, I'd go home."

"Home?" Talisa asked. "To Rina and Bart's?"

"No. It wouldn't be safe, for me or them. Anyway, it's best I'm not there. I just cause fights. I meant home to the hills." He sighed. "But I know that's impossible."

"So where *will* you go?" Garth repeated.

Talisa looked at him and felt the same warmth wash over her as she'd known earlier that night. He seemed to care as much about the welfare of an unknown fugitive from the queen's justice as he would have about that of a lifelong friend. He, the wealthy grandson of an important wizard.

"I don't know. Freybourg perhaps."

Garth frowned. "If they don't find you here, that's the next place they'll look."

"Maybe." Cory shrugged. "I have to go *somewhere.*"

"Uglessia," Talisa said suddenly.

"What?" Both boys stared at her.

"Uglessia," she repeated. "You can go to Uglessia."

PLANS

CORY STARED AT HER, HIS BROWN EYES WIDE. For a moment, she saw something flicker across his face. Hope? Excitement? Then he shook his head.

"I can't go to Uglessia."

"Why not?" Talisa challenged. She wasn't even sure why she'd thought of Uglessia. But now it seemed like the best solution. The *only* solution.

"What would I do there? I can't even speak the language."

"It's not a bad idea." Garth wore a thoughtful frown. "The army wouldn't think of looking for you there."

"*If* I got there," Cory pointed out. "What about the guards on the tunnel that connects the two lands? They'd stop me."

"They'd have no reason to. I doubt word would reach them before you got to the tunnel. You'd just have to give a false name and come up with a convincing story of why you want to go to Uglessia."

Cory gazed at Garth as though his words were a promise of water in a barren wasteland. Then his shoulders slumped. "Even if they let me through, why would the Uglessians allow me to stay? I don't belong there. I'd only be one more mouth to feed."

"I'll send a note with you," Talisa said. But even as she spoke, she wondered. Yes, her family would welcome Cory if she asked them to. And their Freyan was fluent. Cory could talk to them. But would her father and grandparents and the rest of them understand why he had to flee Freya, or would they treat him with polite coldness? She could imagine how Cory would react to that.

He must have caught the doubt in her voice. He shook his head again. "It wouldn't work. Thank you, but..." He looked down at the table and moved his mug to and fro. His whole body sagged with weariness. Defeat.

"Then I'll go with you." The words came out before she thought. But why not? If she went with him, she could make her family understand. And...

And she would walk the mountain paths again, feel a fresh wind on her face, see stars that seemed close enough to touch, be with her family at Midwinter.

Cory's head jerked up. "You can't do that! What about your music?"

"What about it?"

"You've just begun to learn. You can't stop now."

"It doesn't matter."

"Of course it does! Remember what you said to me tonight about my carving?"

"Remember what you answered?" she retorted.

"I won't let you sacrifice so much for me."

"It's not such a sacrifice. And it's not just you. I want to go home."

Cory's eyebrows drew together in a fierce frown. "No.'

Garth was frowning too. "You can't forfeit your music, Talisa. Could you go with him to introduce him to your family, then return?"

She considered this. "No. It's too late in the season. Even on our way there we might meet storms. By the time I returned, the hills would be clogged with snow. And I'm not forfeiting anything. I can sing in Uglessia." She thought about the exercises Master Coyne had set her, how they were strengthening her voice. Well, she could do them at home. As for the lute and harp and all the other instruments she hadn't begun to play... She thrust the picture aside. "And I can make up songs better in Uglessia than I ever did here."

"What about the Coynes?" Garth asked.

She winced. They wouldn't let her go, she knew that – partly because of the contract she'd signed with them and partly because they felt they needed to protect her. The idea of breaking her contract, of sneaking away... They'd been so good to her.

"I'll leave them a note."

"You won't have to," Cory said. "I'm not going to Uglessia."

She looked at him. His hands were clenched on the table in front of him. His mouth was set. All the reassurances in the world wouldn't sway him.

She forced herself to speak calmly. "Very well. I think you're making a mistake, but if you want to risk capture by staying in Freya, it's your decision. *I* am going to Uglessia. Tomorrow."

He stared at her. She stared back. Garth started to say something, then stopped.

"Are you serious?" Cory asked.

"Yes."

He was silent a long time. Finally he said, "All right. If you're sure."

"I'm sure."

He rubbed a hand across his eyes. "But how will we get there? I have no money. We'll need horses. Food. Blankets."

"My grandparents left me some money." Enough for one person to get home. But two? She bit her lip.

"I can lend you some money," Garth offered.

Cory smiled wryly. "And when would I be able to pay you back? Thank you, but no."

"You don't have to repay me. I can spare it."

"No."

Was Cory's stubborn pride going to stop them from reaching safety? Talisa looked at him and realized it was.

Then she remembered. "Your carving! I still have it. You can give it to Garth in exchange for the money."

Cory scowled. "Not a very fair exchange. It wouldn't fetch much. None of my work does."

"Master Fletcher must think it's worth something, and he should know."

His scowl vanished. "All right." He looked at Garth. "Thank you."

The other boy smiled. "You're welcome."

Talisa rose. "I'd better go now before the Coynes send soldiers out searching for *me*. I'll meet you just before dawn tomorrow, at the Portby Square end of Gleeman Street."

Cory nodded.

"Where will you stay tonight?"

"Here."

"Here?" She glanced around. The man in the corner had fallen asleep, his head on the table, his mouth ajar. The tavern owner, a round, bald-headed man, was watching them. Shadows crouched beyond the reach of the dim glow of the candles.

He shrugged. "It's warm and it stays open all night. I might even sleep. If not... Well, I slept earlier this evening. I'll meet you on Gleeman Street."

"I'll be there too with the money," Garth promised, getting to his feet. He didn't look very happy. Neither did Cory. But she couldn't worry about that. What mattered was Cory's safety.

IN THE FROSTY PRE-DAWN DARKNESS, it was harder to shake off doubts and worries. She had slept little, and writing a note to Master and Mistress Coyne had proved very difficult.

They hadn't scolded Garth and her when they'd returned so late last night. Garth had gallantly assumed the blame, saying he'd had trouble tearing himself away from the music. Master Coyne had shaken his head reprovingly but said nothing, and Mistress Coyne had simply clucked her tongue and told Garth to go straight home before his mother's hair turned white.

"And you'd better head for bed, my girl. You look dragged out."

They were kind, the Coynes. They cared. It was hard to leave them. To leave them this way. They would think she was ungrateful. Untrustworthy. An apprentice who broke her contract, just as she'd given away coins that didn't belong to her. She sniffed, then reached for a handkerchief and blew her nose firmly. This was no time for tears. She gathered her bundle and slipped out of her room and down the stairs, cringing every time one of them creaked. The house was quiet except for the sound of snores coming from the boys' room. Probably Lem. He often snored.

She inched the back door open and crept out. Her eyes fell on the rose bush, with its bare, prickly stems. She would never see the roses in bloom again. Silly to think of such things now. She shook her head and set off briskly down the street, past sleeping houses.

Cory and Garth were waiting on the corner. Cory's bundle of clothes was strapped on his back. His face looked as grey as the morning and he was shivering. Talisa glanced at his worn, thin cloak and hoped Garth's money would stretch far enough to allow the purchase of a warmer one.

She reached into her pocket and took out the figure of the small boy. Garth accepted it respectfully.

"There's a place on Eastside Road that sells horses for a reasonable price," he whispered, then glanced around the deserted street and cleared his throat. "They won't be great, but they'll get you to Uglessia," he said in a low voice.

"That's all we need," Talisa said. She frowned, suddenly worried. "You won't get into trouble, will you? For helping us?"

"I doubt that anyone will ever know I *did* help you. I'm certainly not going to tell anyone. What did you say in your note to the Coynes?"

"Just that I'm homesick and leaving now before snow makes it impossible. That I'm sorry." There were no lies in her message, only gaping holes.

"I could mention that we heard 'The Rains of Uglessia' last night and that you seemed sad afterwards," Garth offered.

"No! You've helped me enough. More than enough. Don't lie for me too."

He sighed. "All right."

"Thank you, Garth. Thank you so much."

"Yes," Cory said. He hesitated, then burst out. "But *why?* Why are you doing this? Oh, I know you're a friend of Talisa's, but... Your family has wealth and power. You know I'm against everything you stand for. So why?"

Garth looked startled. "I don't know." He thought for a minute. "I might not be if it weren't for Cat. She found out what it was like living on the streets of Freyfall without money or friends." He looked about him and shivered. "And that was in summer." He paused, then added slowly, "I'm not sure you're doing the right thing in not giving away the names of those who set the fire. What if they do it again? But

I think I understand why you won't. And I admire what you're doing with Alain Swanson. I hope I'd have the courage to do the same. Besides –" he grinned suddenly – "Cat would never forgive me if I didn't help you."

"When will you see her again?" Talisa asked.

"At Midwinter. I'm going to Frey-under-Hill for a while then."

She smiled. "I'm glad."

A cart loaded with turnips and winter squash lumbered by, on the way to Portby Square, no doubt. It was time to go.

"May Freyn smile on you," Garth said.

"And on you."

Then they were off, leaving Garth alone on the corner. The sky had turned a dove-soft grey.

HOMECOMING

"SO THOSE ARE THE BROKEN HILLS," CORY SAID. He gave a long, slow whistle.

Talisa turned her head and looked back at him. He'd halted his horse and was staring at a mass of rugged boulders, loose scree, and jagged cliffs to their right. She reined in her horse.

"I'd heard how the wizards created them at the end of the Uglik War to bar your people from Freya, but I never pictured anything quite like this."

She nodded, remembering her own first glimpse of the grey, desolate wasteland at the foot of the only pass that allowed entry into Freya. "You see why we built the tunnel."

"How far away is the tunnel?"

"Not far. We should reach it in a bit over an hour."

She prodded her horse into motion. Behind her, she heard Cory sigh before he too moved on. They rode along the narrow ledge in silence.

Was Cory as anxious as she was about the guards at the tunnel?

They'd seen no sign of pursuit in the three weeks they'd been on the road, Talisa reminded herself. Cory had suggested they ride cross-country, but she'd insisted they take the fastest route possible to reach the high hills before snow came. The only soldiers they'd seen had been a small band riding the opposite way.

She thought back on their journey, and smiled. She'd felt shy as they left Freyfall on their newly purchased mounts. What would it be like to be alone with Cory for so long? At first she thought it was the same sudden shyness that caused Cory to be silent for long stretches, staring into the distance. Then she realized it was unhappiness at leaving Rina and his home. But their days had soon fallen into a pattern as natural as the rhythm of their steps had been as they'd walked around the Coynes' neighbourhood. They respected each other's privacy and silence, but there was never a shortage of things to talk about as they sat around the evening campfires. Often, gazing into the flames, she sang. As they approached the hills, the last of Cory's depression lifted, and he sometimes joined in the songs. His voice wasn't *quite* as bad as Rina and Bart said it was.

Ahead, the track narrowed even more. A precipitous cliff hung on the right. Talisa roused herself from her memories and concentrated on her riding.

Dusky clouds filled the western sky as they descended into a dell, partially cleared but still tangled with bushes and undergrowth. Through the naked branches of a tree, she saw the gaping mouth of a cavern. She stopped and waited for Cory.

"The tunnel," he said.

"Yes."

He took a deep breath. "Well, let's see how convincing my story is."

She nudged her mare closer to him and rested her hand lightly on his. "There won't be any trouble." She hoped. How she hoped.

As they drew closer, Talisa smelled boiled cabbage and frying onions coming from a small hut beside the path. Some of the guards must be inside, cooking supper. Only two stood in front of the tunnel. Both had bows slung over their shoulders and heavy broadswords at their sides. Talisa's mouth was dry.

It's all right. They have no reason to stop us.

"Your names?" demanded one guard, a sandy-haired man with square shoulders and a raspy voice.

"Talisa Thatcher."

"And your business?"

"I'm returning to my home in Uglessia."

"I remember you," said the other man, stepping forward and squinting at her. "You came through here last summer."

"Yes."

"Been away a while, haven't you?" He was short and heavily muscled, with a scar from what looked like a knife wound running down his right cheek. Talisa recalled him too. He liked to ask a lot of questions. She suspected he was bored.

"Yes."

"And you're coming back now? None of our Freyan boys caught your fancy?" He grinned, then looked at Cory. "Or maybe they did. Who's your companion?"

"Mallory Meadows," Cory answered for himself.

"What brings you here? Where do you live and what do you do to earn your keep?"

"I live on a farm near Dale, where my father has a dairy herd, but I've also been taking a few lessons from the local wizard. He knows Alaric Thatcher, Talisa's grandfather, and says I could learn a lot from him. I've always wanted to travel, so when Talisa came through Dale on her way home, I asked him to introduce me to her. She thinks her grandparents will teach me some of their magic in return for my help with their ursells." Cory looked a little pale, Talisa thought, but his voice was easy. She held her breath.

The guard scratched his chin. "Magic, is it? I can't say I'd want to be a wizard myself. Too much book learning for my taste." He glanced at Talisa. "But then maybe there's other motives for your trip." He winked.

"How long will you be there?" the first soldier asked.

"For the winter at least."

"Sooner you than me. Or maybe not." The short man winked again.

Talisa cleared her throat. "May we go now? I want to be in Uglessia by morning."

"Certainly." The sandy-haired guard stepped aside.

"Got your candles ready?" asked the second man.

Talisa nodded and reached into her saddlebag. Cory did

the same. They lit their candles and advanced into the yawning darkness.

She'd forgotten how low the roof was. How narrow the walls. How weak the glow of the flames in the blackness. Forgotten the smells. Dirt. Dust. Old, stale air.

Her horse was trembling. She patted the sweating coat and crooned softly. Behind her, she heard Cory murmur reassuringly to his gelding. They plodded on. After a while, her mare seemed calmer. Better than Merisha, last summer, who'd jerked and shivered so much that Talisa had dismounted and led her most of the way.

"I've never really known what darkness was like before," Cory said. His words echoed, haunting, eerie. Talisa jumped, then laughed shakily.

They stopped briefly to eat, then went on. At some point, Talisa suggested they should try to sleep. There was no way to tether the horses, but she doubted they'd run. They seemed to want to stay as close to their riders as possible. Talisa and Cory wrapped themselves in their blankets and lay down on the ground. Talisa closed her eyes.

The ceiling seemed to press down on her. Close. Getting closer.

She shuddered and opened her eyes. In the flickering light of the candle, she saw the roof of the tunnel. No nearer than before. She shut her eyes again.

She thought she dozed, off and on. Every time she came to and turned over, she heard Cory shifting in his blankets. Finally, as she stirred once more and sighed, he stood up. "This isn't working."

"No," she agreed.

They rode on, and on, and on. Lit new candles from the stubs of the old ones. The light was so feeble.

This will end. It ended last summer.

But she could *feel* the walls drawing in.

She started to sing. Her voice seemed frail against the overwhelming black night of the tunnel. She faltered.

Cory took up the tune. His voice was definitely off-key, but it was strong. It pushed the enclosing rock walls further away.

Talisa smiled. The journey would end. By morning, they'd be home.

"Magnificent," Cory breathed.

Talisa nodded without taking her eyes off the mountains that rose, peak after peak, in front of her. It was one of those days that sometimes came to Uglessia in late autumn or early winter, when the air was so pure images seemed to stand out with crystal clarity.

"We're home," she said. Laughter bubbled up inside her.

"Yes." Cory was still gazing at the mountains. "How long will it take to reach your home?"

She glanced at the sun. It must be mid-morning. "We should be there by sunset." She gave one last look at the tunnel they'd just emerged from, and gathered her reins, ready to ride on.

"Hmmm." Cory didn't seem to be in any hurry. She glanced at him. He was frowning.

"Cory?"

"Yes." He made no move to go. "How will your family react when you bring a Freyan fugitive home with you?"

"They'll welcome you."

He said nothing. In the silence, the distant shriek of a hawk was very clear.

Talisa looked down at her horse's dark brown mane. Cory's question echoed in her mind. *Would* her family welcome him? Oh, she was sure they'd believe he hadn't set the fire. But he *was* a Freyan fugitive. For generations, her family had worked to improve relations with their neighbour. Would they worry that sheltering Cory would jeopardize that relationship?

Would they be right?

No. Of course not. The only one who knew Cory had fled to Uglessia was Garth, and he wouldn't tell anyone.

But a number of people knew she and Cory were friends. Was it possible that they would connect his disappearance with her sudden decision to return home?

Surely not.

But if they did...

All that had mattered to her, that night in the dingy tavern, was Cory's safety. She hadn't thought about the possible consequences to Uglessia.

And she hadn't thought about how she would feel when she returned to a place where magic, not music, was the centre of their lives, when she was once more confronted by her own inadequacy in the middle of her gifted, dedicated family.

No. Don't think about that. It will be all right. And Cory gave a false name and story to the guards at the tunnel. No one will suspect he's here.

She looked up. Cory was pleating his horse's mane, but she didn't think he was conscious of what he was doing.

She had been silent too long. She took a deep breath. "They'll welcome you," she repeated.

They rode away from the tunnel, along the path that wound its way along the mountainside. They rode in silence.

THE SUN WAS RESTING on the horizon when Talisa crested a ridge and saw, below her, the hut where she'd lived all but the last six months of her life. Like all Uglessian houses, it crouched low to the ground, its grey stone walls one with the stones of the mountain. She reined in.

Cory drew up beside her. "Your home?"

"Yes." What did he make of the meagre house, the small shed that leaned against it, the usit field beyond? In spring and summer, the field was a green patch on a grey robe, but now there was nothing but brown stubble to mark its existence.

"Who's that?" Cory asked.

Her gaze followed his pointing arm. A little below them and to the right was a flock of ursells. Among them, her head a pool of sunlight, was a young woman. Talisa's stomach knotted in – what? Excitement? Joy? Apprehension?

"It's Welwyn."

She felt his eyes on her face. "I'm sorry."

Her head jerked towards him. "Sorry? For what?"

"For making your homecoming difficult."

"It's not difficult. Why should it be?" She heard the sharpness in her voice and bit her lip. "Let's go meet her."

The sun was at their backs. Talisa saw Welwyn turn and shade her eyes to see them. She dropped her hand.

"Talisa!" She was running, the ursells scattering before her. "Talisa! You're home!"

Then she was beside them, laughing, panting, her blue eyes shining. Talisa slid down from her horse and her sister flung her arms around her.

"I'm so glad to see you. It's been too long. I've missed you so, even with Melton...even with the Freyan wizards here with all their new books and ideas. I thought we'd have to spend Midwinter without you. Father, Aunt Gwynne, everyone will be so happy." Welwyn stepped back to examine her, then hugged her again. Talisa returned the hug, feeling her nerves relax and her earlier joy bubble up.

"I've missed you too. Oh, Welwyn, I've been so homesick."

"Is that why you're home early? No, don't tell me now. Father must hear, and I see you've brought someone with you."

Talisa turned. Cory had dismounted and held the reins of both horses.

"Welwyn, please meet Cory Updale, a friend of mine. Cory, this is my sister Welwyn." She spoke in Freyan so Cory could understand.

Welwyn immediately switched to Freyan too. "Welcome, Cory. I'm happy to meet you. Please forgive me for speaking in Uglessian." She smiled at him.

He smiled back, a bit shyly, Talisa thought. "That's all right. And I'm glad to meet you too."

"Please come to the house. Father should be home by now and heating the porridge."

"Where was he?" Talisa asked as they started walking down the hill.

"At Grandmother's. That's where we all gather to learn from the Freyan wizards. You knew they were here, didn't you?"

"Grandmother told me two of them would come here as part of the exchange," Talisa said slowly. She had forgotten about them. She glanced at Cory, saw his worried frown.

"They've taught us so much and have so many ideas. They say they're learning from us too, but I think they're just being polite. We meet with them every day."

"But you were tending the ursells."

"We take turns leading them to pasture. We've combined our flock with Aunt Gwynne's and Uncle Wendell's so that none of us has to waste too much time."

"I see." If she'd been here to help, no one need have wasted any time. She looked at the flock. She should have realized there were twice as many as usual. But where was Merisha? Her eyes scanned the animals without success.

"Has something happened to Merisha?"

"A slight sprain a week ago. Don't worry. We left her behind all week, but she should be ready to head up the mountain tomorrow. She'll be delighted to see you. But not tonight. I'll take the ursells into the pen. Someone else wants to greet you."

Talisa followed her gaze. There, in front of the house, stood her father. Something caught in her throat, seeing the familiar tall, lean form, the grave face, pale red hair, grey eyes under level eyebrows.

Davvid was a quiet man. He didn't cry out or run to meet her, as Welwyn had. But in the last rays of the sun, Talisa saw joy leap to his eyes and a slow, rare smile illuminate his face. Then she was in his arms and he was holding her close.

"Now tell us why you came home," Gwynne commanded.

Talisa glanced at her aunt, then scanned the faces in the room, partly to give herself time to gather her words, but partly just for the pleasure of seeing them all.

The straw bedding had been pushed against the walls to make more room, but even so the hut was crammed. Cory and her cousins sat cross-legged on the tightly packed dirt floor. Her eyes rested for a moment on Jared and Taran. Their hair was just as long as hers, and an even brighter red. The twins weren't absolutely identical – Taran's mouth was a touch wider, Jared's nose a shade longer – but after being away for six months, she'd mixed them up when she first greeted them. And they'd grown while she was gone. Already they were as tall as their father and topped Cory by half a head.

Her grandparents were seated on the bench by the hearth, and the rest of them crowded around the table. Her uncle

Wendell's long legs were stretched out in front of him, his hands folded comfortably over his stomach, but Gwynne was leaning forward eagerly, her green eyes – the eyes both she and Talisa had inherited from Alaric – bright with interest.

As soon as supper was over, Welwyn had ridden off to spread the news. Her grandparents and her aunt and her family had arrived as quickly as ursells and the dark mountain trails allowed. They had filled the room with talk and laughter and hugs. But now was the time for explanations.

Talisa cleared her throat. "I missed you all."

"Of course you did," Welwyn said.

"But what about your studies?" Alaric asked.

Talisa looked at her grandfather, then away. "They're important to me. I'm glad I spent the time with Master Coyne and learned what I did. I'm sorry I couldn't complete my contract. But I had to leave."

"Because you were homesick?"

"Partly." She stopped. How to explain?

"Partly?" Gwynne prompted.

"She left because of me," Cory said.

Everyone's head swung to face him. He had said very little at supper and even less when Talisa's relatives came streaming in. They had all greeted him politely and switched to Freyan for his benefit, but after the first curious glances, they had almost seemed to forget him. Now they stared.

"What do you mean?" Davvid asked. He had gone still, the way ursells did when they scented danger.

"She felt I should come to Uglessia and that she should come with me. I needed to leave Freya. Soldiers were after me." Cory spoke quietly, but there were two hectic patches of colour on his cheeks.

"My," Wendell said in his deep, mild voice. He always spoke mildly and moved slowly. People who didn't know him thought him less intelligent than he was. "And why were soldiers after you?"

"Because they believed I set fire to their barracks."

Talisa closed her eyes. Did Cory *have* to tell his story so baldly? She heard him take a deep breath. "Two men died in the fire."

She didn't like the silence that followed. She opened her eyes. The look on the faces around her was worse than the silence. "Cory didn't do it. In fact, he tried to stop it. Maybe...maybe I should tell you how come I know Cory."

"Maybe you should," her father agreed.

"I met him at Midsummer. I didn't tell you then," she said to her grandparents. She hadn't wanted them to know about her cowardice. She hadn't wanted anyone to know. But she told them about it now, and about Cory's rescue. She went on to explain how they had met again and what had happened after that, stumbling occasionally over her words, trying hard to make them understand.

"Cory's with a group of people who are trying to make life better for those who've been thrown off their land and have almost nothing. But they're trying to do it peacefully. He had nothing to do with the burning of the barracks."

"But I know the men who *did* do it," Cory said. "And I was seen hurrying away from the fire."

Alaric frowned. "Why were you there?"

"I heard that some men – men I knew – were going to burn it. I thought...I hoped I could stop them. But I was too late."

There was another silence. Then Alaric said, "And you won't tell the authorities who did it." It was a statement, not a question.

"No."

"And will these men set another fire? Cause more deaths?" Redelle asked.

"I don't think so."

"No?" She raised her eyebrows.

Cory met her eyes levelly. "They didn't intend to kill anyone. Now that they have... I ran into one of them afterwards. He was...shaken."

Another pause.

"If you want me to leave – leave this house, leave Uglessia – I will."

Talisa gasped. She felt as though she'd been kicked.

"No."

She turned her head and looked at her father. He spoke again, his voice as quiet and firm as before. "You tried to stop the fire, at some risk to yourself, I imagine. You saved Talisa's life. You are welcome to stay here as long as you wish."

"I didn't really save her life," Cory protested. "At least... I'm not sure there was any real danger."

"Perhaps not," Davvid conceded. "But perhaps there was. There often is, with an angry mob. You are welcome to stay," he repeated.

There were murmurs of agreement from around the room. Welwyn nodded vigorously. Talisa wanted to hug every member of her family.

"Tha...thank you," Cory stammered. "But will this cause trouble for you? For Uglessia? I don't think anyone knows I came here, at least not anyone who'll tell, but..."

Redelle and Alaric exchanged a glance.

"There was no pursuit," Talisa said quickly.

"And with winter setting in, they couldn't do anything until spring anyway. By that time they may well have forgotten you," Wendell said comfortably.

Talisa was watching her grandmother's face. It wore a small, worried frown.

"How did you escape when the soldiers came for you?" Taran asked. He was eighteen months younger than Talisa, and his voice still teetered on the edge of boyhood when he was excited.

"Did you have to fight?" his brother asked eagerly.

Their mother shook her head at them. "Your questions will have to wait. It's time we went home. Talisa and Cory have had a long journey and need their rest."

Despite her words, it was a while yet before they all filed out with more laughs and hugs. As Redelle left, she kissed Talisa's cheek. "I'm glad you're home, child."

But Talisa noticed that her forehead was still puckered by that small, worried frown.

TENDING URSELLS

"I S IT TARAN'S OR JARED'S TURN TO TAKE THE ursells to pasture?" Davvid asked the next morning.

Talisa looked up quickly from her plate, with its slice of usit cake. "There's no need for either of them to do it, now that I'm back."

"But you've just arrived. Surely you want to rest or visit."

"I'm not tired. And I'll meet others soon enough."

"Ursells can't be that different from sheep. I'll help with them and any other work that needs doing," Cory offered.

Davvid looked pleased. "Very well. If you're both sure. It *will* help. The Freyans are only promised to us till spring, and we have so much to learn from them."

"But you must meet Mel– I mean, Master Granton and Master Ford," Welwyn protested. "I'd hoped you could come with us today."

"Later." There was nothing she wanted less than to sit around feeling as useless as one more rock on the mountain.

And she wasn't sure it would be wise to meet any Freyan right now.

Talisa watched Welwyn and her father ride off. They turned in their saddles to wave, then set their faces eagerly forward. They would stop at Gwynne's to let the twins know they were free to study. All her family would be at her grandmother's today. Today and other days. All but her.

"They're good people, your family," Cory said from beside her.

"Yes." Talisa shivered. The sun was edging its way above the eastern mountains, but so far it wasn't producing any warmth. "Let's do the washing up and other chores, then get the ursells."

Cory went with her to the side of the house, where she scooped water from the rain barrel. "You don't have a well?"

"No. All our water comes from rain or melted snow, or from a creek on the mountainside." She peered into the barrel. "We might have to go there soon. There's little water left." She frowned. "I hope it snows soon. We need the moisture for our usit crop even more than for drinking and cleaning."

"I guess the shortage of rain the last few years would have affected Uglessia even more than Freya," Cory said slowly.

"Yes." It always did.

"How far away is the creek?" he asked after a moment. "Here. Let me carry the water inside."

She watched him pour it into the pan she'd set on the table, then started washing. "About a mile. Sometimes it dries up and we have to fetch water from further away. We've done that several times lately at the height of summer."

Cory dried the dishes in silence. "I'd always heard that life in Uglessia was hard," he said as he wiped the final plate. "But I never realized just how scarce water is here."

"Grandmother says it's much better than it used to be. She remembers what it was like before Freyan wizards shifted the winds."

Cory shook his head wordlessly.

Merisha remembered her. When Talisa and Cory entered the enclosure where the ursells were kept, she lifted her head, sniffing, then ran to Talisa and butted her gently in the stomach. Talisa laughed and fondled her soft ears.

"Did you miss me, girl?"

Merisha rubbed her head against Talisa's hand. Talisa stroked her head and scratched behind her ears, crooning a Uglessian lullaby. Cory watched, smiling.

"Enough," Talisa said with mock sternness. "I have work to do."

Cory raised his eyebrows when she produced a milk pail. "You milk your ursells as well as using them for riding and for their wool?"

"Oh yes. Our ursells give us everything, even their meat and hides."

"You breed some of them for slaughter then?"

"Of course not!" Talisa couldn't keep her shock out of her voice. She tried to modify it. "Ursells are our sisters and brothers. We would never kill them, but we know they wouldn't object to us making use of them when their time has come."

"Hmmm." Cory grabbed another pail. The ursell he chose sniffed him suspiciously, then settled down under his deft fingers.

Milking done, they herded the animals out of the pen. The ursells were eager for their freedom. The enclosure was a bit small for the combined flocks.

To her chagrin, Talisa found that her legs had grown unaccustomed to steep climbs. Cory shared her discomfort.

"I've been out of the hills too long," he panted.

"Me too."

The ursells were soon ahead of them, but Talisa wasn't worried. They knew the way and were sure-footed on mountains. Only Merisha stayed with them all the way to the small grassy plateau that was their destination.

"Do we get a rest now?" Cory asked.

She laughed. "For a while."

A teasing wind lifted some strands of hair from her forehead and made Cory wrap his cloak more tightly around himself. Talisa frowned. Garth's money hadn't stretched to a warm cloak for Cory. One of her first tasks must be to make him one.

The wind continued to dance and whistle through the grass, but the sun shone brightly in a cloudless sky. At this time of year, it gave little heat, but the rocks at their backs offered shelter. They sat quietly, legs outstretched to catch the sun. An eagle circled overhead. She watched it, and heard a song begin to form in her head. After a while, she sang it softly.

She felt Cory's eyes on her face, but when she glanced at him he turned his head and gazed at the mountains in the distance.

In late afternoon, they gathered the flocks and headed down the mountain. She pointed out some kala bushes beside the path. Cory viewed them with interest.

"So that's where kala comes from. You don't plant it in fields near your houses?"

She shook her head. "The bushes grow wild on the mountains. Whenever anyone has tried to transplant them, their roots soon wither and die. Anyway, if we grew them near our homes, there wouldn't be any room for our usit crops."

Welwyn came out of the hut as they approached. "Dinner's almost ready," she announced, smiling. She walked with them to the enclosure and watched as Talisa gave Merisha a few last pats.

"It was such a good day," she said on the way back to the house. "I wish you'd been there, Talisa. Melton – Master Granton – has an idea that he told me about. He wanted to see my reaction before he tells everyone." Her voice throbbed with excitement.

Talisa glanced at her sister. Her eyes were bright, even in the dim twilight. "You like this Master Granton, don't you?"

Welwyn nodded, a smile trembling on her lips. "But it's not just that. He's such a good wizard, and he thinks of so many ways to help Uglessia."

Talisa stiffened. *Such a good wizard. Ways to help Uglessia.* Welwyn judged everyone by how well they could use magic to aid Uglessia. She always had.

"Oh, Talisa, I'm so glad you're here to talk to!" Welwyn flung her arms around her. Flushing, Talisa hugged her back.

They went in, to be greeted by the smell of usit porridge and Davvid's welcoming smile. She was lucky to be home. She knew that. If only...if only.

THE DAYS SPED BY, quiet but busy. Talisa led the horses back to the tunnel and left them with the guards on the other side, for they weren't like ursells, who could scramble safely about the mountains in search of grass. Cory offered to go with her, but Talisa refused, much as she dreaded the long, dark trip through the tunnel. It was better he be forgotten by the guards. Anyway, he was needed to tend the ursells while she was gone. The journey wasn't quite as bad as she'd feared. The ursell she rode had steady nerves, and the memory of Cory's voice on their earlier trip helped.

Life fell into a familiar pattern. Her legs lost their initial stiffness and she took pleasure in climbing up and down the mountain paths.

Cory seemed to delight in his new life. The bitterness that had sometimes sharpened his voice and tightened his face softened, even when he spoke of Freya. Not that he mentioned it often; he was too busy learning about Uglessia, talking and laughing and asking questions. She began to teach him Uglessian.

They didn't always talk. There were long stretches when they would sit quietly while the ursells cropped the grass nearby. Words and melodies danced through her mind then. Words about Cory, the hills he had loved, his eviction from them, his life in Freyfall. Tunes of busy city streets. Songs of the mountains.

Sometimes, during those silences, she would feel Cory's eyes on her, as she had the first day, and turn her head only to find his gaze averted. She wanted to say something then but didn't know what.

During the evenings, she made cheese or usit cakes or worked on Cory's cloak. Sometimes visitors arrived. Talisa was touched, knowing that many of them had ridden long distances simply to welcome her home. Cory tried to melt into the stone walls of the hut during those visits, though none of the guests gave him more than a friendly word and curious glance. Uglessians had long since accepted the fact that Redelle and Alaric's family had Freyan friends.

One night her great-uncle Urwin arrived with his three sons, two daughters, and all their children. They crowded into the hut till there wasn't an inch of floor left to sit on or wall to lean against. "How's my favourite skylark?" Uncle Urwin asked, throwing his arms around her and demanding a song.

He wasn't the only one who wanted one. As she sang, Talisa sometimes could almost hear an accompanying lute or harp and would ache, just a little, for the music that had surrounded her in Freyfall.

She didn't realize just how badly Cory missed carving until one morning, on their way up the track, when he stopped. Stooping, he picked up a rough, pockmarked rock and stood looking at it. "I wonder..."

"What?" she asked when he said nothing more.

"Whether I could carve stone."

Talisa winced. The only trees in Uglessia were the thin, scraggly pines that stubbornly clung to hillsides, and a few seedlings that had sprouted in recent years. Wood was only used for essentials. There was certainly none that could be spared for Cory to carve.

He had said nothing, but she should have known. How could she have been so blind? She, who felt such joy now that songs once again sprang in her heart?

Cory stowed the rock in his pocket.

After that, he often had a stone in his hands, both up on the plateau and in the hut at night. He would turn it around and around, trying, he said, to discover what it wanted to be, then take out a chisel he had made and start chipping. Most attempts he threw away after a few hours of work, others he kept longer before discarding. But he never seemed discouraged or frustrated, merely intent. After a few evenings, Davvid offered him a better chisel. Cory accepted it the way a hungry man accepts food.

Talisa often wondered what her father thought of Cory. He had welcomed him and seemed to like him well enough, but sometimes she saw him look at Cory with a thoughtful frown.

So the weeks went by, and she was happy – or almost so. Then came Midwinter and her meeting with the Freyan wizards.

FREYAN WIZARDS

"THIS WILL BE THE BEST MIDWINTER EVER," Welwyn said. She took a bite of usit cake. "Just a while ago, I was worried it would be dismal with you gone, Talisa. But now you're back, and Melton and Master Ford will be with us at Aunt Gwynne's tonight. And you, Cory." She smiled at him.

Cory looked down at his plate. "I'm not going."

Talisa was holding a cup to her lips. She set it down so quickly that kala splashed onto the table. "Not going?"

"It wouldn't be safe. Not with the Freyan wizards there. What if they carry word back to Freya that I'm here?"

"Half of Uglessia knows you're here. If the wizards haven't already heard, they soon will."

"They know," Davvid said. Cory raised his head and stared at him. "It seemed better to tell them ourselves that a friend from Freya was with us than to have them find out accidentally," Davvid explained.

"Yes," Cory agreed after a moment. "It's still best I stay away from them, though. It's one thing knowing I'm here, but it's another to actually see me."

"You can't stay hidden till spring," Talisa protested.

He just shook his head, as stubborn and mute as an ursell that had found a particularly tasty patch of clover and refused to leave.

She opened her mouth, but her father shook his head. She closed it again. He was right. Cory wouldn't budge. At least not here. She had a much better chance of reasoning with him when they were alone in the mountain meadow.

Was it only fear of the Freyans that was stopping him from participating in Midwinter festivities? She glanced at him as they climbed the path behind the ursells. He had been strangely quiet the last few days. Sometimes when she spoke to him, he would jerk, as though startled out of a dream. Twice, she'd asked him if something was wrong. He'd instantly denied it and started talking about other things.

Well, if he didn't want to share what was bothering him with her, she'd leave him alone. But not to come to Aunt Gwynne's for Midwinter, not to be with her as they ate and sang and told stories and laughed...

Frost glazed the grass in the meadow. Talisa walked among the ursells, stroking backs, scratching behind ears. Merisha pranced beside her.

"No, no," Talisa told her. "You need to eat the grass while you can. Already it's scarce; soon it will be very hard to find. Eat your fill."

But Merisha wouldn't. She preferred to keep step with the girl. Finally, Talisa went and sat on the boulder where Cory was slumped, a stone and chisel in his hands as usual. He wasn't carving, though. He was staring at nothing.

"Cory..."

He started. "Yes?"

"Something's wrong. I know there is. Won't you tell me what it is?" She hesitated, then added softly, "Please."

For a moment, she was afraid he wouldn't answer. Then he said, his voice a bit cracked, "It's just...this will be the first Midwinter Rina and I will be apart. Last year...last year was hard, with Mother and Father dead. But at least Rina and I were together. And Bart, of course."

She reached over and touched his arm gently. "I know how you feel. I felt so alone at Midsummer."

"That was different. Oh, I know you missed your family," he added quickly as she withdrew her hand. "But at least you knew you could go home. I'm not sure I'll ever see Rina again. And she doesn't even know where I am or how I am."

If only she could ease some of the pain she heard in his voice. She hesitated, as she'd hesitated before, not knowing whether the news would help or hurt, then said, "Cory, Rina's having a baby in the spring."

A slow smile spread across his face. "A baby!" he said. "She'll be so happy. If only I could see her."

"Someone's sure to be going to Freya come spring. You could send a message then."

"I hope they're all right," Cory said. "At least now Rina doesn't have to listen to me and Bart fight all the time."

Talisa thought about what Rina had said. "Cory, Bart *does* care for you."

"I know." He smiled crookedly. "I sometimes think that's why we fight so much." His smile disappeared.

She touched his arm again. "Cory, *please* come to Aunt Gwynne's tonight. You can't be alone at Midwinter."

"Yes I can."

"But –"

"I'll be all right."

"Cory..." She stopped. It seemed he didn't want to be with people. With her. Very well. She walked to the edge of the plateau and stood looking at the rocky path that wound its way to their hut at the bottom of the hill.

This will be the best Midwinter ever, Welwyn had said.

They gathered the ursells a bit earlier than usual and herded them silently down the mountain in the grey winter dusk.

Welwyn had stayed behind that day to brighten the house for Midwinter and bake for the feast. Talisa's spirits rose as she smelled spicy nut cakes and saw dried usit blossoms and crimson berries arranged in bowls and scattered around the hearth. But as she changed into her green festival dress, all she could think of was the last time she'd worn it. The night she'd met Cory.

It was a short ride, under a sky that seemed especially clear, stars that seemed especially bright. Davvid looked up and shook his head. "Still no sign of snow."

Her aunt and uncle's hut was no bigger than Davvid's and just as simple, but that night it was transformed. The sleeping mats must have been stowed in the shed to make more room. The table was covered by a flame-red cloth and laden with dishes. Green banners streamed from the ceiling.

Gwynne greeted them with exuberant hugs and a bubble of words. Talisa returned her smile and hug and began to relax. Then Jared asked, "Where's Cory?"

Her smile evaporated. "He stayed home."

"Oh." His face fell. Talisa wasn't sure whether her cousins viewed Cory as a hero or a rogue, but whichever it was, they found him exciting.

Her grandparents arrived soon after they did, and with them came the Freyan wizards. Redelle introduced them.

"Talisa, you haven't had a chance to meet our guests yet, Master Leonard Ford and Master Melton Granton. Leonard, Melton, please meet my granddaughter Talisa."

Leonard Ford was a man in his late thirties or early forties with a lean, intelligent face. He and Talisa exchanged smiles and greetings. Then she turned her attention to the second man, whose name always brought a sparkle to Welwyn's eyes and warmth to her voice.

He was worth looking at, Melton Granton, with thick dark hair swept back from a wide forehead, a thin, high-bridged nose and a formidable chin. His eyes were his most arresting feature, though. They were the colour of a summer sky that holds no trace of rain, the bluest and brightest eyes she had ever seen. He was younger than his companion, perhaps in his mid-twenties.

"I'm pleased to meet you, Mistress Thatcher. I had heard of your arrival and expected to see you before this."

His voice was rich and commanding, easily dominating the room. Talisa murmured something about being glad to meet him too, very conscious of the fact that everyone else had stopped talking and was looking at them.

"You will be joining us soon, I trust. I realize you've needed to relax after such a long journey, but time is of the essence when magic is involved."

She gaped at him. "Magic? But... I'm sorry. I won't be joining you."

He raised his eyebrows. "No? I would have thought a member of your family would be eager to learn."

Her face felt hot, her hands cold. "I'm not able to perform magic." *Why* hadn't someone – her father, her grandmother, her sister – told him that already? Were they ashamed of her deficiency?

He looked surprised. Then he smiled. "Perhaps your gift isn't as strong as your sister's. However, anyone who possesses even a trace of talent can master the art of wizardry if he or she is prepared to study hard and learn the nature of things and the words that bind them to a wizard's will."

"I can't," Talisa said. She tried to keep her voice level.

He raised his eyebrows again. "No? Surely –"

"Talisa's gift is for singing," Alaric interrupted.

"Oh?" Melton Granton raised his eyebrows yet once more. She was beginning to hate those thin, dark arcs that seemed to rise so naturally. "I see. I do hope you'll honour us with a song tonight, Mistress Thatcher." He gave her what she felt was a patronizing smile and turned away.

She hated him. She *detested* him.

No. That wasn't fair. It wasn't his fault that he had assumed she could work magic. It wasn't his fault that she lacked even that trace of talent that he spoke of. It wasn't even his fault that he so obviously considered singing far less important than wizardry. But Talisa felt as raw as a newly plucked bird as she sat down to the feast.

And a feast it was, with stuffed grouse, wild onions, berry sauce, and Welwyn's nut cakes. At any other time, Talisa would have devoured it as eagerly as her cousins were doing. Tonight the meat tasted tough, the sauce bitter. She kept glancing at Melton Granton, seated between her aunt and her grandmother. She noticed that Welwyn darted frequent glances at him too.

The meal ended finally. Gwynne waved aside offers of help with the washing up. "Midwinter is a time for stories and songs. Taran and Jared can help with the dishes in the morning."

The twins groaned.

The table was pushed back and chairs drawn up around the fire. Melton Granton leaned forward. "Before we begin telling stories and listening to songs, I have something of a more serious matter to share." He smiled. "Serious, but I hope pleasant. Welwyn thought tonight would be an appropriate time to bring it up."

Talisa's eyes shifted to her sister's face. Welwyn looked very beautiful tonight, with her hair shining like early morning sunlight, her eyes glowing with happiness, and a smile curving her lips. Talisa's stomach lurched. Surely they weren't...surely he wasn't going to announce their betrothal.

He wasn't. "I think I have found a way to help Uglessia."

Talisa could almost see excitement leap into the faces of those around her.

"How?" Redelle asked.

"Through kala. The taste for it has grown tremendously in Freya over the last forty years. If you could grow it rather than just gather it, you could buy far more Freyan goods – food, clothes, furniture, books, things you only dream of now."

Wendell frowned. "To do that, we'd have to move the kala bushes to more fertile ground. And we can't do that."

"Because the roots are too fragile. I know. But I think I've found a way."

"Melton's come up with a combination of spells that should succeed," Leonard Ford said. The two wizards explained. It was technical talk that Talisa couldn't follow. She didn't try to.

"So you see, it should work," Melton concluded.

"Perhaps." Alaric wore a thoughtful frown. "But it's not just a matter of transplanting kala bushes. They have roots that spread and take up a great deal of ground. If we moved the bushes to the level land near our homes, where would we plant our usit crops?"

"You'd have no need for usit."

"No need? It's our basic food."

"With the money you'd get from selling kala, you could buy plenty of flour as well as other Freyan food."

"That would make us very dependent on Freya," Redelle said slowly. "What if relations between us went wrong?"

"You and your family have worked extremely hard over the years to make sure things *don't* go wrong. I am sure you will continue to do so. And excuse me, but are you not already dependent? What could be more vital to Uglessia than the rain sent here by Freyan wizards?"

There was silence.

"There are long stretches of time when supplies couldn't get through," Gwynne said. "Freyans don't travel through their hills in the winter."

Melton shrugged. "I'm sure wizards can eventually find a way to change that. In the meantime, you can build storehouses to preserve the flour and other goods."

"Melton's thought of everything," Welwyn said. Pride rang in her voice.

Melton looked around. "Think of all the things you'll be able to buy with the money you'll get for your kala. And if you wanted to increase your profits, I'm sure there'd be those willing to lend you money to buy land from your neighbours so you could grow larger crops. You could become as wealthy as the richest Freyan landowner."

A spark flew up from the fire. Talisa jumped.

"Why would any of our neighbours want to sell their land?" Davvid asked.

"To get more money to purchase Freyan goods," Melton said. Talisa thought he sounded like a teacher trying to explain a simple fact to a backward pupil. "And they'd continue to have money because they'd then work the land for you."

"That doesn't sound much like Uglessia," Wendell said. His voice was even milder and slower than usual.

"Not as it is now, perhaps." Melton glanced around, then shrugged. "Well, that part isn't important, at least for now. But the rest... Surely you see how this could help your people."

"It's such a wonderful plan. It will make as much difference as the shifting of the winds did forty years ago." Welwyn's voice trembled with excitement.

"It would certainly make a difference," her grandmother agreed. She rubbed her forehead. "I'm not sure all the changes would be good."

"But –"

"I'll think about it. We'll all think about it. If we agree the idea is worth exploring, we'll call a circle so that all the people of Uglessia can make a decision. Now, however, is the time for songs and stories. It is Midwinter, after all."

It was. Talisa tried to smile. If she couldn't be happy, she should at least *pretend* to be so. And maybe it was just her dislike of this blue-eyed wizard that made her distrust his scheme so much.

But as she listened to tales and songs and sang herself – not as well as she should have, she felt – she couldn't ignore the cold worm of worry that wriggled inside her.

SPEAKING OUT

TEN DAYS AFTER MIDWINTER, DAVVID AND Welwyn rode home from their studies and announced that the family had agreed to call a circle to discuss Melton Granton's plan.

Talisa's hands dropped from the loom. "Oh."

"I'm sure everyone will agree to it," Welwyn said. Her cheeks were rosy from the cold air. Her eyes were bright.

"Yes," Talisa said after a moment. She got up and went over to the hearth. "The porridge is ready. We'll eat as soon as Cory arrives with the ursells."

"You stayed home again today?" Davvid asked.

"Yes. There's so much work to do, and it doesn't really take two people to mind the ursells. I don't know why I didn't think of it before."

He said nothing, just went to the washing alcove to clean up. Talisa picked up a spoon and stirred the porridge vigorously.

"What's wrong?" Welwyn asked.

"Nothing."

"Yes there is." The sparkle had left Welwyn's face.

"No there isn't." Talisa got four bowls from the chest and placed them on the table. She felt her sister's eyes on her face.

"Is it... Do you mind that we made the decision without asking for your opinion?"

"No!"

"It's not... We would have liked to have it. But the rest of us were all together and it seemed best to come to a decision quickly."

"Of course. I told you I don't mind."

"Talisa –"

"I hear Cory and the ursells now," Talisa interrupted. "Good. I'm hungry."

She wasn't, but she managed to force the porridge down. She talked brightly about the weather, and the ursells, and her weaving. The others were quiet. Welwyn kept giving her worried glances. So did Cory.

The next day was cloudy, with a chill in the air that made Talisa shiver. Davvid looked at the sky and smiled. "It might snow," he said as he climbed on his ursell.

Cory hovered in the hut after they'd finished the morning chores. "Are you coming with me today?"

"No. There's too much work to do." She bent to the bag of uncarded wool at her feet. She'd used up all the stock of carded wool. If she'd been here last summer, or if Welwyn and her father hadn't been so busy studying, the tangles and burrs would be out of it all.

"That's what you've said every single day since Midwinter!"

The anger in his voice jerked her head up. "Well, there is. There's your cloak to finish, for one."

"Freyn's curse on that cloak! I never asked you to make it."

She flinched as though he'd slapped her.

"Oh Freyn," Cory groaned. He rubbed his face. "I'm sorry, Talisa. I didn't mean... I know how hard you've been working on that cloak. I'm grateful. Really I am. For that and everything else you've done for me. But what does it *matter?*"

"Matter?" she echoed. "What do you mean?"

"I... Oh, never mind." His shoulders slumped. He turned away.

She stared at his retreating back. He was halfway out the door before she found her voice. "Cory! How dare you say something like that and then just walk away? You can't say that and then not explain what you mean. You can't..."

She spluttered, out of breath and out of words.

He laughed.

Talisa looked around wildly. The pan they baked usit cakes in rested on the hearth. She rose. Took two quick steps. Picked it up. Aimed it.

"No, no!" Cory held up a restraining hand. "I'm sorry. I wasn't laughing at you. Honest. It's just that I've never seen you so angry before and...well, I like it."

"You like it?" She gaped at him, pan still poised.

"You're natural again. You're you. For the last little while, ever since Midwinter, you've been...different. You've avoided me. You haven't talked to me – not really talked. I keep trying to ask what I've done wrong, but there isn't anyone there to ask. Just a polite mask."

"Oh," she said in a small voice. The rim of the pan was digging into her palm. She put the pan on the table and stared down at it. "I haven't been that bad, have I?"

He said nothing.

"You started it. For days before Midwinter, you wouldn't tell me what was wrong. Then when you finally did, you wouldn't let me help."

"There was nothing you could do," he said quietly.

"But..." Was that why she'd been so upset? Because there was nothing she could do to help, and she hated feeling useless?

"I'm sorry I didn't go with you to your aunt's. I know you wanted me to."

She nodded, still looking down. Then she raised her head and smiled, a bit wryly. "Maybe it's just as well you didn't. I wish I hadn't."

He frowned. "I knew something was wrong. What happened?"

She looked past him. The sky hung like an opaque grey mirror over the bleak mountainside. She wrapped her arms around herself. Cory started, as though just realizing he was standing in the open doorway. He stepped back inside and closed the door.

"Wrong? I don't know that anything's wrong. Maybe Welwyn's right. Maybe the plan's a good one. Maybe it will help."

It was possible that the idea bothered her simply because it came from Melton Granton. It was the wizard's scorn, not his talk of transplanting kala bushes, that made her squirm inwardly at night as she lay staring into the dark, unable to sleep. But she didn't tell Cory that. Instead, she sat down and tried to reconstruct the discussion around the hearth on Midwinter night.

Cory leaned against the wall, listening intently. A frown darkened his face when she mentioned her grandmother's worry about becoming too dependent on Freya. When she repeated Melton's words about Freyans lending money to Uglessians for the purchase of their neighbours' lands, he erupted.

"No!"

"No one liked that part of the idea," she assured him. "But as for the rest of it —"

"No. You mustn't do it."

She hadn't expected this vehement reaction. "I'm uneasy about the plan too. You must admit, though, it does have some merit."

He shook his head.

"But —"

"No. Without usit crops, people would be totally dependent on the money they'd get from Freyans for kala. What happens if there's a bad year and they don't make enough to purchase Freyan products? Then they'd *have* to sell their land to a neighbour — or even to some Freyan."

A cold finger trailed down her spine. She tried to ignore it. "We wouldn't buy our neighbours' lands if they needed money. We'd help them, the way we always have. And why would Freyans want to come here?"

"To make a profit," Cory said grimly. "As for Uglessians... Maybe your people wouldn't change the way they do things. Not at first. But as they got more money from kala and began to be able to buy not just what they need, but what they *want*... Things would be just as they are in Freya."

"But no one would be thrown off their land," she protested. "Not even if they no longer own it."

"No?"

She looked down at the bag of wool at her feet. She should be carding it. She picked up a handful, then dropped it back.

"A decision hasn't been made about this yet, has it?"

"No. That will be done in two weeks, at the circle."

"What will they decide?"

"I don't know."

Cory pulled a rock from his pocket. His thumb instinctively investigated the bumps and ridges in the rough granite while he frowned down at the floor. Talisa waited.

He raised his head. "Anyone can speak at these circles, can't they?"

"Yes," she said after a moment.

"Will you speak?"

"Me?" She stared at him.

"Yes. You've lived in Freya. You know the danger."

She shook her head. "I can't."

"Why not?"

"I don't even know that there *is* danger. If there is, it's only a possibility."

"So? You can present it to them as a possibility for them to consider."

"I can't," she said again.

"Why not?"

She wished he'd stop asking that. "I can't go against my family."

He frowned. "They're in favour of this plan?"

"They liked it well enough to call a circle."

"Then talk to them. Convince them that —"

She laughed.

"What's so funny?"

"The idea of my convincing my family."

He stared at her.

"They consulted every member of the family about whether or not to hold a circle. Everyone except me." She looked away. "And why should they ask me, when they know I have no magic and can't help Uglessia?" Tears blurred her eyes. Angrily, she blinked them back.

"I'm sorry," he said gently.

She stood up and walked to the window. Davvid's wish had come true. Fat, lazy snowflakes were floating to the ground.

"I don't think you're right," Cory said. "I think your family respects your opinions. But if they won't listen to you, will you speak out at the circle?"

She thought of speaking to her grandparents, her father, her aunt and uncle and cousins and sister. Of the glow in Welwyn's eyes and the catch in her voice whenever she mentioned Granton. Of speaking at the circle against the combined will and wisdom of her family.

She couldn't. She *couldn't*.

Just as she had not been able to defend the innocence of Uglessians before an angry crowd on Midsummer.

She closed her eyes. A picture came to her of a singer standing on a corner, feet blue with cold. Was it snowing in Freyfall too? Was the woman still there, still without shoes?

"Talisa?"

"I don't know," she told the falling snow. "I'll think about it."

She turned. Her eyes fell on the bag of wool. It needed to be carded. Then she glanced at Cory. There were other needs. "It's time we took the ursells to pasture."

TALK TO YOUR FAMILY. *Convince them,* Cory had said. But how could she talk to Welwyn about the wizards' plan? All her father said, when she brought up the subject, was that it was up to the circle to decide. Her uncle and grandfather were away, carrying word of the meeting throughout Uglessia. She could, she knew, have ridden to her aunt's or grandmother's in the evening. She didn't. She was a coward. She knew it.

As the time for the circle grew closer, she found it harder and harder to sleep.

She was conscious, always, of Cory's attention focused on her, even when his eyes were elsewhere. He didn't say anything, though, till the last day.

"What have you decided?"

It was cold. She huddled in her cloak and watched clouds scud across the sky. "I don't know."

"Maybe you won't have to speak," he said after a long silence. "Maybe they'll vote against it without any warning from you."

"Maybe."

Even if she did speak, what could she say? Why should they listen to her? She scooped up a handful of snow and let it sift through her fingers. Snow coated the ground like the flour Mistress Coyne sprinkled on the table before she rolled out pastry. Freyan flour. Wouldn't it be good to be able to buy flour with the money they'd make from kala crops? Her mouth watered, remembering the taste of bread.

She gazed down the hill to where their hut stood, a larger mass of stones amidst the surrounding ones. It had taken her parents a long time to build it, she knew, chiselling each stone to fit, cementing them with dried ursell dung. It had taken them even longer to haul away rocks so they could plant usit. Would her father ever sell his house and land?

No. Of course not.

But what would happen if he didn't have enough money to buy Freyan flour, Freyan oats? Without usit...

And what about other Uglessians, clinging so stubbornly to their patches of land on the sides of the mountains?

She gazed at her home for a long time, then raised her eyes to the slopes and crags beyond it. Everything looked gentler today, softened by the sheet of snow. But life in this country was harsh. If things changed, if people didn't help each other...

"Will you come with me to the circle?" she asked.

"With you?" Hope leaped into Cory's voice. "Does that mean you'll speak?"

"Will you come?" Her gaze was still on the mountains.

He hesitated. "I don't want the Freyans to see me."

"Please."

This time his pause was fractional. "All right."

IT SNOWED THAT NIGHT, but the next morning the only clouds were those formed by their breaths in the still, cold air. They rode the short distance quickly.

The circle was to be held on the small plateau behind Redelle and Alaric's home. Cory whistled when Talisa told him it was the same place where her great-grandmother Yrwith and Kerstin Speller had convinced Uglessians forty years ago to give up their dream of invading Freya, and trust Freyan wizards to shift the winds and bring much needed rain instead.

Those from nearby were still riding in when they dismounted, but many who came from longer distances had arrived the day before. Campfires dotted the hillside. Ursells were everywhere. So were people.

The circle began at mid-morning. Talisa stationed herself and Cory as far from the centre as she could, even though that meant she had trouble seeing over everyone's heads. She could hear her grandmother clearly, though, as she opened the meeting. The plateau worked as a natural amphitheatre.

"Greetings," Redelle said. "Thank you for coming. We are here today to consider a proposal brought forward by Melton Granton and Leonard Ford, the two Freyan wizards who are staying with us as our teachers and guests."

She went on to outline the plan, clearly and dispassionately. When she'd finished, there was a brief silence. Then someone called out, "What do you think of the idea, Redelle?"

"The magic should work," she said carefully. "As for the rest... It has merits, but I can also see potential problems. It is for you to discuss and decide."

Something tight and painful in Talisa's chest uncurled. Her grandmother wasn't supporting the plan, simply presenting it. And the two wizards weren't fluent enough in Uglessian to be able to argue their case convincingly.

But Welwyn was, and Welwyn did. She talked with passion and conviction, her voice trembling slightly with the intensity of her belief in this project that would make life better, make life easier, make life richer, for all Uglessians.

Talisa saw hope blossom on the faces around her, and felt Cory's eyes on her. She wasn't sure whether he had understood all of Welwyn's words, but he had obviously grasped the force of her argument.

She didn't move. How could she speak now, right after Welwyn? How could she speak against what her sister had said at all? Cory couldn't expect it of her. Surely others would debate Welwyn's words.

They did, but hesitantly. They had questions. They had doubts. They were unsure. But others spoke too, of how hard life was here and how good it would be to have more. "Why shouldn't we live like Freyans?" they asked.

Talisa had never seen the ocean, but she had heard of the tides that surged in, sweeping all before them. It was like that now. She could feel it.

Cory must have felt it too. "Talisa..."

"I know."

And she did. But she couldn't oppose her sister. Her family. And who would listen to her anyway?

Coward. Coward. Are you going to be silent now, just as you were at Midsummer?

My silence hurt no one then.

No. But it might have. It might have led to the deaths of innocent people.

Her legs didn't want to move. It was the hardest thing she had ever done to walk forward and step into the middle of the circle.

She couldn't look at anyone. She fixed her gaze above all their heads. "I wish to speak against this proposal."

She had a strong voice, a singer's voice. It was not strong now. She cleared her throat, trying to loosen the tight band that choked her words.

"I understand why many of you support this plan." *Oh, Welwyn, please understand why I do not.* "But I feel it presents too many dangers. What if Freyans become hostile? What if they become unwilling to pay high prices for kala? What if the kala crops fail and we have no money to buy Freyan food? We will not have usit to fall back on."

Others had raised these same questions. What was she doing, tossing her words into the crowd like a child throwing rocks into a pond, only to have them sink without a trace?

A man in front of her stamped his feet to warm them. Someone coughed.

Talisa took a deep breath. "Master Granton has said that Freyans would be willing to loan money so that some Uglessians could buy their neighbours' lands and pay them to work for them. It is possible that a day will come when some Uglessians are rich, some poor, when some can be thrown off the land they work but no longer own. It has happened in Freya."

At least this was new. She risked glancing at the faces near her. They were polite, attentive. Nothing more.

How could she make them *see* what might happen?

Cory's song. The song that had begun as they walked the streets of Freyfall together and grown and developed in the days and weeks they'd spent tending ursells.

She glanced at her family then. Welwyn looked troubled, not angry. Beside her, Melton wore a faint, scornful smile. Davvid gazed back at her with steady, unreadable eyes.

The song was unpolished. She had never sung it out loud, only heard it in her mind. Mixed in with Cory's tale were the rocks and mountains and ursells of Uglessia, all stitched unevenly together with a melody that sighed like the wind blowing through the grass in the mountain meadow and soared like peaks that tried to pierce the sky. At one point, she could almost see Master Coyne wince at the patchwork nature of the song. But she sang it with sorrow and anger and joy. And maybe its very roughness and jagged edges gave it power.

There was a hush when she finished. Perhaps this rock would not sink but create ripples, even waves. Blindly, she walked back to her place by Cory's side. All the way there, she felt the hot bright glare of Melton Granton's eyes.

After the Circle

I T WAS HARD TO FOCUS AFTER THAT. TALISA KNEW others spoke, but she couldn't concentrate on what they said. Welwyn's words reached her, though, like a long knife penetrating the fog to find its victim. "Do not let my sister's bitterness stop you from grasping this opportunity." After that, Talisa deliberately wrapped the fog around herself.

After a while, there was a pause. Then she heard her grandmother call for the vote. She closed her eyes.

Cory nudged her. "It's all right," he whispered.

She opened her eyes. Hands were in the air. Many of them. But not enough. Surely not enough.

"Those opposed," Redelle said.

Hand after hand rose.

"It would seem the majority is not in favour of this proposal. Thanks to all for coming, and to all who spoke. Thanks also to Master Ford and Master Granton for conceiving this idea. I know they had Uglessia's well-being in mind, and hope they will continue to think up ways we can improve our lives. Twilight is coming. It is time to eat and rest."

In ones and twos and small groups, the crowd dispersed, talking, laughing, blowing on cold fingers to warm them, going down the hill to camps or waiting ursells.

Cory grinned at her. "You did it! You won!"

Her answering smile was weak. She should feel relieved. She *was* relieved. But...

Her eyes searched for Welwyn. They didn't have far to go. Her sister was striding towards them, her face sharp and white against the pale blue of the late afternoon sky.

She stopped in front of them. "Why?" Her voice shook.

"Why what?" Talisa asked. But that was a foolish response. She groped for an answer to give her sister.

"Why did you speak against it? Or no. You didn't speak, did you? If you had merely spoken, used facts, used reason, it wouldn't have mattered. But you wrapped your words in a song. Why? So you could prove you have more power through your singing than I do through my spells?"

Talisa stared at her. She couldn't speak.

"That's it, isn't it? You didn't like the idea because it involves magic, magic you can't use. So you decided to wreck the plan, using the gift you do have."

No! She's wrong. All wrong.

Is she? asked a cold, judging voice inside her.

"That's not fair," Cory said angrily.

Welwyn whirled to face him. "And you! You're even more to blame. Do you think I don't know who's behind this? You're so embittered over losing your land that you try to ruin everything. Not content with killing soldiers in Freya, now you destroy our hopes for making life better here."

She spun on her heel and ran. Talisa watched her go, feeling sick.

Then she noticed Melton Granton, standing not five yards away. He was staring at Cory, his eyes narrowed into thin blue slivers of ice. Talisa froze. How much had he heard? How much had he understood, with his limited Uglessian?

Leonard Ford came up and touched his arm. "Come on, Melton. Time for supper. We've been invited to share it with the family of that young man who's studying at the College of Wizards, and it's a long time since breakfast."

Melton continued to stand there, staring.

The other wizard followed his gaze. He smiled. "A fine song, Mistress Thatcher. I couldn't understand all the words, but I recognize a good song when I hear one. It certainly had an impact."

"I'm sorry," Talisa mumbled.

"For what? Opposing our plan? Don't worry. It was an idea, that's all. I think it was a good one, but it seems the majority didn't agree. We'll come up with a new one, I hope. Come along, Melton."

The younger wizard continued to stare at them for a moment, fists clenched. Then he turned and stalked away.

Talisa watched him go, stomach churning. "Maybe you shouldn't have come."

Cory grimaced, then shrugged. "Oh well. It was probably fated that we meet sooner or later." He grinned at her again. "Let's go. Master Ford was right. It's been a *very* long time since breakfast."

It had been, but Talisa didn't feel hungry. Redelle had asked the whole family to supper. How was she to face them? What would Welwyn say this time?

"It will be all right," Cory said gently.

They met several curious glances as they made their way towards the path that led down from the plateau. Talisa flushed. Had they all heard her sister's outburst? But then someone smiled. Someone else called a greeting. Several people stopped to talk, but they only asked about her stay in Freya or complimented her on her singing. Their progress was slow.

Davvid was standing at the top of the path, waiting for them. He looked tired, Talisa thought. She wanted to say something, but what? Should she apologize? Explain? Ask how he felt? They descended the hill in silence.

Welwyn wasn't in the hut. Everyone else was: Redelle stirring soup, Alaric cutting a round of cheese, Gwynne placing bowls and plates on the table. They all turned around and looked at Talisa when she entered. She stopped.

"Congratulations," Redelle said.

"Congratulations?" Talisa echoed. She blinked. "But –"

"You spoke well. And sang beautifully."

"It was a marvellous song." Gwynne put the bowls she was holding down and came over to hug Talisa.

"But I thought... Weren't you all in favour of the plan?"

Redelle shook her head. "I thought it had enough merits to draw it to everyone's attention. But it would make such a difference... I wasn't at all sure."

"I thought we should try it," Alaric said. He smiled. "Or I *thought* I thought that. I voted in favour of it, but I must admit I felt relieved when it was defeated."

Gwynne nodded. "I was going to vote for it too, before I heard your song. Not after."

"I was against it from the beginning," Wendell said from the corner where he and the twins had seated themselves to keep out of the way.

Davvid said nothing.

Talisa rubbed her eyes. Tears were trying to form in them. "I was afraid you'd be angry."

"Why would we be angry?" her grandmother asked. "Even if we'd all badly wanted this idea to go ahead, we wouldn't be upset with you for honestly expressing your opinion."

"You reminded me of two other young people, arguing for what they believed in," Alaric said softly. Talisa knew he was thinking of himself and Kerstin Speller, pleading for Uglessia forty years ago against the mighty ones of Freya.

The flames in the hearth were leaping and crackling, but they weren't the only things that made her feel warm.

Then she remembered. "Welwyn –"

"She too spoke well for what she believed in," Redelle said.

"Where is she?" Davvid asked.

"I saw her ride off on her ursell," Taran volunteered from his corner.

Davvid frowned. "I'll go after her."

"No," Gwynne said. "She needs some time alone. She'll be all right, Davvid," she added as he hesitated. "Sit down. You need your dinner."

The soup was tasty, the talk and laughter around the table easy. But Talisa's mind kept flickering back to her sister's pale face and angry words. Had Welwyn only lashed out at her because she was bitterly disappointed in the results of the vote? Or had she truly meant what she'd said?

Was there some truth in what she'd said?

Clouds had moved in again. As they rode along the dark trail, Talisa tried to decide what she should say to Welwyn when they reached home. None of the words she came up with seemed right.

She needn't have worried. Welwyn wasn't there. Davvid stirred up the ashes of the fire, a troubled frown between his eyes.

"Should we try to find her?" Cory asked.

"She knows her way home." Davvid buried himself in the book he'd been reading all week, yet another treatise on the theory and practice of magic that he'd borrowed from the Freyans. After a while, though, he put it down and slipped outside. Talisa hesitated, then joined him.

"Do you think she'll come home tonight?" she asked.

"Where else would she go?"

"Aunt Gwynne's, perhaps."

"Perhaps. Well, if so, Gwynne will send one of your cousins with a message."

They were silent. Talisa watched a cloud drift away from the crescent moon.

"I'm sorry."

He sighed. "It's not your fault. If it's anyone's, it's mine. You tried to talk to me, but I didn't want to listen. I knew how strongly Welwyn felt about this."

"You're not to blame," Talisa said quickly.

"Hmmm."

It was cold. She thought about going inside, but didn't.

When Davvid spoke again, his voice was so low she had to strain to catch his words. "I was never good at talking. Your mother was. If she were alive... But you both seemed to do so well, even so. I always took great comfort in how close the two of you were."

"We still are," Talisa said firmly. She closed her eyes. *Please, mountain spirits, make it be so.*

They were silent again. Finally he said, "If it weren't for Melton, she wouldn't feel so strongly about this."

"No."

He shot her a sideways glance. "And you? You're fond of Cory, aren't you?"

Blood rushed to her cheeks. "We're good friends."

They stood quietly for a few more minutes, then he turned to go back in. With his hand on the door, he stopped. "I was very proud of you today."

She stayed outside a while longer, breathing in the cold night air, breathing in his words.

Welwyn returned late, when everyone had gone to bed and the fire in the hearth had burned down to low embers. She slipped in beside Talisa so quietly that the straw matting scarcely stirred. Talisa turned to her, wanting to say...something. But Welwyn's back was to her, and it was very stiff.

She was subdued the next morning and in the days that followed. Talisa and Cory walked around her on tiptoes for some time, but Talisa thought she wasn't really angry, only tired. It was as if the sparkle inside her had sunk into grey ash. She only flared up once, when Jared said something about Melton being a sore loser.

"What do you expect? He spent a great deal of time and thought coming up with a plan to help us, only to have his work thrown back in his face."

Cory suggested privately that Granton might have had more on his mind than pure helpfulness. "There are merchants who would pay well to have a larger supply of kala."

Talisa considered this, then shook her head, a bit reluctantly. Much as she disliked the wizard, she didn't think he'd had an ulterior motive. "He's just reacting so badly because his pride is hurt."

More snow came, and with it, bitter cold. They huddled around the fire at night. Talisa's hands grew chapped and stiff. So did Cory's, but he continued carving, not just in the evenings but also when they were on the mountain with the ursells. One day, shyly, he handed her a small stone cut in the shape of an ursell. But not just any ursell, she saw with a catch at her heart. It was Merisha.

She raised her eyes to his. "Oh, Cory. Thank you."

"You're welcome," he said gravely.

They gazed at each other. He reached out to touch her face. Then a sudden, startled bleat jerked their heads around. An ursell had slipped on the snow. She teetered precariously close to the edge of the cliff. They rushed to her aid and the moment passed.

Those winter days were good ones, despite the cold, despite Welwyn's misery, despite the distance that lay between them. Talisa ached for their old closeness to return. She wished she could remove the strain she sometimes saw on her father's face. But she could not be unhappy, because Cory was there to talk to and laugh with and be silent with. Songs seemed as natural as breath, those days.

The cold moderated, but snow continued to fall. Although it made walking and riding difficult, even treacherous, they rejoiced, knowing the life it nurtured.

But winter couldn't last forever. The days grew longer, the air warmer. Welwyn brightened with the lengthening days. Talisa worried that the coming departure of the Freyan wizards would cast a grey haze over her spirits once more, but it didn't. In fact, a burden seemed to lift from her as the time grew nearer.

Everyone but Cory gathered at Redelle and Alaric's the day the wizards left. Talisa would have liked to stay home, but that would have been rude. Thanks and good wishes were exchanged.

"We may be back, if you'll have us," Leonard said.

"Of course," Redelle replied promptly.

Melton said nothing.

Welwyn's eyes rested a long time on his back as he rode away, but when she turned back to the others, her face looked calm, even serene.

There would have been no time for study even if the two men had remained. Spring was birthing and planting time, and they were very busy. With all the snow they'd had, the ground was easy to work. Talisa ran some moist soil through her fingers with a sigh of satisfaction.

Four ursells were born that year, including a son to Merisha. Welwyn and Talisa worked on that birth together, and shared a delighted smile as the small creature rose on his wobbly legs. Talisa crooned a song to him, the song they sang to all baby ursells.

Little one, brother grey
Grow up strong, that soon you may
Run and climb, but never stray.
Follow in the ursell way
And know that life is good.

Life *was* good.

And then, on a day of boisterous wind and skittish sunshine, Jared came galloping up to them as they crouched planting usit seeds, and told them that Freyan soldiers were on their way, hunting for Cory.

SOLDIERS IN THE HILLS

TALISA STARED AT JARED. HE HAD JUMPED DOWN from his ursell. His face was flushed, his long red hair swirling in the wind. Both he and his ursell were breathing heavily.

Davvid straightened up slowly. "Where are the soldiers now?"

"At Darwent and Jada's. They stopped to ask directions, and little Owen slipped away to warn you. I saw him and said I'd come since I thought I'd be faster."

Darwent and Jada's. They'd be here soon. Talisa's hands felt icy. "Are you sure they're after Cory?" she whispered.

"Yes. They can't speak Uglessian, but they mentioned his name, Owen said. And they must know he's staying here, since they gave your name, Uncle Davvid, when they were flinging their arms about to ask for directions."

A cruel hand twisted something inside her.

"Melton," Welwyn said. Talisa looked at her. Her face was the colour of bones bleached too long in the sun. "He knew. He must have told... It's my fault." She closed her eyes for a moment. Opened them. "He asked me about Cory, the night of the circle, and I...I told him. I was so angry, so... It's my fault," she repeated.

Talisa started to raise her hand to touch her sister's arm, then dropped it.

"Where is Cory?" Jared asked.

"With the ursells."

Jared followed Davvid's glance up the mountain. "I'll go warn him."

Talisa tried to speak. Couldn't. She wet her lips and tried again. "No. We must say we don't know where Cory is. Pretend we didn't know they were coming. If they saw you there...they'd be suspicious. I'll go."

Davvid shook his head. "You'd be the first person they'd suspect. You must be here, calmly planting usit, when they arrive." He looked at Welwyn. "Will you warn Cory?"

She nodded. Jerkily.

"Tell him he must hide in the hills until they leave." He looked at Jared. "You'd better not be here when they arrive."

Jared sighed. "I suppose not. I'll spread the word about what's happening." He mounted and rode off, almost as fast as he'd come.

"What will Cory eat?" Talisa managed to get out. There were no berries or roots at this time of year.

"Make up a bundle of food for him. If they stay long..." Davvid paused. "We'll leave food near the pasture. Tell him to keep checking." He sounded calm, but the frown between his eyes dug deeply into his skin.

Talisa ran for the house. Food. Usit cakes – but there were so few of them – cheese, salted meat. She placed them in a cloth and tied it clumsily, then thrust the package at Welwyn, who was standing waiting.

Welwyn took it. "Oh Talisa..." She stopped.

Her face was an ashen mask of despair. Talisa couldn't bear it. She threw her arms around her sister and hugged her fiercely. Welwyn returned the hug. Then she was gone, out the door, up the path, her hair a shimmering net of pale gold.

Talisa took a deep breath. Another. Another. They didn't help. She forced herself to walk back to the usit field, kneel, plant seeds. Wait.

She didn't have to wait long. Perhaps fifteen minutes later, she saw a troop of green-uniformed men ride over the crest of the western hill and descend towards the hut.

Davvid stood up. "We'd better go greet them." He looked at Talisa as she rose, then gripped her shoulder for a moment. "Steady."

The soldiers turned their heads and watched them as they approached. There seemed to be a great many of them, and a great many tall, big-boned horses, snorting and stamping the ground.

"May we help you?" Davvid asked politely.

A man leaned forward in his saddle. "You speak Freyan. Good. Are you Davvid Thatcher?"

"Yes."

"We're here looking for a man we've been told is staying with you. A Freyan named Cory Updale."

"Cory? Why are you looking for him?"

"You admit that you know him and that he's been staying here?"

"Admit?" Davvid's eyebrows rose. "Certainly. He's here as our guest."

The soldier's head snapped towards the house. "Is he inside?"

"No."

"Where is he then?"

"I'm not exactly sure." Davvid paused, then added, "Won't you come in and explain what this is all about? You and your men might need a drink too."

The other man hesitated, then swung down from his horse. He was tall for a Freyan, about Davvid's height, and lean. He had big hands. His uniform, which bore the insignia of captain's rank, was not as clean and neat as the ones Talisa had seen on the streets of Freyfall. Nor were his men's.

"I do owe you an explanation, I suppose. But no drink. We have no time to waste." His voice was polite but clipped, brooking no argument. He turned to his troop. "Dismount, but stay by your horses. I won't be long."

Once inside, the captain sat down without waiting to be asked and removed his cap. Talisa leaned against the wall as far from him as she could. Her knees felt so weak she would have liked to sit, but all the chairs were too close together. Davvid seated himself and waited.

"My name is Captain Wellwood. I've been sent here to find and arrest Cory Updale and take him back to Freya to stand trial."

"What is he accused of?" Davvid asked after a moment.

"I think you know. At least, your daughter does. Both daughters, I imagine." His eyes, pale blue under straight dark eyebrows, inspected Talisa. "Are you Welwyn or Talisa Thatcher?"

"Talisa." She was ashamed of how small her voice sounded. She cleared her throat.

His eyes sharpened. "So you're the one who met this man in Freya and brought him here."

"Yes." She cleared her throat again. "You said we knew, but I don't. What is the accusation against Cory?"

"Arson, treason, and murder." The words slapped the air, flat, stark. Talisa pressed harder against the wall and wished she'd sat after all.

The captain continued, his voice hard. "He set fire to a barracks in Freyfall. Two soldiers died."

"Cory didn't set the fire."

"No? Then he needn't fear returning to Freya and facing trial, need he?"

She said nothing.

"Where is he?"

She met his eyes levelly. "I don't know."

"You don't know? You bring him to Uglessia, keep him here in your house, but now you don't know where he is?" The captain's eyes were narrow slits, his voice a sneer.

"I would appreciate it if you did not speak to my daughter in that tone," Davvid said. He spoke quietly, but Talisa heard a rare note of anger in his voice.

Captain Wellwood's head swung his way.

After a moment, Davvid added, "We really have no idea where Cory is at the moment. He was here earlier today, but he went out by himself after breakfast. I imagine he's somewhere on the mountain."

"Where's your other daughter? Welwyn?"

"With the ursells, in the meadow at the top of the path."

"Very well," the captain said curtly. He rose and walked out. Davvid and Talisa followed. "Mount up," he called. "I want this area searched, and searched thoroughly."

"Wait," Davvid said.

Captain Wellwood looked at him impatiently. "What is it?"

"You can't take those horses on the mountains. They aren't as sure-footed as our ursells. They'll slip."

The other man hesitated, scanning the steep cliffs all around him. Then he shook his head. "We need speed. And they've travelled through the Freyan hills and over the trail from the tunnel. They'll do." He turned back to his troops. "Carver, choose five men to stay here with you. Keep a close watch in case Updale returns. The rest of you, spread out over the mountainside. Go in pairs."

Talisa watched the soldiers file out across the hillside and start to climb. Captain Wellwood took the path that led to the pasture. Did he think Welwyn would reveal Cory's whereabouts?

"Come," Davvid said gently.

They returned to the usit field, leaving the six soldiers guarding the house.

Usually, songs and wordless tunes came into Talisa's mind as she worked the soil and planted seeds. Today, all she heard was the thudding of her heart and the gusting of the wind.

Would Cory be able to keep ahead of the soldiers? Could he stay hidden?

He was wearing the cloak she'd made him, she remembered. The grey wool would blend in with the rocks.

Her eyes kept leaving the ground in front of her to search the stones above.

Dusk brought Welwyn and the ursells, and a grim-faced band of weary soldiers.

"May we camp here overnight?" Captain Wellwood asked.

"Certainly," Davvid said courteously. "And would you and your men like some supper?"

Talisa thought of their stock of food, always low at this time of year, and winced. But her father was right. The Freyans were their guests, even if unwelcome ones.

"No, we have rations," Captain Wellwood said. "Thank you," he added as an afterthought.

Talisa didn't suspect the guards outside the house of deliberate eavesdropping, and she knew they didn't understand Uglessian. Nevertheless, their presence placed a muffling hand over her mouth. Her sister and father seemed to feel the same way. The three of them said very little as they ate their meal and went about their evening tasks.

It wasn't till they were in bed that Talisa dared to ask Welwyn, "What did he say? What is he doing?"

"Hiding, I hope, though even if he's not he should be safe. I put an invisibility spell on him." For a moment, pride surged in Welwyn's voice. Then it died. "It will only last a day."

They were silent. Talisa tried, as she'd been trying all afternoon, to remember if there were caves with hidden openings near the pasture.

"He said to tell you not to worry, that he'll be all right." Welwyn was silent a long time. "He thanked me. He... Oh, Talisa, I'm sorry. I'm so sorry." Silent sobs tore through her, racked her whole body.

"Hush," Talisa whispered. She stroked her hair and back. "Hush. The soldiers won't stay long. It will be all right."

She prayed to all the mountain spirits that she was right.

THE SOLDIERS STAYED. Each morning, they saddled up and rode off, hunting for Cory. Each morning, Welwyn led the ursells to pasture. Talisa ached to go in her place, but knew it was better this way. The Freyans were less suspicious of her sister. She could leave food for Cory to retrieve after dark, when the soldiers returned to their camp by the house.

Then, on the fourth day, Captain Wellwood stationed some of his men on the mountain overnight. Talisa could see their campfires, sparks of light against the dark sky. One spark came from the plateau.

"I'll try to slip away tomorrow and leave the food else-where," Welwyn promised. "Close but not too close."

She nodded when she returned the next day. But the following day brought bad news. "The food's still there," she said quietly. "Either Cory didn't see where I hid it, or it wasn't safe for him to get it."

Oh Cory. Cory, what will happen to you?

On the seventh day, Talisa and Davvid watched a lone horseman ride back to camp, his companion stretched face down over his horse's neck. The soldier called to the sentries on guard.

"Trouble," Davvid said.

Talisa nodded. They left the field and hurried to the camp. By the time they arrived, soldiers were gently lowering the unconscious man to the ground.

"What happened?" Talisa asked.

The man who'd just ridden in turned to her, his freckles standing out vividly against his blanched skin. "He fell. Over a cliff. We were riding... It was steep, but I thought... There must have been a loose stone. He just...fell." He swallowed. His Adam's apple bobbed. "I heard... The horse screamed. I climbed down as fast as I could, but it took ages, it was that steep, that slippery. By the time I got there..." He swallowed again. "I had to use my knife on the horse. There was no help for it. But Lance... He's not dead, but he hasn't moved, no, nor opened his eyes. Not once."

"And we don't even have a healer with us," muttered one of the guards.

"Perhaps I can help," Davvid said quietly.

"You?"

"I'm a wizard. I know something of healing."

The Freyans glanced at one another. "Maybe we should fetch the captain," one of them said uncertainly. But they didn't. They stepped back from the injured man, making room for Davvid. He knelt beside him.

Talisa's hands clenched and unclenched. *Why*, she wanted to cry. *Why help him? He's hunting Cory. He's hurting Cory.*

She gazed at the man on the ground. His arm was twisted at an unnatural angle. His skin was as grey as the mountains, his face contorted with pain, even in his unconscious state. She couldn't hate him. Nor could she hate his freckle-faced companion, who had so bravely climbed down to rescue him. It would have been easier if she could.

After a few minutes, Davvid raised his eyes. "He has internal injuries as well as a broken arm. He's badly hurt. Talisa, will you ask Welwyn to come here? I'll need her help."

Help only another wizard could give. At one time – and that a short time ago – his words would have hurt. Now they didn't. Talisa hurried off.

Welwyn was sitting on a boulder, looking unhappy. She jumped up when she saw Talisa. "What –?"

"Father needs you. There's been an accident. One of the soldiers fell over a cliff."

Welwyn nodded. As she went past Talisa, she slipped a small package into her hand. "I haven't been able to hide it," she murmured. "There are too many Freyans close by." Then she was gone.

Talisa put the packet into her pocket and glanced around. A green uniform met her eyes. The man wasn't far away, but he wasn't looking in her direction either. Perhaps... But no. If Welwyn, with her ability to cast the illusion of invisibility around herself, hadn't felt it safe to hide the food, she couldn't. Talisa sat down on Welwyn's rock and waited.

It was an overcast day, with raw edges that whispered of rain. The ursells, with their thick coats, didn't seem to mind, but she hunched her shoulders against the cold and shivered.

If *she* was cold, what about Cory? Did he have a cave to shelter in? A crevice between two boulders? How tantalizing it must be for him at night, watching soldiers huddle around their fires.

Hungry. He must be so hungry.

And tired. Was he forced to run from place to place, to dodge from rock to rock?

If only Melton Granton hadn't disclosed Cory's whereabouts. If only Welwyn hadn't told Melton that Cory was a suspect in the arson. Resentment stirred, like the ashes of a spent fire. Then it subsided.

If only *she* hadn't begged Cory to come with her to the circle.

It could go on and on, Talisa thought. If only Cory hadn't been seen near the barracks. If only he hadn't become involved with the men who set the fire in the first place. So many if onlys. Enough to seed their entire usit field.

She glanced at the spot where she had seen the soldier. He wasn't there. Her breath caught. Surely, if she couldn't see him, he couldn't see her. She rose.

Several of the ursells looked up as she passed. "Stay," she said firmly. They did. Thanks be that Merisha was down below with her baby. If Talisa left the meadow, Merisha would have followed.

Please, please, mountain spirits. Let Cory be close by. Let him see where I put the food, Talisa prayed as she scrambled up the steep hill. Cory must know they would try to leave food for him. But with so many soldiers around, he might have been forced to leave the area. He might be miles away. She bit her lip. *Please.*

There was a small hollow, not far from the pasture but hidden from it. She reached it quickly and delved into her pocket.

"What are you doing?"

Her heart jumped into her throat. Very slowly, she turned. A soldier stood behind her, his eyes slitted with suspicion.

Of course. They hunted in pairs. If one were nearby, the other would be as well. She had forgotten.

"What are you doing?" he repeated.

"I... Tending the ursells."

"Your ursells are down there." He pointed.

"Yes. I..." Frantically, she searched for an answer. *Think, Talisa, think.* "I...I need to relieve myself. The plateau seemed too open. With so many soldiers around..." She trailed off and held her breath.

"Hmmm." His eyes were still slitted. "You're not the one who's usually here. Where's the other girl?"

"She had to help Father. One of your company fell over a cliff and was badly hurt. Welwyn and Father are trying to heal him."

"Fell over a cliff?" He looked around the rocky mountainside and turned a faint shade of green. Good.

"Yes. Now, if you'll excuse me..."

He withdrew to a discreet distance, but she knew he'd be back. She didn't leave the food.

Oh Cory. I'm sorry.

DIRE CONSEQUENCES

CAPTAIN WELLWOOD CAME TO SEE THEM THAT evening, just as they'd started supper. Welwyn and Talisa put their spoons down. Davvid rose.

"Thank you for helping Private Lance."

"You're very welcome," Davvid said gravely. "He should be all right, though it will take some time for the bones in his arm to heal."

The captain nodded. Talisa thought he'd leave then, but he didn't. He stood just inside the door, cap in hand, but didn't speak for several minutes.

"Would you like to stay for supper?" Welwyn asked politely. "We'd be glad to have you."

He glanced at her. "No, thank you." A smile flickered across his face. Then it disappeared as he turned back to Davvid. "You warned me that our horses weren't suited to these hills. You were right. This is the first accident, but we've had several near mishaps. I came to ask if we could borrow your ursells while we're here."

"I'm sorry. No."

"We wouldn't expect you to lend them to us without compensation. We'd pay a fair price."

"I'm sorry."

Red washed across the captain's face. "Look –" He stopped, and resumed in a milder tone, "We'd take good care of them."

"I'm sure you would," Davvid said quietly. "The answer is still no."

Captain Wellwood was silent. In the light slanting in through the window, Talisa thought his face looked tight. His voice was equally tight when he spoke. "Please give me the courtesy of an explanation."

"Certainly," Davvid said levelly. He paused for a moment, then said, "My daughters and I will do all that we can to make sure that you and your men are safe and comfortable while you are here. The laws of hospitality demand that. They do not demand that we lend our ursells to those who are hunting a man who has been a guest in this house."

Talisa's breath caught. None of them had spoken so frankly to this Freyan soldier before.

The captain's hands clenched on his hat. He took a half step forward, then stopped. When he spoke, his voice was as level as Davvid's, but Talisa heard barely controlled rage in it. "I have told you that Updale burned the barracks in Freyfall and killed two Freyan soldiers. Refusing to help us in our pursuit might be viewed as less than friendly towards Freya. Hostile, even."

After a moment, Davvid said, "I feel nothing but respect and friendship for your country."

"But you refuse to help."

"Yes."

There was silence. Beyond the hut, Talisa heard one of the guards call to someone further off, and the answering shout. Her hands dug into the stone edge of the table.

When Captain Wellwood spoke again, his voice was very soft. "Your actions may lead to indignation and anger in Freya."

"We would regret that," Davvid said. Talisa marvelled that he still managed to keep his voice so quiet, so even.

"You would," Captain Wellwood agreed. "The consequences could be...dire. Winds can be shifted again. Rain can cease."

The captain glared at Davvid. Minutes crawled by. Then he spun on his heel to leave. As he did, his eyes fell on Talisa. He stopped.

"And what do you make of this, Mistress Thatcher?"

She stared at him.

"It was you, after all, who brought this man here. You must take some responsibility if relations between our countries...deteriorate."

He stalked out.

Talisa stared down at the porridge in her bowl. The dried berries in it seemed to look up at her like dark accusing eyes.

"What ingratitude!" Welwyn spluttered. Talisa raised her head. Her sister's cheeks were flushed, her eyes bright. "We save the life of one of his men, and he turns around and threatens us!"

"He was frustrated and lost his temper," Davvid said. He sat down heavily and rubbed a hand across his face. "It will pass. For the last forty years, conditions between Freya and Uglessia have swung this way and that. We've always managed to right them in the end." He smiled faintly. "Don't look so worried, Talisa."

"That's right," Welwyn said. "And remember, we're in this together." She squeezed Talisa's left hand. Her right hand was still gripping the edge of the table.

Forty years. Forty years of working hard to make sure Uglessia's relations with Freya were good. Now they might fall apart. Because of her.

The consequences might be dire, Captain Wellwood had said.

Freya need not even send an army. All it had to do was shift the winds back to their original pattern, to the way they had been before Kerstin Speller came. Deny Uglessia the rain it needed so badly.

Her hand was going numb. She opened her fingers. Red lines marked her skin like scars.

THE NEXT DAY the Freyan soldiers, looking glum, stretched out across the mountainside on foot. Captain Wellwood rode off down the track.

"Probably seeking help from other Uglessians," Welwyn said. "Little good it will do him."

Talisa nodded.

"I'd better be off with the ursells." Welwyn gave her a

sideways smile. "With the soldiers less mobile, I should be able to steal away and leave food for Cory."

"I hope so." How long had it been since he'd eaten?

As though to make up for its miserable mood yesterday, the weather produced one of those perfect spring days where the sun and breeze and the air itself seemed to laugh with the joy of returning life. But Talisa knew no joy, no laughter. She worked in the usit field in silence, as did her father. At one point, he left to inspect the injured man and returned, looking pleased. Talisa tried to feel pleased too, but couldn't.

As evening fell, the Freyans returned, complaining loudly about sore feet and aching muscles. Welwyn descended with the ursells and gave Talisa a reassuring nod. For the first time that day, Talisa smiled.

Captain Wellwood was the last to come back to camp, riding in just as the red rim of the sun sank below the western mountains. From the look on his face, Talisa didn't think he'd enjoyed his day.

"They'll have to leave soon," Welwyn said as they got ready for bed. "They still haven't found Cory, and Captain Wellwood must realize now that he won't receive any help. Besides, I don't think the soldiers are very happy now that they're having to use their own legs." She laughed.

She might be right. Please let her be right. But if she were, if they returned to Freya, mission unfulfilled... Talisa stared into the darkness, no more able to sleep than she had been the night before.

The next day was identical to the one before. Welwyn took the ursells to pasture, Davvid and Talisa planted seeds in the usit field, and Captain Wellwood and his soldiers went their separate ways. Talisa worked doggedly, but her mind failed to register what her hands were doing.

What could she do?

Could they say Cory was dead? But the Freyans would demand to see his body.

Could she convince them that Cory was innocent? But Captain Wellwood would only say, as he'd said before, that if so, Cory need not fear returning to Freya for trial.

Think. Think.

But her thoughts went nowhere. They were like the rain that collected in the cracks of rocks. Stagnant. Useless.

She had felt useless before, knowing she lacked any talent for magic. But that had only wounded her pride.

Surrounded by the smell of damp earth, she dug holes, deposited seeds, covered them, over and over, while her mind battered itself until it felt bruised.

"That's done then," Davvid said.

Startled, she glanced up. He stood beside her, dusting off his hands. They'd started at opposite ends of the row and met in the middle. The usit was planted.

"Now all we need is a good rain," Davvid said. He sounded cheerful, but Talisa was sure she saw a worried frown cross his face before he looked away. She rose slowly, rubbing the small of her back.

Later, while Davvid prepared supper, she stood outside the hut, watching the soldiers return. One was limping badly.

"What happened?" one of the sentries called.

"Fell on some loose stones. I think my ankle's sprained. Freyn's curse on this mountain! On all Uglessia!"

The guard shook his head. "We're sure to get more twisted ankles and broken arms before we're done."

Another Freyan muttered something, too low for Talisa to hear.

Her heart lifted. If the injuries increased and the muttering grew louder, surely Captain Wellwood would be forced to withdraw. His departure wouldn't end their problems, but at least Cory could have shelter. Food.

Some food he already had. Welwyn brought the reassuring news that the package she'd left the day before had disappeared. She'd hidden another one in the same place today.

Talisa helped Welwyn put the ursells in the enclosure. Merisha rubbed her head against her. Talisa patted her.

"Did you enjoy your day on the mountain? And did your little one behave himself?" For the first time, Merisha and her baby had climbed to the meadow.

Welwyn laughed. "I had to run after him several times. He's as high-spirited as his mother."

Before entering the hut, they stood to watch the sun descend in a fiery arc. A lone horseman rode up the track, back straight, face set. Captain Wellwood. A smile trembled on Talisa's lips.

She turned to go in.

Someone shouted behind her. She spun around.

At first she couldn't understand what had caused the shout. Then she saw a soldier's upraised arm, pointing.

Soldiers started to run.

Shadows were thick on the mountainside, but she could see a man, walking slowly but purposefully down the path the ursells took to pasture.

Her heart pounded. Her eyes strained to make out his features.

Then the sun flared in a final blaze before it disappeared, bathing the man's face in a crimson glow.

It was Cory.

PRISONER

"NO. OH NO."

Her words were a moan, a prayer. She should be screaming, telling him to turn, to flee. She took a breath that shuddered through her and opened her mouth.

Too late. Far too late. Soldiers had spilled out of the camp and surged up the hill. In a minute – less than a minute – they would seize him.

Cory stopped. "I surrender," he called. "I'm coming to give myself up. Let me walk in on my own."

They paid no attention. They grabbed him and hauled him down the path. Roughly.

"No! Don't!"

Talisa started to run. A hand gripped her arm. She whirled. Davvid had come out of the house. He held her arm tightly.

"Don't, Talisa," he said quietly.

"But they're hurting him!"

"There's nothing you can do. Captain Wellwood will stop it."

"Captain Wellwood," she spat.

But Davvid was right. The captain shouted an order to his men to take their hands off the prisoner. By the time Cory reached the foot of the trail, he was walking unhindered among the pack of green-uniformed men.

"I must talk to him. I must."

"Later."

"But –"

"Later. Now is not the time."

It hurt to do nothing, only watch, only listen. Talisa bit her lip hard and stood still.

"You are Cory Updale?" Captain Wellwood demanded. He had dismounted and come to meet the band of soldiers and their prisoner.

"Yes." Cory's voice sounded calm. How could he be calm?

"You are surrendering? You will offer no resistance as we take you to Freya to stand trial for arson, treason, and murder?"

"No."

"We will have to bind you nevertheless, but you may wish to eat first."

"Food would be welcome." Was there a hint of laughter in Cory's voice? Surely not.

Captain Wellwood nodded and walked off towards the campfires. So did Cory, still pressed as closely by his captors as was the dung that cemented the stones of the house together. He glanced over his shoulder. Talisa strained, but the light was too dim, the distance too far. She couldn't make out the expression on his face.

"Come inside," Davvid said. "You must eat. You too, Welwyn."

Under her father's watchful eyes, Talisa tried to eat, but the food clogged her throat till she felt she would choke. She put her spoon down.

"Why?" Welwyn burst out. "He can't be that desperate. He had the food I left for him."

Talisa shook her head mutely. No one spoke. The silence went on and on.

"Try to eat," Davvid said gently.

At least Cory would be full tonight. And warm, with blankets over him and a fire nearby. Talisa managed to choke down a few mouthfuls. Welwyn ate even less. Talisa looked at her face, then away. She had no comfort to offer. She stared at the flames in the hearth, that flickered and danced quietly.

At last she said, "Do you think... May I go and talk to him now?"

Davvid hesitated. "Morning might be better."

"They may leave first thing tomorrow." And how could she bear to wait any longer?

"That's true." He rose. "We'll go ask Captain Wellwood's permission."

"No. I have to do this by myself."

After a moment, he sat back down. Talisa headed for the door.

"Don't forget your cloak," Welwyn said quietly.

She snatched it from the hook and left.

There were no sentries around the house. Talisa supposed they felt no need of them. Not now.

The moon had just begun to rise above the rim of a mountain, and the sky was a deep, soft purple. It would have been a clear night had it not been for the fires ahead of her and the smell of acrid smoke.

A few soldiers looked up from the plates they held as she approached the first fire. They said nothing, but their eyes were curious. She gazed past them. No sign of Captain Wellwood. Her steps faltered. Should she ask them where he was or seek him out herself? She glanced about.

Her breath caught. Beyond the ring of light from another fire, Cory sat in the shadow of a boulder. His head was bent, his arms bound behind his back. She started towards him.

"Here, where are you going?"

She stopped and turned. A heavy-set, bearded soldier had risen from his log by the fire.

"I want to talk to Cory."

His eyes narrowed. "Why?"

"I..." Why indeed? To ask him how he was? To ask him why he'd surrendered? To say...what?

"He was a guest in our house. I need to speak to him."

"Hey, Birdsell," someone called. "It's obvious why she wants to see him, Why not let her?" Loud smacking noises were followed by louder laughter. Talisa's face flamed.

The bearded man hesitated. "I don't know."

"What is it, Birdsell?" Captain Wellwood's voice came from behind her. She turned to face him.

"I wish to speak to Cory."

He studied her. She held her breath and waited.

"Very well. He's over there." He pointed.

"I know. May we have some privacy?"

His pause this time was longer. "Very well," he said again. He turned to his men. "Move back. Far enough that you can't hear but not so far you can't keep an eye on him."

The smacking noises came again. This time Talisa saw the soldier making them, a man with a silly sheep's face and a sillier grin. The grin faded as Captain Wellwood's eyes rested on him.

She waited till the soldiers had retreated to a discreet distance, then walked forward. Cory rose awkwardly, his arms stretched tightly behind him. She stopped.

It was hard to see clearly in the light from the newly risen moon and the unsteady flames of the fire, but she thought he looked pale. And haggard, with enormous dark shadows beneath his eyes. His clothes were wrinkled, and his uncombed hair fell in clumps across his face. Despite all that, he looked...peaceful. Content, even.

They regarded each other for what felt like a long time. There were so many things Talisa wanted to say, so many questions to ask, but her words seemed blocked by a huge lump in her throat. He spoke first.

"You came. I hoped you would."

She swallowed. "Cory –"

"There's so much I want to say to you, and so little time."

So little time. Yes. She swallowed again. "Cory –"

"I think what frightened me most, when I was hiding on the mountain, running crouch-backed from rock to rock, was that they'd find me and haul me away before I had a chance to talk to you, to say..." He stopped. She stared dumbly at him.

"To say thank you."

She shook her head.

"Yes. I owe you so much, Talisa. Not just for bringing me here, for risking... But before that. For encouraging me to talk about the farm. For looking for me when you weren't sure I hadn't set the fire. For...for caring enough."

He fell silent. She wanted to say something but couldn't. Behind her, she heard soldiers moving about. Someone laughed.

"But most of all, I want to thank you for these last few months, for this winter here. For the first time since we were driven from our farm, since I watched my parents die, I've felt...happy." He shook his head. "No. More than that, though that too. I've felt...at home. At peace." He smiled, and the smile tore at her heart.

She couldn't speak, but she must. She took a deep breath, then another. "Cory... Cory, *why?* Why did you give yourself up? Oh, I know you were cold, cold and hungry, though we tried to get food to you."

"You did," he said softly.

"But they were growing discouraged. A few more days..."

His eyes left her face, wandered in the direction of the hut and the mountains beyond it. "And then what?"

She stared at him.

"What would have happened after they left?"

"I...don't know."

"Nor do I. But I thought about it. Oh, not at first, when I was as frightened as a panicked hare, when all I could think about, if I thought at all, was how to keep out of their hands. But later, when it began to seem as though they might not catch me after all. What would happen to you, to your family, to your people when those with power in Freya – the queen, the court, the army, the wizards – learned that a Uglessian girl had brought me here and other Uglessians had helped me escape? I could not bear it."

Out in the darkness, a horse neighed.

"This is for the best, Talisa."

"No! That is... I know why... But do you think *I* can bear it, to have you taken away, put on trial, put..." But she couldn't say it, though the words beat in her head like a drum roll, going on and on and on. *Put to death. Put to death. Put to death.*

"I'm sorry, Talisa. I'm so sorry."

She shook her head fiercely, denying, not his words, but the future facing them, the future that seemed as inevitable as the coming of night.

"Mistress Thatcher."

She jumped. She hadn't heard Captain Wellwood walking up behind her.

"You have had as much time as I can allow. You must go now."

No! No! She turned. "Please... A little longer."

There may have been a trace of pity on the captain's face, but there was no relenting. And his voice was as unyielding as granite when he repeated, "You must go."

She turned back to Cory. He smiled at her.

"May all your mountain spirits go with you, now and always," he said softly.

She tried to smile too, because it was something she could give him at least. "And with you. And may Freyn smile on you." And then, despite Captain Wellwood's presence, she added, because it was something else she could give him, and because it was true, "I love you."

The sky was black now. Flames leaped and twisted against it, like spirits writhing in agony, as she stumbled back through the camp.

JOURNEYS

THEY LEFT EARLY THE NEXT MORNING, breaking camp as the sky began to lighten and riding away even before the sun appeared above the mountains. Cory's arms were still tied. Talisa wondered if they ached, or if they were numb by now. He looked back once. She thought he smiled, but was too far away to be sure.

She had not been able to speak when she'd returned to the house last night. Nor could she speak now. Davvid and Welwyn said nothing either as they stood with her, watching the troop ride away, but she felt their sympathy like supporting arms holding her upright.

The horsemen disappeared behind a dip in the hills, appeared again, then rode out of sight.

Davvid sighed. 'We'd better have breakfast."

She shook her head.

"Try, Talisa," Welwyn said gently.

For their sakes, she did, and managed to eat a couple of mouthfuls before pushing her plate aside.

"I'll take the ursells to pasture today."

"There's no need," Welwyn protested.

"I want to."

With the four new young ursells, it was a job that required concentration. That was good. Talisa watched them as carefully as their mothers did on the trip up the path. Most stayed close, but Merisha's baby tended to wander. He gave her a reproachful look the second time she herded him back into line. Two minutes later, he strayed again. He glanced over his shoulder at her as he did so. If he'd been human, he would have grinned.

"You are a child of mischief," Talisa informed him. "And no, I will not run after you. I'll let your mother tend to you this time."

She did, nipping his shoulder sharply as she nudged him back to the track. Talisa almost smiled, watching them.

They would have to give him a name that reflected his impish nature when the time came. Cory had been surprised when she'd told him that no babies, human or ursell, were given names until a year after their births.

"Why not?" he'd asked, stroking Merisha's baby.

"So many die that first year. If they survive that, they're likely tough enough to live on."

He had been silent a long time. "Life's hard, here in the mountains of Uglessia," he'd said at last.

"Hard, yes. But that makes it all the more precious."

The dirt and stones of the path blurred. Life was precious anywhere.

All day, she scurried after the young ursells as frantically as the clouds scudded across the sky. It kept her from thinking. When she stood still, all she could see was a troop of soldiers riding westward towards the tunnel, towards Freya, towards death.

No! She shook her head violently. She would not think that. She looked around, but the youngsters were all grazing quietly beside their mothers. There was nothing to distract her from her thoughts, or from the sight of the rough-hewn boulder against which she and Cory had leaned so often, or the patch of loose stones by the path where he used to crouch, hunting for just the right rock to carve.

She shouldn't have come here. Everything reminded her of Cory. She heard his whistle in the call of a bird, saw his shadow in the windswept grass, felt his presence everywhere.

If only he had become apprenticed to Master Fletcher. Then there would be people to speak on his behalf: his master, other carvers, the whole weight of a guild.

But he hadn't. Who would there be to speak for him now? His sister? His brother-in-law? Master Swanson? They had no more power or influence than she did.

She stared down at the ground, scuffing the dirt with the toe of her shoe. It was still soft and moist from the winter snows. The wind brought the notes of a far-off lark. She listened, half unwillingly, to the song that echoed and changed, lifted and fell in her mind.

Song.

She wasn't powerless. She had swayed her people with her song. Cory's song.

She looked up, eyes wide.

She could add verses to it, verses that told how a young man hurried to stop a fire but came too late.

Could she sway Freyans?

She was trembling with sudden hope. She wrapped her arms around herself.

He might not have the Carvers' Guild behind him, but might there be others who would speak for him?

Garth? Garth's grandfather?

Perhaps. If someone went to them, persuaded them. And what about Kerstin Brooks and her husband Jem? Wouldn't they fight on his behalf if they heard his story?

Maybe even the Coynes. They knew Cory. If someone talked to them...

It might not work.

But it might. The power of influence and the power of song.

She gazed about. Below, she saw the hut, crouched low to the hillside, and a bright dot that she knew was Welwyn's head. Beyond them stretched the peaks and valleys of Uglessia, bare, grey, rocky, with here and there a flash of blue that marked a life-giving stream.

The mountains of Uglessia had given her back her songs. They'd given her Cory's song.

But it was in Freya, now, that she must sing it.

Two DAYS LATER, just as night eased into pre-dawn pallor, she headed west, not on Merisha, who needed to stay with her baby, but on an older ursell with a placid disposition.

It had not been as difficult as she had feared to convince her father that she should once more travel to Freya. The difficulty had come in persuading him she must go alone.

"You'll need help. Support."

"I'll ask Grandfather to write a letter to Kerstin Brooks. I'm the best one to talk to the Coynes and Garth. And Garth is the best one to speak to his grandfather."

"Why?" Welwyn asked. "Do you want to prove you can do this by yourself?" She was watching Talisa steadily.

Welwyn always had known her too well, Talisa thought. Perhaps she was the only one who had understood why Talisa had insisted on going to Freya last year. At one time, her sister's knowledge of her would have made Talisa flush and turn away. Now she just shook her head.

"No. I would welcome help. From both of you. But this must not seem like a dispute between Freyans and Uglessians. Cory surrendered so that there wouldn't be conflict." Her voice shook for a second. She looked down, then back up. "My actions will simply be seen as those of a girl in love." She blushed slightly. "But if you came, or other Uglessians..." She stopped.

Davvid was quiet for a long time. Finally, he nodded. "You're right."

So here she was, setting off on a journey by herself, just as she'd done last year. But how different her mood then, how different her motives. How different *she* was. Then, she'd been jittery with excited apprehension and filled with an aching need to prove herself. Now she no longer needed to prove anything, either to others or to herself. But her apprehension had turned into fear, a fear that was a constant pain in her stomach. If she didn't succeed...

Talisa straightened her shoulders. She had her grandparents' letters in her saddlebag. They had written not just to Kerstin but to other wizards they knew.

And she had her song. And her determination.

The sun came up over the tip of an eastern hill, gilding the rocks ahead of her. She rode on into the deepening morning, her journey begun.

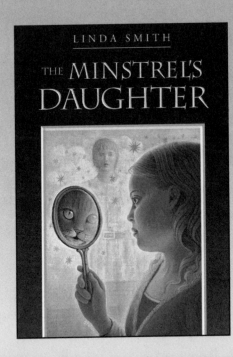

PHOTO: CATHERINE MCLAUGHLIN

ABOUT THE AUTHOR

LINDA SMITH is the author of *The Minstrel's Daughter*, Book 1 in the "Tales of Three Lands" trilogy. Titles from her first series, The Freyan Trilogy, which includes *Wind Shifter*, *Sea Change*, and *The Turning Time*, were finalists for a number of book awards, and another recent title, the 2003 picture book, *Sir Cassie to the Rescue*, was highly recommended by *CM Magazine*. She has also published poetry and short fiction in a number of anthologies and periodicals, and has had her work broadcast on CBC Radio.

Born in Lethbridge, Linda Smith grew up in Alberta, and has lived in Truro, Nova Scotia; Saskatoon; and Boston. Since 1984, she has made her home in Grande Prairie, where she worked as a children's librarian until 2001, and now writes full-time.